THE ROAD
TO HER

What Reviewers Say About KE Payne's Work

365 Days

"One of the most real books I've ever read. It frequently made me giggle out loud to myself while muttering, 'OMG, RIGHT?'"
—After Ellen

"Payne captures Clemmie's voice—an engaging blend of teenage angst and saucy self-assurance—with full-throated style."—Richard Labonte, *Book Marks*

me@you.com

"A fast-paced read [that] I found hard to put down."—C-Spot Reviews

"A wonderful, thought-provoking novel of a teenager discovering who she truly is."—Fresh Fiction

Another 365 Days

"Funny, engaging and accessible."—*Kirkus Reviews*

Visit us at www.boldstrokesbooks.com

By the Author

365 Days

me@you.com

Another 365 Days

The Road to Her

THE ROAD TO HER

by

KE Payne

2013

THE ROAD TO HER

ISBN 10: 1-60282-887-3
ISBN 13: 978-1-60282-887-2

This Trade Paperback Original Is Published By
Bold Strokes Books, Inc.
P.O. Box 249
Valley Falls, NY 12185

First Edition: July 2013

Credits
Editors: Lynda Sandoval and Ruth Sternglantz
Production Design: Susan Ramundo
Cover Design By Sheri (graphicartist2020@hotmail.com)

Acknowledgments

Creating a book doesn't just happen by magic, and so I have some fabulous people to thank for getting this, my fourth novel, through the publishing process and onto book shelves. Firstly, the lovely people at Bold Strokes Books who do such a brilliant job: Radclyffe for welcoming me to the BSB family in the first place, to Lynda Sandoval and Ruth Sternglantz for guiding me through the editing maze, and to Sheri for going with my choice of cover and turning it into something even more amazing. I'm also truly grateful to each and every other person who works tirelessly behind the scenes at BSB and who made publishing this book such a pain-free journey for me. Thank you all.

I'm indebted to Sarah Martin, for not only being an awesome beta reader and giving up her precious time to read my work, but also for her constant encouragement and support. I'm always telling you how grateful I am, Smartie, but seriously—thank you! A massive thanks also to Emma for your funny and encouraging e-mails over the last few months that have all driven home to me just how important it is to never let the buggers get me down and to always persevere with my goals. PS: Tell your gran to keep reading the PFs too!

To BJ—no words will ever be enough to let you know how much I appreciate everything you do for me. Without your constant love and support, I would never be able carry on with what I love doing, so thank you.

Finally, a huge thank you to all the readers who continue to buy my books, and who take the time to contact me to say how much they enjoy them. I greatly appreciate every e-mail, Facebook comment, and Tweet that you send me, and your continued support is immensely important to me. Thank you all so much.

CHAPTER ONE

S o, Holly, what do you think?" Kevin Driffield sat back in his chair, his small speech over. "We reckon having a lesbian character is going to really bump up the ratings this year." He steepled his fingers and looked at me from across his desk, the flicker of a smile on his round, nondescript face.

"We're thinking this could be the most popular gay storyline since Martin and Dexter in *The Escape* two years ago." Kevin's assistant producer, Susie Abecassis spoke before I'd had the chance to answer Kevin's question. "Are you up for it?"

"And Jasmine Hunter's been chosen to be that character?" I met Kevin's continued look and mirrored his smile.

"Having an already-established character such as Martin fall in love with a newcomer like Dexter was an instant hit with the fans," Kevin said. "People are still talking about it, even now."

"And now we want to recreate that success in *Portobello Road* with you." Susie spoke animatedly.

My name is Holly Croft, and I guess if you're older than twenty-five then you'll possibly never have heard of me, but I'm an actress in a well-known early evening soap opera which half of the UK's teenage population go absolutely crazy for. It's set in and around the Portobello Road area of West London and is called, appropriately enough, *Portobello Road*.

Well, over the years, *Portobello Road* has totally changed my life. I'm twenty now, but I've been in it since I was just twelve. I play a character called Jasmine Hunter, and fans of the show have followed her through thick and thin: through her school years, all the way through her parents' long and bitter divorce, to her first day at university, and right through to her now apparently falling in love with a girl.

"We thought it was time Jasmine came to the fore," Kevin was now saying, tilting back on his large plush leather chair—the sort that executives are fond of using—and leaning back so far I was convinced he'd topple over backwards and clatter to the floor. "She's been too long just in the background, but we feel she has potential…"

"More potential than she's being given at the moment," Susie said, cocking her head to one side and smiling so much her eyes crinkled. "We think *you* have potential, too, Holly."

I looked down at the sample script on the table in front of me and chewed at the inside of my lip. Jasmine was being taken in a totally different direction, and to be honest, I couldn't decide whether I was nervous or excited at the prospect of her having such a major storyline after years of just being "that Hunter kid." Just recently, the most exciting thing that had happened to Jasmine was her passing her driving test and her parents divorcing last year after her father was caught in flagrante delicto with his secretary. But this? This was something else.

"Well, I'm flattered," I began, "uh, flattered that you'd give me such a huge storyline, and that you think I can handle it." I looked down at the script again.

"We want this storyline to run for at least the next year." Kevin leaned forward in his chair. He placed his arms on the table and looked at me intently, then picked up his copy of the script and ran his eyes over it. "It's going to be a terrific love story, a real heart tugger. We don't want it to be just a token piece, shoved in somewhere between Shane's hair transplant and Hazel's nervous breakdown."

"Casey Fletcher—Jasmine's love interest—is a brand-new character," Susie said, reading from a printed sheet in front of her. "She's eighteen—the same age as Jasmine—and they'll meet at university."

"They'll be friends to begin with," Kevin continued, "but then they'll both begin to realise that they want something more than just friendship."

"We want Jasmine to struggle with her feelings, deny she likes her, all that sort of stuff," Susie said, glancing up at me then looking back down at her sheet of paper, circling something on it with a pen. "We'll keep the viewers hanging on a good while with the classic *will they, won't they* scenario before they both confess their feelings for each other."

"And Casey certainly won't just be a flash affair for Jasmine," Kevin added. "It'll be a proper, long-lasting, and loving relationship."

"The Martin and Dexter storyline will pale into insignificance compared to what we've got in store." Susie nodded in agreement.

I looked from Susie to Kevin and back again, adrenaline beginning to fizz inside me.

"It sounds awesome!" I looked back at Susie and then tried, unsuccessfully, to sneak a glimpse at what was written on her sheet of paper.

"So are you up for it?" Kevin finally asked. "You think you can handle the pressure?"

"Up for it?" I said. "My God, yeah, I'm up for it!" I tried to contain my excitement. "And, yes, I can totally handle the pressure."

I was more than keen to be involved in the process right from the off as well. I was protective of Jasmine. Of course I was. I'd grown up with her, so it was important she got the right girl, and it was important that the writers did the whole story perfectly. I loved Jasmine and I loved the show. *Portobello Road* had given me a good life for the last eight years; it had given me money, and perhaps while it hadn't given me as much fame as it had some of the other cast members, it had given me security and many loyal and fantastic friends and colleagues. I was very lucky. It had also given me the opportunity to move from my parents' home in the countryside and buy myself a small but fabulous modern apartment overlooking the Thames. I was so privileged and I knew it; there weren't many twenty-year-olds out there that could afford their own place, let alone one in the centre of London.

Yes, I loved *PR,* I loved Jasmine, and right now I totally loved Kevin and Susie.

"Excellent!" Susie reached over and pulled out a small pile of papers from a blue file and absent-mindedly flicked through them. "Now we know you're happy to go ahead, we'll contact some agents and get some auditions going for the part of Casey," she said, putting the papers back into the file. "Then get whoever we choose to do a screen test with you, okay?"

"We'll get the ball rolling this afternoon if you're okay with that." Kevin gathered his papers together and stood up to leave.

"I'm more than okay with that," I said, already thinking ahead to how fabulous it was all going to be.

❖

The next week passed by in a flurry of the usual routines, during which I didn't hear any more about the new plotline. Instead, my days mainly consisted of hours passed in the green room and canteen at the *PR* studios, which were located in a large complex around five miles outside of London, where I would learn my lines and chat with my co-stars while I waited to be called on set. This was usually followed by a few brief scenes shot with my on-screen family, particularly my on-screen mum, a lovely, vivacious, and totally scatty actress called Bella Hamilton, who was currently Soaps' Favourite Mother, according to *Just Soap* magazine.

But it was shortly after lunchtime—ten days after I'd first heard about my new storyline and just as I was packing my things together, ready to leave again for the day—when Susie came into the green room with a file under her arm and a look of importance on her face.

"So we chose our Casey last week," she said, sitting next to me on the sofa and taking a piece of paper from her file. "She had her audition on Thursday and we're really pleased with her."

I put my bag to one side, interested. My scenes over the last few weeks with Bella had been fun enough, but the thought of now doing something completely different was more than appealing.

"We interviewed four actresses altogether." Susie shuffled herself back on the sofa and crossed one leg over the other. "Elise was, by far, the best of them all."

"Elise?"

"Elise Manford," Susie said. "Seems very nice. I think you'll like her."

"I hope so," I said, suddenly nervous.

"We'd like you to do a screen test with her this afternoon, make sure the chemistry's there," Susie said. "We're very keen for you to be involved in every stage of the process."

Elise Manford. I said her name to myself, racking my brains as to whether I'd ever heard of her before. I hadn't.

"Be back at three, can you?" Susie asked.

"Sure," I said, glancing at the piece of paper still in her hand.

"Have a read of this," Susie said, handing me the papers, "so that you're not coming in completely blind this afternoon."

I took the script, an excited tightness building in my chest at the thought of what might be written in it.

"It's a short sample scene between Jasmine and Casey, nothing too long, just about five minutes' worth," Susie said, hauling herself up from the sofa.

I glanced at it and saw that the scene had been split fifty-fifty between Jasmine and Casey so that we each had around twenty lines each. It looked like meaty stuff at first glance, an argument or a fight, something for us both to get our teeth into. Seeing it reaffirmed that this was really going to happen caused a brief moment of panic that I wouldn't be up to not just this scene, but the whole story.

I sighed, annoyed with myself. I was being ridiculous, I knew. Okay, so I'm not academically gifted, I'm never going to be an astrophysicist or an Olympic sportswoman or discover a cure for some deadly disease. But one thing I'm sure about is I can act, and I have an unstinting confidence in my abilities as an actress. Of course I could do the story justice. I was only daunted, perhaps, by the prospect of doing a good job on this particular storyline. I wasn't fazed by the storyline itself—why would I be? Unlike Jasmine, I was happy with my sexuality and knew exactly what I wanted from life. I'd had a girlfriend once, you see. It was a while ago when I was at school, studying part-time at the same time as acting, and she had been my first and only girlfriend, but I'd loved her and she'd been The One. At the time, at least.

Grace. That was her name. We were together for around eighteen months, towards the end of my time at school. And we were a proper item, not just experimenting. We were madly in love. We'd pass by each other in the corridor exchanging knowing looks, linking hands briefly as we walked by. We'd go to one another's homes, telling our parents we were studying in our rooms, but of course studying was the last thing on our minds. It was all very secretive and clandestine because we were both so far back in the closet we'd shut it, locked the door, and thrown the key away. It's how we both wanted it. Her, because she didn't want her parents to find out. Me, because, I don't know…because I figured it was no one else's business. Okay, so a small part of me also didn't want the press to find out and bandy my personal life around in the papers because I was only sixteen and I knew I wouldn't be able to handle it. But the main reason was because Grace and I were special. She was my adorable little secret and I wanted her to stay that way.

Anyway, I needn't have worried about getting found out because, despite us apparently being madly in love with each other, Grace eventually dumped me. So that little problem was soon sorted. She went to Spain for three weeks as part of her Spanish language qualification, staying in a small town just outside Madrid with a local family. And then somehow managed to fall in love with the daughter of the family (yes, within three weeks) and decided to return to Madrid and move into an apartment with her new love the minute her exams were over.

I know. You couldn't make it up, could you?

The one thing I was grateful to her for—and still am—is that she never outed me to anyone. Not to my family, my friends, the press, no one. Her parents found out about her a couple of years later, but to her credit she never told a soul about us. And for that I was always grateful. It could have been so easy for her to go to the papers and do a kiss and tell, but nearly four years on, still no one knows about us.

So Grace was my first and only girl. I never heard from her again after she moved to Madrid, and I've never got over her. Crazy, hey? She left me over two years ago and I still can't move on because she's all I think about, all I want. Knowing I can never have her sometimes near kills me, and I'd do anything—*anything*—to have her back in my life again right now.

I've flirted with girls in clubs since, and even a few guys as well, but nothing has ever really happened, and certainly nothing has ever matched up to the feelings I had with Grace. I knew I needed to accept the fact she was never coming back and that I had to get on with my life, as hard as that was.

So instead of looking for my next Grace, I concentrated on doing the best job I could in *Portobello Road*, and I guess it paid off in the long run because now, here I was, holding in my hands probably just about the most exciting-looking script I'd seen in years, on the verge of becoming a major player in one of the soap's biggest-ever stories.

Of course, the fact I liked girls in real life and that the *PR* people had decided to make Jasmine gay was pure coincidence. But that had to make my job easier, right?

I couldn't wait to get started...

CHAPTER TWO

I jumped when I heard a voice behind me and jerked my head up, looking far more startled than I should have done. I was in the green room, waiting for "Casey" to arrive so we could do our screen test together. I'd read the script through thoroughly, wanting to do a great job and impress everyone immediately, and now, knowing I'd learnt my lines, I slumped on the sofa, idly surfing the net on my phone and thinking about what to have for dinner later.

"Hey," the newcomer said, lifting her chin in greeting.

"Hey," I replied, putting my phone down.

"So we're reading together later," she said, walking towards me and extending her hand. "I'm Elise."

"Holly." I sprang up from the sofa and shook her hand.

We stood and looked at each other for a moment, each of us assessing the other in those brief seconds. Elise had an air of superconfidence about her, filling the room with her presence the second she walked in. She was taller than me and, I figured, older than me. Slightly slimmer, too. She was dressed in what looked like designer jeans and a battered leather jacket—the sort you'd pay a fortune for—with an equally battered brown leather messenger bag strung across her shoulders. She had dark blond hair, cropped short against her suntanned face; with her fine bone structure and expressive dark blue, almond-shaped eyes, the haircut worked really well. Better than it ever would have done on me, anyway. It looked a classy cut—the kind done at a hideously overinflated price in the centre of London, not just down at your local suburban salon.

"It's been a while since I had a screen test in England," Elise said. I was struck at just how nice her teeth were, too—expensive looking, just like the designer jeans, leather jacket, and haircut. "I'm kind of nervous."

"Oh?" I absent-mindedly reached down for the script, which was on the table next to me.

"Yeah," Elise went on. "I've just come back from LA, you see?"

"I see," I said, figuring that was where the tan was from. "What were you doing there?"

"This and that." Elise smiled, revealing deep dimples in her cheeks. "Interviews, auditions, pilots. Same old."

For some, maybe, I thought, making a mental note to Google her later and find out just exactly what "this and that" really meant.

"Right," I said, nodding. "How long were you there for?"

"About fifteen months or so," Elise replied.

"And now you're back here," I confirmed.

"Yup." She walked past me and sat down on the sofa, in the place where I'd been sitting just before. "Susie'll be here any minute," she said. "Shall we familiarise ourselves with what we're going to be reading before she comes?"

"Sure."

She delved into her bag and pulled out a piece of paper, shifting along slightly as I came to sit on the sofa, too, angling my knees so I was facing her more. "They just gave me this now," she said, waving the piece of paper at me. "Haven't had a chance to look at it yet."

"Me, neither," I lied, not wanting her to know that I'd just spent the last half an hour scrutinizing it to death.

"So you play Jasmine, uh, Jasmine Hunter, yes?" Elise peered down at the papers. "And I'm going to play someone called Casey Fletcher."

She seemed to be talking more to herself than to me, so I stayed quiet.

She traced her finger down the paper, her lips moving silently as she read her lines to herself, occasionally frowning, sometimes smiling.

"Wow, this is heavy stuff!" She looked up and grinned, peering at me through her fringe, which had flopped down over her eyes.

"They did tell you in the audition why your character was being brought in, didn't they?" I asked, puzzled by her reaction to the sample script.

"They told me my character will be a…what was it they called it?" Elise took a pen out of her bag and started underlining parts of her script. "A *distraction*. That's it. Casey will be a distraction to Jasmine." She looked up at me.

"To begin with," I said. "Then it gets serious."

"Then it gets serious, yes." Elise arched one perfectly plucked eyebrow.

"It's going to be so exciting for Jasmine," I said, holding my script limply in my hands. "It's about time she had some fun, I think!"

"You've been in the programme long, then?" Elise asked, underlining something else on the paperwork on her lap.

I briefly wondered why she hadn't bothered to find out more about me before our screen test together. I'd have thought she would have wanted to come fully prepared, but perhaps that wasn't her style.

"Eight years," I replied. "Been in it since I was twelve."

"Double wow!" Elise's head snapped up in surprise.

"Sorry?"

"Wow that you've been in it so long, and wow that you're twenty!"

"You think I look older?"

"Younger." Elise's eyes scanned me up and down, immediately making me uncomfortable.

"Oh."

"You seem younger, too." Elise shrugged. "No offence meant."

"None taken," I lied, wondering just why she would think to say something like that, bearing in mind she'd only just met me. "How old are you, then?"

"Nineteen."

Elise was nineteen! I'd imagined her to be four or five years older, I'm not sure why. Maybe it was the positive, assured attitude she had, and the nice teeth and make-up and designer gear. Or perhaps it was because she'd been to America, I don't know. The furthest away I'd ever been in my twenty years was Morocco, and even then my parents wouldn't let me go until they knew the names and addresses of every—and, my God, I mean *every*—single person that came with me. I suddenly felt very immature and naive.

"I don't really think eight years is that long to be in a soap, to be honest. Not over here, anyway. Michael Adams has played James Morris in *Portobello Road* for over twenty-one years," I said uncertainly. "And he seems to be doing all right for himself."

Elise nodded. "I'm sure it's not long to some, but I can't imagine staying that long in one thing." She crossed her long and expensively clad legs. "I have so many other things I'm going to do."

I opened my mouth to answer her, but just at that moment, the door to the green room swung open and Susie breezed in, bringing with her the smell of freshly made coffee from the canteen next door.

"Hiya, you two!" She practically bounded over to the sofa. "Great that you've met each other already."

I shot a glance over to Elise but she wasn't looking at me.

"Ready to roll?" Susie rubbed her hands together excitedly and motioned for us to both follow her.

I hopped up and followed her to the door like an obedient spaniel, casting a look back over my shoulder to see Elise slowly pack her bag up and rise to her feet. She tweaked at her fringe, tucking a few stray hairs back behind her ear, smoothed her hands down her jeans, and sauntered over to where I was still standing, holding the door open for her.

"Thanks, Eight-Year." She winked as she passed me in the doorway and followed Susie down to another room just off one of the main sets.

Feeling slightly miffed at the Eight-Year quip, I followed them both down the corridor, finally entering the room, too. I nodded at Graham, *Portobello Road*'s casting director, sitting on a cream sofa in the corner, glasses perched on the end of his nose.

"Girls, welcome." He rose and gestured for me and Elise to stand on a marker in the centre of the room, just in front of a camera.

"You've met and had a chance to get to know each other a little, I hope?" he asked, sitting back down on the sofa.

Elise and I nodded in unison.

"Okay, so we'd like you to read through the scripts you've been given." Graham waved a hand at a pile of papers he now had on his lap. "Just to make sure you gel, you know?" He raised his hand to the cameraman, waiting patiently behind a camera, to indicate that we were ready to go.

I looked across at Elise and jerked my head, indicating that I was ready when she was. This was something new for me, and I fluttered inside. I'd had screen tests before, but usually with other members of my character's family present, too. This was different. This was just me and her, and that huge, overbearing sense of responsibility hit me in the guts again the minute I heard Elise read her first line.

And she was good. Boy, was she good! As she read her lines, I could see looks of approval passing between Graham and Susie, as if their initial decision to conditionally offer her the part was absolutely the right one. I read really well, too, even if I do say so myself. It was as if Elise was bringing the best out of me. Either that or the quality of the sample script and the whole excitement of my new storyline were giving me a renewed verve.

Whatever it was, the room positively crackled with atmosphere, the hushed silence around us punctuated by our voices, which both echoed round the near-empty studio. They'd thrown us both into the deep end with an argument scenario where Elise and I had to row with each other over a boy, and it was damn good stuff. It was packed with one-liners and quick-fire reposts, and I was psyched at how totally in the zone I was when I was reading it.

Elise was incredible; just as I'd felt her strong presence in the green room earlier, now the whole set was feeling it, too. A runner, passing through on his way to who knows where, stopped in his tracks and stood to the side of the set, listening to her, watching her, mesmerised. I could sense Graham and Susie sitting, engrossed, as

Elise spoke her lines, and the more intense she became, the more passionate and powerful my delivery was, too.

If this was an indication of the sort of stuff I'd be required to do as Jasmine, then I couldn't wait to get filming properly.

❖

"Whoa!" Susie sprang to her feet and walked quickly over to me and Elise, her hands stretched out in front of her. "You… two…were…*amazing*!" She placed a hand on each of our arms and beamed at us.

We'd just finished our screen test after five or so minutes of absolutely spellbindingly solid acting from the pair of us—a scene where no one interrupted us, no one had to prompt us, and no one asked us to read lines again. It was, in short, the perfect single take.

I was elated. It had been the most exciting thing I'd acted out since a one-to-one scene I'd done with my "mother," Bella, six months earlier. That had been good, but this was a hundred times better.

Graham and Susie seemed to think so, too, judging by the looks on their faces. Of course they were elated—Elise would be perfect for the show. She was everything *Portobello Road* was constantly aiming to be: smart, sassy, and confident.

Graham slowly took his glasses off and placed them in his shirt pocket, then got to his feet and slow-clapped Elise and me, while Susie remained rooted to the spot in front of us both, her hands still on our arms.

"Did you feel it, girls?" he asked, coming to stand next to Susie. "I hope so because, my goodness, Susie and I felt it!"

"I loved it, yeah," I said, turning to Elise and raising my eyebrows. "Would we use this script in filming? Because I thought it was amazing stuff."

"We'd use something similar, yes," Susie said. "We wanted to keep the sample as close as possible to what we'd use in the soap itself, to see how you'd both play it."

"Then I can't wait!" Elise said. "If the part is still offered to me, of course." She glanced at Graham.

"Elise, my dear, if I didn't offer you the part after that screen test, I think Susie would take me outside and shoot me right now." Graham rolled his eyes. "I thought you were outstanding."

"You both were," Susie piped in.

"Holly, meet Jasmine's new love interest, Casey Fletcher." Graham walked back to his chair and picked up a file. "In the meantime, here's your scripts for your first scenes together." He wandered back to us, handing us each a blue plastic folder.

"And we'll see you both bright and early Monday morning," Susie said, making for the door. "I can't wait," she added, holding the door open and allowing Graham to pass her before leaving the room herself.

I remained standing in the middle of the room as the camera was wheeled away and off to another part of the studio.

"So how was it for you?" I asked Elise when everyone else had left us.

"It was good, yeah," Elise replied. "You read well."

"So did you," I said truthfully.

Elise shrugged. "I guess," she said airily, walking away.

"Neat writing, huh?" I called to Elise as she wandered over and collected her jacket from the back of a chair.

"Very." She glanced back over her shoulder.

"You excited?" I asked, still holding my script in my hand.

"Yuh-huh," Elise said, shrugging her jacket on and running her hand through her hair.

She reached down and picked up her bag, hauling it over her shoulders. "Anyway, I'm outta here." Elise pulled her mobile from her bag and ran her thumb over the front of it, reading something on the screen. "See you Monday, I guess," she said, lifting the phone to her ear and sauntering from the room, one hand in her jeans pocket, leaving me standing there, feeling deflated after all the intensity and excitement that had gone on before.

CHAPTER THREE

I was pretty gutted at Elise's actions after our screen test, if I'm honest. I was absolutely buzzing from the whole thing, but her muted reaction, shrugging it off and strolling from the room like she'd just finished reading the daily paper after her coffee break, had stung. I was cross with her for diluting the atmosphere when I'd been so keyed up about it all, even if she hadn't meant to.

Her indifference had thrown me, when I—and Graham and Susie—had thought the whole screen test had been outstanding. Before it, I'd been so excited about the storyline, but now I was feeling apprehensive about what Monday would bring. We were going to film our initial scenes together when Jasmine meets Casey for the very first time at university, and it niggled away at me over the weekend as to whether Elise would be more enthusiastic off-camera when the time came.

As it turned out—to my relief—she was more animated when we got together again on that Monday. I'd spent the entire weekend reading my script over and over, pacing up and down my apartment, reading my lines aloud, varying how I said them each time. I felt like a kid about to start at a new school—excited, but nervous at the same time.

And Elise was as brilliant as she'd been three days before. We successfully filmed our first scenes together by lunchtime, and it was as though we'd been acting together all our lives. She was effortless in her delivery of her lines, and if she was nervous on her first day of filming, she sure as hell didn't show it. I thought that we bounced off each other perfectly, just as we'd done before, and I couldn't help but keep getting a thrill of excitement, knowing that we would get to film more scenes like these—and better ones still—in the months ahead.

Kevin had told me that morning that Elise had been offered a twelve-month contract for the show, with a view to extending if she proved a hit with the viewers. He told me, in a tapping-his-nose kind of way, that he and Susie were confident she'd be a sure-fire hit. They both thought she was awesome and would be a real addition to *PR*.

I had to agree, and I told Elise as much that same morning.

"Thanks, yeah, that's a neat thing to say," she said as we wrapped for the day, our very first scenes together in the bag.

We walked down the corridor to our respective dressing rooms. I shared with Bella—and had done for the last three years—and Elise had been allocated a room further down the corridor from mine, sharing with one of the slightly lesser-known actresses on the show. I wished we'd been allocated a room together, though. I figured it would make learning our lines easier and more fun if we were, but The Powers That Be had seen fit to keep us separate.

"You must be pleased, too," I said, "to get the contract signed and sorted."

Elise nodded.

"Kevin told me this morning," I added hastily.

"Yeah, we signed it last Friday after the screen test," Elise replied. She paused. "Listen, you want to come to my room after you've changed?" She jerked her head towards her door down the corridor. "We can go over tomorrow's lines."

Perhaps it was the cute way she jerked her chin, or just how she'd been standing, bag hitched over one shoulder, a hand buried deep in her pocket, looking cool and self-assured. I don't know. But the second she looked at me and asked me to her room, an image of Grace flooded my mind, instantly flustering me.

"Your room?" I mumbled. "Yeah, sure."

I left her briefly and went off to change from Jasmine's on-set clothes back into my own, and then headed straight down to Elise.

I found her already changed and lounging in a small leather chair, idly flicking through a fashion magazine. Her room was neater than mine, but that wasn't a surprise. Bella wasn't the tidiest of people, and it was a frequent source of irritation to me how she was unable to remove empty polystyrene cups from her dressing table or piles of magazines from the soft upholstered sofa that we had in there.

Elise's room was like an oasis of calm and tidiness in comparison. I immediately liked being there.

"So, how long have you been back in England?" I asked as I sat down on the sofa, trying to ignore the sight of her long, jean-clad legs dangling over the side of her chair.

"A few months," Elise said. "I came back just after Christmas."

She wore a loose-fitting top, casual but expensive looking, the colours of which really suited her, and a string of long beads hanging perfectly down the front. Her faded jeans seemed to cling to her legs, and her feet were just socked, the pair of boots she'd been wearing just before, during our filming, discarded on the floor next to her. Added to all this were numerous cloth bracelets and bangles on her wrist, which looked lovely against her still-bronzed skin. Her fantastic LA tan, which suited her so well would, I thought, soon be a thing of the past.

"London weather's not quite what you've been used to, huh?" I asked, thinking about the colour of her arms.

"Not really, no."

"How was it? LA, I mean," I asked. "I've never been."

"It was okay, yeah," she said.

We didn't speak for a second, and I started racking my brains for something to say to her or ask her. I'd finally gotten round to Googling Elise over the weekend—of course I had! Are you telling me you wouldn't have done the same thing?!—but it hadn't told me that much, which was annoying. All I'd managed to find out was that she'd been acting since she was fifteen, had done some youth theatre, a few adverts on TV, and that she'd left the UK for the States a week after her eighteenth birthday. I couldn't find any websites that would tell me anything of her time in LA other than that she'd tried her hand at the pilot season, so I figured it hadn't been a successful time there. That would at least explain why she'd come home after only fifteen months.

"I've never been," I said.

"You said," Elise replied, the hint of a smile on her face.

"And, you, uh, you're getting on okay with everything here?" I asked, flustered by her nice smile. "It's kind of straight into it here, hardly any rehearsals, isn't it?"

"Yeah." Elise looked down at her bag as she heard her phone beep, then slowly leant over to retrieve it.

"I guess it can be a bit strange coming back and starting on a new show, so I understand if you're feeling a bit overwhelmed by it all."

"Yeah, I'm getting on okay," she said pleasantly, looking briefly at her phone, and then putting it back in her bag. "And I'm not overwhelmed, no."

Why was she making me ramble on? My eyes were pulled towards her legs again, so I immediately glanced around her room, looking at some photos pinned to her mirror and the few Good Luck cards still scattered around her table.

"So you live close to here?" Elise asked, jolting me from my thoughts of her legs.

"South Bank," I replied. "Near The Eye."

"Nice." Elise nodded her head approvingly. "I'm renting myself a place further up the Piccadilly line. Guess it'll be a while before I can afford something on the South Bank, huh?" She grinned lazily at me, crossing her legs at the ankle.

"I've not been there long," I mumbled, suddenly embarrassed.

"You live alone?" Elise asked. "Or with someone?"

"Alone," I replied simply. "You?"

"Alone as well." She paused. "No boyfriend, then?"

My face coloured, either from the question or from her sexy eyebrow—I wasn't sure which. "No boyfriend, no," I said lightly. "You?"

I saw Elise's face cloud slightly. "No," she said firmly. She thought for a moment. "Better that way, I always say," she said.

"You think?" I asked.

"I know," she said, hauling her legs over the side of the chair and sitting upright. "Weren't we supposed to be going over our lines for tomorrow?"

Her sudden change in attitude surprised me, our conversation about boyfriends apparently over.

"Lines, yes," I said, slightly flummoxed. "How do you think it went this morning, by the way?"

"I thought it was great," Elise said slowly. "You?"

"Yeah," I said. "I'm very happy with what we did."

"Although…" Elise hesitated.

"Although?" I asked.

She looked thoughtful. "Sometimes you seemed a bit, um, stilted, y'know?"

I put my head to one side and frowned. "Really?" I laughed. "That's a new one on me, I have to say!"

"Like, you didn't get it." Elise shifted in her chair.

"Didn't get what?"

"The vibe."

"Jasmine and Casey's vibe, you mean?"

"Yeah."

What the…? How had this gone from polite conversation to a criticism in ten seconds?

"Of course I get their vibe," I said tersely. "I'm so into this storyline, you've no idea! I've known about Jasmine and Casey for ages. I've been living and breathing them for weeks now. I go to bed thinking about them, I wake up thinking about them."

Elise nodded. "But sometimes this morning I thought you were a bit hesitant in the delivery of your lines," she said carefully. "That's all I meant."

"Hesitant?" I heard my voice rise an octave.

"Hesitant," Elise repeated. "But that might just be your technique, I don't know." She shrugged, almost dismissively.

"Well, I thought I did a good job with it, if I'm honest." I shifted uncomfortably in my seat.

Brilliant! So one minute we're being friendly, talking about apartments and boyfriends, and the next she's slating my acting ability. Exactly who was this girl again?

"I wasn't being critical," Elise said, as if reading my mind. "You asked me how I thought it went, so I told you." She looked cautiously at me.

"You said I can't act." I looked at her incredulously, immediately thinking about Googling Elise again. Sod trying to find out what work she'd done—now I wanted to find some reviews of her work, and I just wanted to read the crap ones.

"No, I didn't," Elise said.

"Yes, you did. You said I was stilted," I said, trying not to sound hurt.

"You were sometimes," Elise replied bluntly. "I didn't say you couldn't act, though. That's totally different."

"And hesitant." I cleared my throat. "You said I was hesitant."

"Mm-hmm."

"No one's ever complained before," I said, folding my arms across my chest defensively.

"What, not once in eight years?" She tucked a strand of hair behind her ear. "I'm not complaining, Holly." Regret flickered across her face. "Sorry if it sounded that way."

"How else was it supposed to sound?" I stared at her, open-mouthed.

"I just said you were a little stilted when it comes to acting opposite Casey." Elise started inspecting her nails. "But if you say you're not like that with other characters, then maybe it's just Casey." She looked at me, head to one side. "But I never said that you couldn't act."

"You so did!" I smiled tightly. Inside I was fuming.

"I so did not." Elise slowly raised her eyebrow again, totally throwing me.

"And...and...as for not getting the so-called *vibe*," I blustered, dropping my eyes, "well, I think we bounce really well off each other, to be fair."

I wanted to let it go. I did. I just couldn't seem to. An actor's worst criticism is for stilted acting. I'd never—*never*—been accused of such a thing, and it stung. I paused and stared down at my feet, not wanting to make any more eye contact with her. I was unsure how to answer her now, the hurt making me tearful, and I desperately didn't want to cry in front of Elise.

I waited for her to reply but she didn't.

"Well, I guess I'd better go work on that, then, rather than going over tomorrow's lines, huh?" I finally said, when it was clear she wasn't going to respond. I lifted myself away from her sofa and made for the door, regretting that I'd even bothered to come and try to be nice to her.

Elise, to my annoyance, still didn't reply straight away. Instead, she picked her magazine up from her lap and started flicking through it again.

"Okay," she finally said.

Nothing else.

Just…okay.

I figured that was her way of letting me know the conversation was over, so with a final look her way, I left her room. Outside in the corridor, I wandered a little way down towards my own room, then stopped and leant against the wall, thinking about everything she'd just said.

The cheek of it! So she thought I was stilted, did she? Didn't she realise if I was—*which I wasn't*—then it had to be because of her. I'd never been stilted with Bella or anyone else I'd ever acted with, so then it had to be Elise's fault, didn't it? I clenched and unclenched my jaw, replaying our conversation, saying her words over and over. Yes, that was it. It was Elise. Her superior attitude, unfriendliness, and detachment from me, right from day one, were making any opportunity I had to connect with her virtually impossible.

I turned to return to her room to tell her just that, but something held me back.

And *hesitant*? How could she call me hesitant? What did that mean, anyway? Was she suggesting I was unsure of how to deliver my lines or that I didn't know how to act? Of course I knew how to act!

I stared at her closed door a while longer, imagining her sitting so smugly behind it and, still bristling, quickly walked away from her dressing room and back down the corridor before I changed my mind and barged back in there to give her a piece of my mind. While I walked away from the studios, away from Elise, I vowed to myself that I would have tomorrow's scenes so damn perfected she wouldn't have another chance to tell me she thought I was stilted. Or hesitant. Or a bad actor.

Just who the hell did Elise bloody Manford think she was, anyway?

CHAPTER FOUR

I went straight to my dressing room when I arrived back at the studios the next day, pleased that Bella hadn't arrived yet, and sat down at my table, looking in the mirror. I stared hard at myself—at Jasmine—suddenly dreading having to see Elise again and getting angry all over again, despite calming down overnight after giving myself another talking-to. How dare she suggest I wasn't a good actress? She'd only been working with me for a day, and she thought she knew me well enough to be so disparaging? How *fucking* dare she.

I glared at my reflection, detesting Elise and everything about her. So she'd been in America for fifteen months? Big deal. So she was confident and beautiful? Big deal. I was the established one here, not her. I was the one who lived and breathed *PR*, not her.

How was it that someone I didn't even know two weeks ago could have the ability to make me feel so insecure about everything, all of a sudden? Would she analyse every little detail of my acting now, trying to find fault with the way I said certain lines or the way I stood when I delivered those lines? If that wouldn't make me hesitant, then what would?

I breathed in slowly, staring at my face looking back at me in the mirror.

Just listen to me!

What was it about her that wound me up so much?

Okay, so she was not terribly communicative, and had—I thought—so far been damned rude to me, but there was something else niggling away at me that suggested there was more to it than just that. I wished I could put my finger on it, but I couldn't. Was I jealous of her? Did I secretly want to be just like her? Perhaps it was because she was everything I thought I wasn't—oozing with confidence and sassiness—and didn't appear to give a damn about anything or anyone as long as she was okay.

But, I figured, as long as Kevin and Susie and anyone else who had a say in my acting was happy, then Elise and her stupid comments could just go and bugger off. I also figured her attitude and rudeness were her lookout, not mine. We'd both had our new scripts for the coming weeks delivered to our rooms that morning, and now I was more determined than ever not to let her get to me anymore. Jasmine and Casey had to work, and so Holly and Elise had to work, too, despite all the negative feelings I had towards her.

If only it was that easy…

❖

"Okay, scene four, take one." Our director Stuart Grant pulled his pen out from behind his ear and pointed it at Elise. "And action."

"So, Jasmine." Elise picked up her empty prop cup and drank from it. "You up for it?"

"The gig?" I circled my finger round the edge of my own prop cup. "If you're going, then I might go, yeah."

"For real?" Elise looked over her cup at me. "I'd like it if you did."

It was Wednesday; three workdays since Elise had joined us. Now here we were, filming Jasmine and Casey scenes on the set that doubled as their university, talking over coffee and offering viewers subtle hints that the pair were growing closer.

"For real," I repeated. "Yes." I opened my mouth to say my next line but stopped as Elise held her hand up.

"Cut." Stuart jerked his head towards Elise. "Problem?"

"She said *yes*," Elise said. "*Yeah* would have been better."

"You think?" I asked, frowning.

"I do think," Elise said. "Yeah." She emphasised the yeah.

"Okay, from Casey's *I'd like it if you did*, please." Stuart made a winding motion with his hand. "Action."

I stared at Elise and spoke my lines, adding my *yeah* without taking my eyes from hers.

"I'm glad, Jas," Elise said, not taking her eyes from mine, either. "I like hanging out with you, you know?"

"Well that's fortunate," I replied, suddenly forgetting my lines. "I…I like…"

I sat back as Elise held her hand up again.

"Cut." Stuart's voice was quiet. "*Fortunate*, Holly?"

"No one says fortunate unless they want to sound like the Queen." Elise leant back and ran her hands through her hair. "The line was *That's awesome. I like hanging out with you, too.*"

"I know what the line was," I said. "I just had a mental block."

"So try to unblock it," she offered unhelpfully. She leant over the table towards me. "And maybe when Jasmine's talking to Casey, she could maintain a bit more eye contact."

"I thought I just was."

"Only briefly," Elise said. "I think there needs to be more eye contact throughout, to be honest."

"Okay," I replied sarcastically. "Anything else, while we're at it?"

"Maybe lighten up a little." Elise shrugged. "Jasmine *is* supposed to fancy Casey, after all. It's not all coming from Casey by now."

"From Casey's last line, please." Stuart tapped his pen on his clipboard. "Say your line, Holly, then push your plate over to offer Casey the fries."

On my cue, I delivered my line perfectly, pushing my plate over towards Elise until Stuart indicated that the scene had been shot successfully.

"Okay, that's a wrap, thank you, ladies." He grabbed his portfolio and gestured to Louis, his assistant, to follow him from this set to the next one. "Back just after lunch, please," he called to Elise and me over his shoulder as he left. "If we could get the kitchen scenes filmed before the day's out, that would be good."

I jerked my head in acknowledgement, but my heart sank. An afternoon full of scenes with Elise didn't exactly fill me with excited anticipation, especially after all of that.

With Stuart gone and everyone else on set dispersing, I got up from the table and walked away, brushing past Elise on my way out, bristling with irritation and indignation.

"That took longer than I thought it would," Elise said breezily, following me as I headed for the door to the main corridor.

Without answering, I yanked the door open, not bothering to hold it open for Elise. I got a certain satisfaction at hearing it close and open again a second later, knowing that I'd achieved my goal of letting it shut in her face.

I'd been nothing but nice to her all morning, despite still being annoyed with her for Monday's comments, but all she seemed to want to do was bring me down. I'd had enough of it—and of her.

I headed down the corridor towards the canteen for lunch, just wanting to get away from her. I was aware of Elise's footsteps just behind me and tried to speed up, but however fast I walked, she just kept walking right behind me.

"Something bothering you, Holly?" Elise's voice rang out down the corridor.

"Really? You think?" I said over my shoulder, turning the corner and practically smashing my way through the fire door that separated corridors. Again, I didn't bother holding the door open for Elise, and yes, again I was pleased when I heard it slam and immediately open again.

"Wanna talk about it?" Elise was still behind me.

"Nope."

"I think we should."

I stopped in the middle of the corridor and swung round to face her. "Okay. Did you have to be so condescending?" I hissed.

"When?" Elise asked, frowning.

"Just now. In recording."

She looked perplexed. "You're talking about when I suggested you might like to loosen up a bit?" Elise suddenly looked amused. "You were playing Jasmine like some tight-arsed spinster, Holly!"

"Bullshit!" I lowered my voice as one of the lighting guys came past us.

"You thought that was condescending?" A hint of a smile tugged at her lips. "What's patronising about offering a little advice?"

"As if it wasn't bad enough you telling me I couldn't act, you go one better today and tell me—in front of everyone—how you think I should be playing Jasmine!" I was practically shaking with rage by now; the look of barely concealed amusement on Elise's face wasn't helping. I glared at her. "Were you there when Jasmine found out her uncle was trying to kill her? No. Were you there when she was trapped in the house fire? No. Were you there when she—"

"For the hundredth time, I didn't say you couldn't act," Elise interrupted. "I'm sorry if you've misunderstood me."

"I've been doing this shizz since I was this high," I said, holding my hand out above the ground. "So I don't need you to be telling me how to play Jasmine, okay?"

"It was just advice, Holly, that's all." Elise held my gaze, making me uncomfortable.

"And does this *advice* extend to pretty much telling me how you think Jasmine thinks? Or how Jasmine speaks?"

"Nothing wrong with a bit of flexibility." Elise half laughed.

"And there's no need to laugh at me," I said indignantly.

"I'm not." Elise looked down at the floor then slowly back up to me. "You're kinda sweet when you're angry. It's hard not to smile."

"I'm not angry!" I blurted. "And I'm not sweet!"

"You are," Elise said, leaning on the corridor wall, her arms folded. "And…you are."

I stared at her, mouth slightly open, totally flummoxed. "Anyway," I stuttered, "I've been playing Jasmine since I was twelve years old so I think I probably know her just a teensy bit better than you, don't you?"

"Now who's being patronising?" Elise asked, one amused eyebrow raised.

"I'm not," I said slowly. "I'm just telling you like it is."

"Well, that's me told then, isn't it?" Elise said. Another twitch of amusement on her face as she said it made me feel funny inside this time, rather than annoyed.

She pulled herself away from the wall and walked past me, brushing so closely that our arms bumped. I watched her saunter off down the corridor, then hastily looked away again as she glanced back at me, the look of amusement still on her face, before disappearing around the corner and out of sight.

I was livid. Worse, I was livid about being livid. How was it she was able to wind me up so easily, when I barely even knew her yet? Everything about her just oozed superiority and contempt, and at that moment I knew I should loathe her, but there was something about the way she'd been standing and smiling at me and telling me I looked sweet that…

I shook my head angrily. Sod being sweet. I knew my character inside out, and I sure didn't need some smart-arse like Elise Manford coming in and offering her so-called advice.

She could just go to hell.

❖

Not wanting to go to my dressing room, knowing that I'd stew over things until I was called back on set that afternoon, I grabbed myself a coffee and a sandwich from the canteen and made my way to the green room instead, figuring it would be good to chill out for an hour or so. Secretly I was hoping someone would be in there that I could blare off to, however immature and petulant that might have been, but I didn't care. I was in that kind of mood, thanks to Elise.

I was in luck. Bella was already sitting on the sofa, nursing a steaming plastic cup of coffee, her glasses perched on the end of her nose as she read the latest gardening magazine.

"Hey!" she said cheerfully, looking over her glasses at me when I entered the room.

"Hi, Ma," I replied, as I always did when I saw Bella.

Bella Hamilton was the sort of person who loved life and was everyone's absolute best friend. She'd played my on-screen mother, Anna Hunter, since we'd both joined the show eight years earlier, and had become as close off-screen as we were on-screen. She was my surrogate mother, there was no doubt about that, filling the gap that my own mother had left when my parents had decided to relocate to the countryside from the suburbs, when I'd finally moved into my own apartment in London.

My parents loathed London. They hated the noise, the smell, the crowds, the transport system—everything—and did their utmost to avoid coming to the capital at all costs. My hectic work schedule meant visits to them were few and far between. Bella was, essentially, the only family left close to me, and I loved her almost as if she were my own mother.

"Whoever invented coffee from a machine needs to be shot," Bella now said, waving her cup at me and spilling a drop of coffee down her front. "Bugger it!" She frowned and hastily dabbed at it with her sleeve.

She looked across towards me and shrugged. "Ready for another afternoon at the coal face?" she asked, still dabbing away.

"I guess," I replied, picking my way around the tables and sitting down on the sofa next to her.

If I'm truthful, my second spat with Elise had really gotten to me, and I'd thought about it more than I wanted to. I didn't know why, though, but eventually put it down to the fact that I'd been hurt more than annoyed with her because I'd thought we should be getting on better now, and I didn't understand why she would want to do it to me again. The first squabble that we'd had had irritated me; the one that we'd had this morning had just hurt me, plain and simple.

"Enthusiasm. Love it." Bella gently bumped my arm, spilling another drop of coffee down her top. "For the love of…!" She looked down at her jumper.

"I'm just finding work a bit tough-going at the moment, Bella," I said, getting my script out of my bag and putting it on my lap.

"Heavy workload?" Bella looked sympathetic. "I must admit when I saw your schedule coming up, I thought it was a bit full-on."

"No, the scripts I can cope with." I idly flicked the papers. "It's just, well…I don't know."

"Wanna talk about it?" Bella lowered her voice, aware that a few others were lurking around nearby.

"I don't know." I sighed.

"Is it the new girl?" Bella slurped noisily at her coffee. "I don't see her around in here too much."

"She seems to keep herself to herself a lot," I replied. "In her dressing room mainly."

"You two don't hang out together, then?"

"Nuh-uh." I shook my head. "Not at all."

"Oh." Bella took another slurp from her coffee and grimaced. "It's still early days, Holly," she said, picking up a swizzle stick from the table in front of her and giving her coffee another stir.

"I wondered that," I said. "Okay, I know she's only been here five minutes, but I don't feel like I know her at all. It's almost like she has barriers up."

"So she's shy. Everyone finds starting a new job daunting."

"She doesn't strike me as shy or in the least bit daunted, that's the thing." I watched as Bella licked her swizzle stick and tossed it back onto the table. "She strikes me as…well…a bit superior."

"Hasn't she just come back from the States?" Bella asked. "I thought I heard someone mention that."

"Yeah, LA." I nodded. "Tried to find work there but didn't, so that's why she came back."

"Maybe she sees this as a bit of a backwards step, then," Bella said, waving as Rory Stone, who played her ex-husband—my father—in the show, entered the room. "Maybe she's embarrassed that she failed to crack America and has had to come back to a teatime soap."

"There's nothing wrong with that!" I said, defensively.

"Of course not, pet." Bella patted my arm. "But, well, the money wouldn't be as good, the weather *sure* wouldn't be as good, and, let's face it, isn't it every actor's dream to have a crack at making it over there?"

"I guess," I said, probably more sullenly than was necessary. "It's just that sometimes she makes me feel a bit small, as well, to be honest."

"How?"

"Just picking me up on my acting and stuff."

"Such as?" Bella looked kindly at me over her glasses.

"She said I couldn't act, Bella!" I blurted, sounding about ten years old.

"She said *what*?" Bella put her coffee down and leant closer to me.

"Well, not in so many words," I backtracked. "But she said I was stilted and hesitant."

"Of which you are neither," Bella said warmly. "Perhaps you need to go and have a word with Kevin? Or Susie?"

"I don't want to," I said. "Not just yet." I paused, watching as Bella took her coffee and drank from it again. "She's condescending as well. She seems to think it's weird I've been here for eight years." I laughed quietly, feeling a bit daft.

"Look, I can't comment on Elise 'cos I've not worked with her yet," Bella said, always the diplomat. "But I guess just see how things go on, and if you're still not happy, then go speak to Kevin or Susie about it, even if you're not keen to get them involved."

"I don't really like her, Bella," I suddenly said, an image of her dimpled smile drifting into my mind and back out again. "And I've got to like her, or none of our scenes will be realistic." I thought for a moment. "I was so excited when they told me they'd be getting in a new person for Jasmine to play opposite," I said, "and I liked her the first day I met her, but well, now I'm not so sure." I leant towards Bella and lowered my voice. "Between you and me, she irritates me a bit."

"And between you and me," Bella lowered her voice, too, "Robbie doesn't like her, either. But you didn't hear that from me."

Robbie Turner played my on-screen older brother, Tim. I liked him a lot. He was the sort of guy who was up for a good time, like, *all* the time, if you know what I mean. He was lovely, too, always friendly, always laughing, and always ready for a night out, whatever day of the week, whatever his schedule. I knew that with Robbie, if I told him something in secret, he'd take that secret to the grave with him. I also knew that he was the most laid-back guy I'd ever known. So if Bella said Elise got on his nerves, too, then Elise really must be an irritating person because it sure as hell took a lot to get Robbie riled.

"Robbie's not so keen, either?" I began to feel better.

"Well, not on the acting front because he hasn't done any scenes with her yet." Bella tapped the side of her nose. "But he told me he doesn't like her attitude." Bella paused. "Probably because he asked her out, and—"

"Already?" I interrupted Bella, my voice sounding strangely thick. The mention of Robbie asking Elise out pricked sharply at me. "He didn't waste any time, did he?"

"That's Robbie for you." Bella laughed. "Anyway, he got very—and I mean *very*—short shrift."

"I can well imagine," I mumbled.

Bella looked at me, like my own mother would. "Have you actually tried to get to know Elise?"

"I have, yes." I sighed. "We've chatted in her dressing room."

"Well, that's a start." Bella smiled.

"And that's when she told me she thought I was a bad actor." I gave an ironic laugh.

"Which you're not sure if she meant as it sounded," she said gently.

"How else would she mean it?" I scratched irritably at my hair. The thought of what Elise had said was getting me tetchy again.

"Have you tried to get to know her outside of work?" Bella asked, ignoring my question. "Invited her out for a welcome drink?"

I shook my head.

"How about a night out? With us all?" She raised her eyebrows.

"Well, I…"

Bella gave me another motherly look. "Perhaps she needs to come out with us lot so we can get to know her better away from the workplace, and she can get to know us," she reflected.

"Maybe," I replied, feeling bad.

"So, then, let's invite the poor girl for a night out." Bella's eyes sparkled. "It's been ages since we all went out together. It'll be the perfect excuse."

I looked down at my feet. "Now I feel awful," I said, giving an embarrassed sideways glance to Bella, "for just moaning on about her without actually trying to do something about it."

"Don't." Bella patted my arm. "Sometimes it just takes a mother to see these things."

Chapter Five

A drink?" Elise raised her eyebrows.

"Yeah," I said airily. "We could all go up West Friday night. We thought it would be a nice way for us all to get to know each other."

I smiled amiably over to Elise as we walked from the set that same afternoon. We had just wrapped for the day, having successfully filmed all our kitchen scenes, much to Stuart's relief and satisfaction, and we were now both walking from the studios back towards our cars.

"After your little show in the corridor this morning I'm surprised you want anything to do with me," Elise said slowly.

"Show?" I stopped dead.

"Show, tantrum, whatever."

"It wasn't a tantrum, Elise," I said tersely, starting to walk again.

"You're getting grumpy again, aren't you?" Elise grinned. "Cute."

I breathed out sharply and remembered Bella's advice. "So, do you want to come out with us on Friday?" I asked, ignoring her last comment.

"Of course!" Elise pulled a scrap of paper from her bag and scribbled down her mobile number onto it. "Just let me know where and when and I'll be there."

She handed me the piece of paper, then yanked the fire-exit door open and left the building, me following close behind her. "I'm looking forward to it already, Eight-Year," she called back over her shoulder as she walked away from me.

I watched her as she walked across the car park and got into her car, surprised but suddenly ludicrously pleased that she'd want to come out with us. I dug around in my bag for my keys and wandered towards my own car, parked some way from hers. I heard Elise's door slam, then listened as she tried to start the engine, hearing it turning over and over but not fire. I paused, casting a glance back to where Elise was parked, and waited, hearing her engine labour more and more.

Finally I put my keys back in my bag and walked over to her, tapping on her window and gesturing to her to bring her window down. "Sounds like your starter motor's gone," I said, leaning forwards slightly, trying to sound like I knew what I was talking about. "I think turning it over and over's just going to make it even worse."

"Shit!" Elise brought her window back up and turned the key back towards her, pulling it roughly from the ignition. She sat in her car a while, just staring out the front window as if thinking about what to do, then opened the door and got out, cursing under her breath.

"Guess you'll have to call the breakdown people out," I offered.

She flicked a glance to me then away again. "I don't have breakdown." She sighed. "Just never got round to it when I came back here." She looked back towards me sheepishly.

"You'll need a tow to the nearest garage then," I said, fishing my phone out of my bag.

"Great!" Elise leant into the car and grabbed her bag from the passenger seat. "I have to be in Surrey by six and it's quarter past five already." She slammed the car door.

"How long would the train take?" I asked, looking at my phone to try to find the phone number of the nearest garage.

"Too long." Elise started rooting around in her bag for her phone, too. "Guess I'll have to cancel Surrey, then. That'll be one very upset boy." She cursed again.

"Oh?"

"My nephew's fourth birthday party." Elise shrugged and flicked a finger over the screen of her phone, presumably finding a phone number.

Elise had a nephew? Why did I find that so sweet?

"I see." I paused.

"Stupid piece of junk." Elise turned and kicked at her front tyre, then grimaced. "Why today of all days, huh? Why?" She jabbed at her phone and held it to her ear.

"Wait…" I touched her arm, the physical contact sending a curious but pleasant jolt through my hand. "I can take you to Surrey."

Elise pulled the phone slowly from her ear and cut her call. "You'd take me?" she asked.

"Uh-huh." I nodded, turning back to my car. "But we'll have to get a wriggle on if we're to get there for six."

"Are you sure?"

"'Course." I started to walk back to my car. "C'mon."

As I approached my car, a wry thought came to me. Elise might have irritated me that morning, but I figured it was times like this you had to be adult enough to put your animosity to one side and step up to the plate. I thought about my own niece in Scotland, five years old herself, and of how crestfallen she'd be if her favourite auntie were to miss her party. I glanced back at Elise coming across the car park after me and figured, whatever I thought of her and whatever she thought of me, she was still a little boy's favourite auntie, too.

"It's very good of you," Elise now said as she approached my car. She looked hesitantly at me, as if she wanted to say something else, but instead she just came round the passenger side of my car as I gesticulated with my head that the door was open and she could get in.

"Head for the motorway and I'll tell you which junction to get off at, okay?" Elise said as she buckled herself in and I turned my car around and exited the studio car park.

We drove on in silence for about the first five minutes or so, me trying to ignore my acute awareness of her presence in the car, of her closeness to me, and of her lean legs kicked out in front of her. We exchanged a few comments about the weather, but other than that, we were quiet. It was that awkward, empty silence when you know that you're both struggling to think of something to say but can't manage to come up with a single thing.

"I'm glad I've got a chance to talk to you again today, actually," Elise suddenly said, finally puncturing the quiet in the car as we approached the motorway.

"Oh yes?" I glanced up in my rear-view mirror but not at her.

"Mm," she said, looking straight ahead out of the windscreen.

I waited, but all I heard was the droning of my tyres on the road.

"I just wanted to, well, to say sorry, I s'pose, about being funny with you this morning." Elise shifted slightly in her seat. "And I wanted to say sorry for saying you'd had a tantrum. That wasn't the most diplomatic thing to say."

"Okay," I said cautiously. "Well, apology accepted."

And what about saying again earlier that I looked cute when I was annoyed?

Elise didn't say anything more for a few minutes. Instead, she turned her head and stared out the window, watching the scenery speed past us while I drove on, thinking that I should say something in response but not being able to. I was just starting to get uncomfortable, telling myself I really should try to make conversation with her, when Elise spoke again.

"I think I irritate you, don't I?" she said, turning her head to look at me this time. "When I suggest things to you during takes and things."

I stared ahead, concentrating on the road, but inside I was churning. So at least she was aware that she annoyed me; that was a start.

"There are ways and means of telling someone something, I think," I said. It was the most tactful thing I could think of to say.

"And I guess I haven't really done much to endear myself to you—or anyone else—have I?"

I didn't know how to answer that one, but before I could think of a suitable response, she spoke again.

"I've been told before I'm a bit full-on," she said, reaching down into her bag and pulling her phone out. "And I know it can get people's backs up, so I guess what I'm saying is that I'm sorry I'm the way I am." She bent her head down and started texting, so I wasn't sure if she was expecting me to reply or whether I should just let her carry on texting in peace.

"You're not full-on," I finally said. "But I think you're not afraid to tell someone what you think of them." I paused. "Or tell them what you think of their acting," I added.

"I do like working with you," she suddenly said, putting her phone in her lap and gazing back out the window.

"Really?" I replied, surprised.

"Really," she said, briefly catching my eye then looking away again.

I looked back at her, expecting to see her smirking, but she was still gazing out the window again, her face expressionless.

"But you said I was stilted and hesitant," I said, adding a small laugh.

"Oh, not that again." Elise turned and looked at me, exasperated.

I didn't like the instant change in her attitude and, wanting to keep her in a good mood, didn't reply. Instead, I asked her how long until our exit junction and then drove on in silence again.

My mind was turning over and over. I was totally dumbstruck by what Elise had just said to me, so much so that I began to think I'd misheard her. She'd stunned me by her confession because she'd shown nothing in her words or approach to me over the last week to suggest anything like that, so to hear her actually tell me had shaken me.

"Next junction, then right round the roundabout." Elise's voice jolted me from my thoughts.

She directed me through a one-way system and down some side streets before we arrived at a smart detached house down a leafy avenue. I could see loads of brightly coloured balloons tied to the bushes in the drive and a small banner shouting *Happy Birthday Toby* stretched diagonally across the front door.

"Time to get high on birthday cake and Coca Cola." Elise unbuckled her seat belt and reached down for her bag by her feet. "I'd invite you in but…"

"Not at all," I said. "I wouldn't expect you to."

She turned and looked at me, maintaining proper eye contact for a good few seconds. "Thanks for this," she said. "I'm really very, very grateful."

"No probs," I replied, smiling. "You okay for a lift back home?"

"My father's down from Manchester, so I'll sweet-talk him into bringing me back," Elise said. "He'll grumble about driving into London and the congestion charge like he always does, but he'll do it for me." She opened the car door. "Like he always does." She laughed.

I watched her walk up the drive and disappear through the opened door without turning back to look at me. I sat in my car for a moment, suddenly feeling a little bit flat, before reversing back out of the drive and heading down the avenue again and back towards the motorway.

I replayed our conversation over in my head as I drove, thinking what a curious thing it had been for Elise to suddenly apologise out of the blue. I guess it was even more surprising to me that she must have actually been thinking about our past conversations, just as I had done, if she felt the need to apologise for what she'd said. Embarrassment coloured my cheeks at the memory of being so offhand with her, both that morning and before. Perhaps I'd been paranoid and maybe Elise hadn't been critical of anything I was doing, despite me taking everything she'd said to heart. Perhaps Bella had been right, and I'd simply misunderstood what Elise had been trying to tell me.

And she enjoyed working with me as well! What was that all about? Nothing—and I mean *nothing*—in her behaviour or attitude towards me had ever hinted at anything other than she didn't think much of me, and yet, there she was, telling me she enjoyed working with me. Did that mean she actually liked me? I was convinced that she probably disliked me as much as I disliked her, but her saying that was now making me question everything I'd thought about her. It was baffling, to say the least.

By the time I entered the outskirts of London I must have replayed our conversation over a hundred times and had finally made up my mind to have a proper heart-to-heart with her about it all. Bella could be right about that as well; maybe Elise wasn't as bad as I'd made her out to be, and I just needed to give her a chance.

CHAPTER SIX

Friday, was a day off for me, thanks to our good work Wednesday afternoon which had put us ahead of schedule. After a brief visit to my parents in the countryside, I returned to London the same afternoon, surprisingly refreshed from having a whole day away from the capital.

While I'd been away at my parents', I'd texted Bella, Rory, Robbie, Elise, and anyone else I could think of to arrange a time and place to meet up that night for our planned drinks, so that we could get to know Elise better, and had decided on a club called Bobby's somewhere out in Mayfair. It was a favourite haunt of the *PR* cast and was very generous in doling out free drinks to us all. We loved it there and always made the most of their hospitality. Well, wouldn't you? You're only young once, right?

"Free drinks?" Elise asked when we arrived that night. She followed me out of our cab and into the dark environment of the club. "As in *totally free*?"

She was dressed up to the nines—we all were—wearing a tight jade-green minidress and killer heels, which made her taller than she already was. She looked amazing, towering over me as we weaved our way over towards the bar behind Bella and Robbie.

"Totally, one hundred percent free," I said. "Perks of the job."

We arrived at the bar to find someone from our group had already arranged drinks for us all. Elise took the glass of red wine that was handed to her by Bella and raised it to me. "To Jasmine and Casey," she said, taking a sip from it.

"Jasmine and Casey!" I said, mirroring her action with my glass.

I watched, amused, as Elise drained her drink and looked hopefully at the barman again. When he didn't notice her, she placed her empty glass on the bar and turned back to me. "Dance?"

"Sure." I put my drink down. "You two coming?" I draped my arm round Bella's shoulders and looked at her and Robbie. "Or is this one a bit too fast for you, Bella?"

"You think a forty-something can't keep up?" Bella reached up and grabbed my hand that was around her shoulder. "Watch and learn, kid. Watch and learn."

Laughing, the four of us headed to the dance floor, getting sucked into the swell of people in the darkness. Elise and I managed to get separated from Bella and Robbie, swept along amongst a wave of other clubbers dancing around us. It was only when the music finally slowed down, after around fifteen minutes of constant fast-paced techno music, and when I was just starting to get too hot, that Elise suggested we go back to the bar for another drink.

Elise suddenly grabbed my hand and veered off to the left when she saw Bella already sitting at the bar, perched precariously on a high stool and chatting to the barman. I glanced briefly at Bella, thinking I ought to join her, but followed Elise instead.

"You don't want to sit with the others?" I leant against the bar and jerked my head towards Bella.

"Thought it would be neat to chat with you alone." Elise shrugged. She lifted her head slowly to a barman, effortlessly catching his eye and summoning him over to us, even though he appeared to be busy with other customers. "Got any champagne?" she cheekily asked when he got to us. "Whatever you've got, we're not fussy." She looked at me from the corner of her eye. "Especially if it's free," she whispered.

I watched as the barman fetched a bottle from the chiller, popped it, then poured us a long glass each, the bubbles rushing precariously to the rims of the glasses before settling down again.

"You look warm." Elise's eyes roamed my face, making me self-consciously flick my hair away from my forehead.

"Dancing always makes me hot." My cheeks burned even more as I spoke, wishing I'd said something less ridiculous.

Two glasses of champagne appeared in front of us.

"To Jasmine and Casey," Elise said, lifting her glass to me.

"We already did that, didn't we?" I smiled, taking a small sip, loving how the bubbles pricked my tongue.

"With wine, though," Elise said. "That doesn't really count." She studied me over the top of her glass. "You enjoy playing Jasmine, don't you?"

"I do," I replied truthfully. "I can't imagine her ever not being in my life."

"You're so right for the part of her," Elise said. "I think you totally nail her."

A sound bite of our first conversation when Elise suggested I was stilted entered my head, and I resisted the urge to respond as I remembered her reaction in the car when I'd mentioned it after another compliment from her.

"Thank you," I said instead.

"I mean it." Elise stared down at her glass, running her finger round the edge of it. "You're a lot like Jasmine, you know."

"What, goofy and a bit silly?" I laughed, taking another sip.

"No," Elise said, watching me. "Just nice." She began popping the bubbles from the surface of her champagne. "I think Jasmine's very brave as well," she said quietly. "Casey, too."

"Brave?"

"To both know what they want and not be afraid to get it."

"You mean because they want each other?" I asked, struck by the sudden seriousness of her tone.

"Mm." She studied me carefully. "It must be nice to have the confidence to go for something—or someone—that you want."

"You don't strike me as lacking in too much confidence," I said. "I mean that in the nicest possible way, of course."

Elise dragged her eyes from mine. "Nah, I have buckets of confidence when it comes to my work," she said, still popping her bubbles, "just not so much when it comes to other things."

"Such as?"

"Never mind." Elise drank the rest of her champagne back. "Alcohol makes me think too much sometimes."

❖

Long after Bella had left and Robbie had made out with his third girl of the evening, Elise and I finally fell out of the club at around four the next morning, blinking groggily at the hazy early morning light that took our eyes ages to adjust to. As we made our way unsteadily down the road, still busy with all the West End revellers, I was aware of a flashlight going off just to my right. I swung round and saw some guy standing less than twenty feet from us, with a camera in his hands. As I looked at him again, another flashlight went off, temporarily blinding me.

I stopped in my tracks and looked in bemusement at him, then turned and looked at Elise.

"Did we just get papped?" I asked her.

"I think we did, yeah." Elise peered into the semi-darkness.

I looked at the pair of us, looking slightly dishevelled and more than a bit drunk, and dissolved into a fit of laughter, leaning against Elise for support. How ridiculous was that? That some newspaper would think readers would want to see a picture of us both coming out of a nightclub at four in the morning. What was even more ridiculous was that some paparazzo should have to spend his night sitting outside a club in the hope that he might get one, perhaps even two pictures of some celebrity falling out of it.

I could practically already see the headline:

SOAP STARS IN LATE-NIGHT SHOCKER—
PORTOBELLO ROAD'S JASMINE AND CASEY
CAUGHT HAVING FUN!

Perish the thought!

"What kind of picture did they think they'd get at this time of the morning anyway?" I asked, walking with Elise away from the club, occasionally looking back over my shoulder to see if I could still see him.

"Probably disappointed that we didn't kiss for them," Elise said nonchalantly.

"What?" I turned and looked at her as we walked along.

"Well, c'mon!" Elise rolled her eyes. "That's what they really want in a picture, isn't it? Reality being blurred and all that."

"S'pose," I said, not fully understanding in my fog of drunkenness.

Still thinking about how stupid it had been to find ourselves photographed in the early hours of a Saturday morning coming out of a nightclub, Elise and I walked along the Thames together awhile, chatting about newspapers and the paparazzi and what a weird and wonderful business we both worked in.

It was approaching four thirty a.m. by the time we finally managed to hail a cab back to our respective apartments. We figured we'd share one to my place, then Elise would go on to hers in the same cab after I'd been dropped off, but once we starting moving off, Elise started shuffling uncomfortably in her seat, with a look on her face that suggested she was in pain.

We were both still drunk from the champagne, the night air having done little to sober us up. I looked at her, puzzled, as the cab drove on down to my apartment, which was no more than a five-minute ride from where we'd been picked up. Finally, not being able to stand her wriggling any longer, I spoke.

"Have you got ants in your pants or something?" I spoke slowly, careful not to slur my words.

"No, but I need to pee." Elise frowned and stared out the window, presumably trying not to think about it too much.

"That'd explain the non-stop wriggling, then." I giggled, turning my head and looking out the other window.

"It's another twenty minute drive from yours." Elise grimaced. "At the very least." She started jiggling her knees up and down.

I turned and looked at her, catching her eye. My head, still so full of champagne bubbles, somehow found this extremely funny—like how everything is extremely funny when you're drunk, even if it's not the least bit amusing—making me laugh so hard, it made my stomach hurt.

"Don't make me laugh," Elise hissed, jiggling her knees up and down even faster. "I don't think I'm gonna make it home at this rate."

Through tears of laughter, I was about to answer her when the cab pulled up in front of my block of apartments. Pulling out some money from my purse, I handed it to the driver then turned to Elise.

"Come up and use mine," I said, putting my hand on the cab's door handle. "You can get yourself another lift from here."

"Can I?" Elise's face was a picture of relief.

I nodded, then got out of the cab and waited for Elise to get out the other side. We walked to the communal lift in silence, the only sound puncturing that silence our footsteps on the carpet, and went up the three floors to my level, still not speaking. I let us both in and stepped aside to let Elise pass me, flicking the light switch on as I did so.

"First door on the left." I waved an arm. "Just there."

Elise didn't reply. Instead she hurried down to the bathroom while I switched more lights on in the lounge, giving the apartment an instant cosy look. When Elise returned, a few minutes later, she was grinning sheepishly.

"Sorry about that," she said, pulling a face.

"Don't you ever do as your mother always told you?" I asked, a smile twitching at the sides of my mouth.

"My mother?" Elise adjusted the shoulder straps on her dress and smoothed her front down.

"Always make sure you go before you leave somewhere?" I raised my eyebrows.

"Very funny." Elise came past me, shrugging her coat off and placing it on the back of a chair by the window, nodding approvingly as she wandered around my apartment.

"Nice place," she said, looking back over her shoulder.

"Thank you."

Suddenly thirsty, and, yeah, wanting more alcohol now the champagne was starting to wear off, I remembered the nicely chilled bottle of already-opened chardonnay I had in my fridge.

"Drink?" I took my jacket off and hung it by the front door. "I have wine."

"Perfect."

I thought she might just want to go home, so I was surprised and pleased when she accepted the offer and sat herself down on my sofa while I went into the kitchen to fetch the wine and a couple of glasses.

Kicking off my shoes, which had been pinching my feet for the last goodness knows how many hours, and wriggling my feet into my slippers with a happy sigh, I entered the kitchen and froze. There, on the floor, was the biggest, blackest, meanest looking badass spider I'd ever seen. Now, I hate spiders. Totally irrational, I know, but I do. Now here was one, sitting on the floor, looking like he wanted to fight someone. Preferably me.

"Jeez." I shuddered, shutting the kitchen door tight and walking quickly back to the lounge.

I sat down with a *flumph* on the sofa next to Elise.

"That was quick," she said, absent-mindedly looking up from a magazine she'd picked up from the table.

"The wine'll have to wait." I pulled a face. "There's a spider the size of a Rottweiler in there." I jerked my head towards the kitchen door.

Elise placed the magazine down on her lap and turned slowly to look in disbelief at me. "You're joking, right?" she said. "You won't go in there because of a spider?"

"And?" I said archly.

"Well, it's not going to kill you, is it?" Elise said, incredulity etched on her face. "Just step round it."

"Pole vault over it, more like," I said, casting a glance back at the kitchen. "You haven't seen the size of it."

"Oh, for goodness' sake!" Elise flopped the magazine down on the table and stood up from the sofa, scuffed her shoes off, and, taking one in her hand, padded quietly over towards the kitchen.

"Well, what are you going to do?" I called across.

"I'm going to kill it, you dummy," she called back.

"No, don't!" I leapt up and hurried after her, getting to the door before she did. I stood in the doorway, barring her way with my arm. "Don't kill it."

"Are you kidding me?" she said with a withering glare. "Please tell me you're kidding me."

"I'm not," I mumbled. "I just don't want you to kill it."

Elise sighed.

"I just don't like that sort of thing." I felt my face reddening.

"Softie." Elise dipped her head and looked up at me, making my face go even redder.

I paused. "Can't you just get rid of it for me?" I looked hopefully at her.

She rolled her eyes, but there was a hint of fun on her face as she did it and I sensed my own face cooling off again.

"I'll get it in a tissue and place it gently outside the window, okay?" she said. "Or would you rather I fetched it a coffee and let it watch a bit of TV before I put it out?"

"There's no need for sarcasm," I said, opening the kitchen door and hastily stepping back.

"There's every need for sarcasm when you're being such a— Good God, that's a whopper, isn't it?" Elise's face fell as she spotted the spider/Rottweiler hybrid.

"I told you that two minutes ago," I said, trying not to sound too smug. "There's plenty of toilet paper for it." I waved a hand towards the bathroom and took another step back.

Elise scratched at her chin and pulled a face. "Hmm."

"Hmm?" I repeated, looking at her in amusement.

She pursed her lips and glanced back at me. "I don't think toilet paper is going to be sufficient for this particular one." She cast a nervous look at the spider.

"Not scared, are you?" I asked, thinking how adorable she looked when she was slightly drunk and nervous at the same time.

"No," she shot back at me. Her eyes were slightly wider than they'd been a few moments before, I noticed.

"Casey would get rid of spiders for Jasmine," I teased. "She fancies her, so she'll do anything for her."

Elise looked slowly at me. "I'll trap it and take it outside," she said, ignoring my comment about Casey.

"So if I get you a large container, you'll get rid of it for me?" I asked. "Because there's no way I'm going anywhere near that!"

Elise thought a while. "Make it a very large container, yeah?" She finally said.

I walked back into the lounge and grabbed the lid from a spindle of blank CDs from my bookshelf and returned, waggling it at her.

"Like this?"

"Perfect."

Elise stayed rooted to the spot, still looking at the spider, "just to make sure it doesn't move…"

I went into my bedroom and plucked a large postcard from the cork noticeboard hanging on the wall, returning to stand next to Elise.

"Good luck," I said, handing both the plastic lid and postcard to her.

"Gee, cheers," she said sarcastically, taking them from me.

I watched in both amusement and awe as she then walked slowly towards the kitchen, container and postcard in her hands. She stopped in the doorway, and I watched through my fingers as she took a deep breath and started to approach the spider.

"Would you like a chair and whip to restrain it?" I called out.

"Very funny." She turned and looked at me, a mock-angry look on her face.

I carried on watching her as she finally tipped the spider into the container and, while I held the door open, flung it out, still in its container, into the communal hall outside.

"Don't ever ask me to do that again," she said, shutting the door and glaring at me.

I looked at her leaning against the door, her face flushed, both from the alcohol and the spider. My insides flipped over.

We carried on looking at each other before Elise suddenly broke out into a grin and shook her head. She bent over and put her head in her hands, dissolving into a fit of giggles. Laughing, I came over to her and briefly hugged her, pulling away sharply at the sensation of her body against mine and the realisation of what I'd done.

"Thank you, Elise," I said, shocked at my impromptu affection towards her. "There's no way I could ever have done that!"

"Do you think it's still out there?" she asked.

"Don't know," I replied, quickly stepping back from her. "Do you want to look?"

"No, I flipping don't!" She laughed, finally moving away from the door. She puffed out her cheeks. "Perhaps we'll leave it out there for a bit," she said, glancing at me as she passed me.

We sat back down on the sofa, both of us flopping down at the same time, laughing slightly, and sat in silence for a moment.

"You're funny," Elise suddenly said, breaking the silence. "I didn't realise before."

I shot her a look. "Funny as in *haha,* or funny as in *weird?*" I asked uncertainly, waiting for her to hit me with another comment about how strange she thought I was because I could neither remove a spider from my kitchen nor kill the stupid thing.

To my relief, she didn't come out with any comment at all.

"Funny as in *haha,*" she said, leaning her head back against the sofa. "You're good fun. You make me laugh, and I honestly can't remember the last time I laughed as much as I have this evening."

The minute she said that, I realised that she'd made me laugh all night as well: in the club, in the cab coming home, and now here in my apartment. I guess I'd just never realised quite how funny she was before, but now here she was, still tipsy from the champagne but triumphant in her spider-catching prowess, sitting on my sofa looking…well, human. Human, and lovely, and as sexy as hell.

I quickly turned my head away, making a big show of plumping up the cushions behind me. Anything to distract me from Elise sitting on my sofa, still apparently looking at me.

"There hasn't been much laughter in my life lately, to be honest," she suddenly said, breaking the silence.

"No?" I looked back at her.

She shook her head.

"I thought you enjoyed being on *Portobello Road?*" I asked, suddenly worried.

"Noooo, I didn't mean right now!" Elise laughed softly. "That's what I was trying to say. I've had more fun since I came back to England than I have in months and months."

"Really?"

"Really."

"So LA wasn't a laugh a minute?" I subconsciously shifted my position a little further away from her.

"I had bad experiences there," Elise said, shooting me a look. "Some horrible experiences in shows, in castings, auditions..." She paused. "With men."

"Oh," I mumbled, hoping that she wouldn't start trying to talk to me about men. "Not good."

She laughed. "No, not good at all, Holly."

"So a pretty miserable time all round, really, then?" I offered.

"You could say that," she said, holding my look. "So thanks."

"Well, thank *you* for getting rid of the spider," I said, leaning my head against the back of the sofa.

"Can I let you into a secret?" Elise leant her head back again as well.

I looked at her profile, the soft line of her jaw, her hair falling perfectly around her face. "Hit me."

"I don't really like spiders." She wrinkled her nose.

"My hero!" I clasped my hands to my heart in exaggeration.

We sat, both with our heads leaning against the back of the sofa, and looked at each other for a second before I broke the gaze and lifted my head away. When I glanced back, she was still looking at me, and the look on her face made me feel uncomfortable for a second, but I didn't know why. Her expression was strange, but not in a bad way, and I wondered if she'd misinterpreted my quip about her being a hero for sarcasm.

"Yes," she said finally. "Your hero."

I smiled uncertainly and then pulled myself upright, waving a hand in the direction of the kitchen. "I think you more than deserve that wine now," I said, still thinking about the look she'd just had on her face.

"I'd love to," she replied. "But"—she reluctantly pulled her eyes away from mine—"I really should go. Lines to learn and all that."

Disappointment stabbed at me. I wanted her to stay longer and was urging her to change her mind and stay for another drink, but Elise seemed flustered—embarrassed, even—which was most unlike her.

She got up from the sofa and wriggled her feet back into her shoes. "Sorry."

"It's no problem," I said. "Don't worry."

"Thanks for the offer, though." She looked as though she was about to say something else, but didn't.

"Any time," I replied, reaching over to the chair to pick up her coat.

As I handed it to her, our fingers brushed and, again, I sensed my face reddening. After a few moments I looked at her shyly, hoping she hadn't noticed.

"I'd like to do it again sometime, though," Elise said, standing with her coat in her hand.

"Clubbing with Bella and Robbie?" I made big eyes, making her laugh.

"No," she said slowly. "Drinks with you."

"Sure," I said. "We'll have to arrange something again soon."

"I'll look forward to it," she said, holding my gaze. "Guess I'll see you tomorrow, then." She shrugged her coat over her shoulders.

"You sure will," I said. "Hey, thanks again." I opened the door for her, peering outside into the hallway, relieved that the CD container was now spiderless.

"Any time," Elise said, walking past me and bending to pick up her spider-catching implements from the hallway floor. She paused. "Actually, no. Not any time!" She pulled a face as she handed me the container and postcard. "See you soon." Elise nodded, kind of curtly, before turning and walking off towards the lift. I stood in the doorway and watched her reach the lift and jab at the buttons, turning to look at me one more time as the doors opened.

I closed the door to my apartment and leaned against it, thinking. It was as though I'd seen the real Elise that night for the first time, not the Elise that I'd been working with, and even if it meant she'd probably still drive me crazy at work the next time I was there, it really did seem as though I was finally making progress with the mystery that was Elise Manford.

And I liked what I was seeing. I mean, I *really* liked what I was seeing.

CHAPTER SEVEN

The phone rang shortly after two p.m. the next day, just after I'd finally persuaded my hungover stomach to accept some food. I had no plans for the day, which was probably just as well, considering I didn't feel capable of doing anything more than just chilling out on the sofa and watching a soppy movie on one of the satellite channels.

I saw Elise's name flashing up on the screen at me, sending a rush of adrenaline down my spine the minute I saw it.

"Hey." Elise's voice sounded hoarse, presumably still rough from the previous night.

"Hey." An image of her face entered my head as I heard her voice.

"I wondered if I could come over," Elise was now saying. "I wanted to show you something."

I scratched sleepily at my head. I knew that I was tired, hungover, and scruffy, but I was still ridiculously pleased that Elise wanted to come to my apartment again.

"Sure," I said, trying to hide the pleasure in my voice.

"I think you'll like it," Elise said.

"What will I like?" I clenched my jaws tight, trying to stop a yawn.

"The thing I want to show you!" She laughed.

I texted Elise my address, thinking she'd probably been too drunk last night to remember it, telling her to take the Tube as it was easier to come across town that way. She'd told me she lived up in North London somewhere on our first meeting, but that's all. Wherever she was, it was a darned sight easier to Tube it than try to drive across London.

Once I'd also texted her directions from my nearest Tube station, I pulled myself wearily from the sofa and wandered into the bathroom, pulling a brush through my hair and covering up the tired-looking blotches on my face. I put on a hoodie and sweatpants, not wanting to look like I'd just got up—even though I had—but equally not wanting to look like I'd made too much of an effort for Elise, either. Crazy.

She arrived around forty minutes later, looking as fresh as a daisy and as though she'd been up for hours, not the short time I'd been up. As I saw her standing in my doorway, dressed immaculately, hair perfect, face made up, I looked down at my crumpled sweatpants and fluffy-socked feet and wished I had made more of an effort, after all.

I stood aside and motioned for her to come in.

"I see you got dressed up for me, then," she said, eyeing up my baggy hoodie as she sauntered past me and entered my apartment, flinging herself down onto my sofa. She looked across to me, still standing in the doorway, a huge grin spread across her face.

"Very funny." The sight of her sprawled out on my sofa, relaxed and gazing happily at me, made my insides soften. "So?" I asked. "The thing you wanted to show me is…?"

"This." Elise fished into her shoulder bag and pulled out a magazine. "They're calling us Jasey, you know. Jasmine and Casey. Cute, huh?"

Our storyline was the worst-kept secret in Soapland. All the soap magazines and TV forums on the Internet had talked about how "little Jasmine Hunter" would fall in love with a girl in a future storyline, and people had been posting for weeks, talking about how excited they were about it all. Even though Jasey's confession scenes hadn't yet gone out, the viewing public knew it was going to happen sooner rather than later, and anticipation—certainly if the magazine articles were to be believed—was already building.

"And they're calling you and me Hollise as well," she continued. "Look."

Elise handed me a copy of some glossy magazine for teenagers. On the front was a still from the programme and the headline: *What Next for Jasey...and Hollise?*

"And this is before we've even done any kissing scenes?" I asked, catching her eye. She was looking straight back at me, but now her face wasn't showing any emotion, so it was impossible to know what she was thinking.

"Yuh-huh," she finally said, her face breaking into a lazy grin, making me bite my lip self-consciously and look away.

I hastily opened the magazine and flicked to the page where Elise and I featured. It was a double-page spread talking about Jasmine and a backstory about Casey, plus a brief bio of the pair of us, which surprised me—considering the magazine in question had never even interviewed me nor, to my knowledge, Elise.

I started to read from the article, occasionally pulling a face. *"Portobello Road's new sexy lesbian couple,"* I read, *"are set to make pulses race in the coming weeks when they share their first kiss..."*

I looked up at Elise. "Sexy lesbian couple? Puh-lease!"

Elise shrugged.

"Beautiful brunette Holly Croft, nineteen, told us..." I flicked my hand across the page. "I must be having memory lapses 'cos I don't ever remember speaking to this magazine," I said, frowning and looking at the front cover again.

I read on: *"The two girls, who are even hotter in real life than their on-screen characters...*Oh for goodness' sake!" I flung the magazine down on the coffee table and sat back on the sofa.

"No, no!" Elise laughed, grabbing the magazine and thrusting it back in my hands. "Read on! It's good!"

"You're totally psyched about this, aren't you?" I looked at her, eyes wide, her face lit up, and couldn't help but laugh.

"Damn straight I am! Aren't you?" She looked surprised.

"Well, yeah, of course I love it," I said. "It seems to have gone a bit more mad than I would have expected, but in a good way."

"Mad?" Elise took the magazine back from me. "It's gone stratus-bloody-spheric!"

"But we've only just started with their story," I said.

"I know!" Elise pulled her hand through her hair. "So just imagine what it's going to be like six months down the line." She thought for a moment, then took her iPhone from her bag. "Look at this, too." She flicked her thumb over the screen of her phone, her eyes widening occasionally as she read what was on it.

"Here," she finally said. "I found some fanvids made about you on here, too, uploaded just last night." She handed the phone to me. "None of Casey yet, of course, but it's only a matter of time, isn't it?"

I peered at her iPhone as some tinny music played out, a real nice haunting, slow tune that someone had put some clips of Jasmine to. It had been done beautifully as well, and whoever had put it all together had done it so cleverly, meaning that each small clip matched the mood of the music perfectly. It was, in short, a stunning, perfect video of Jasmine's story so far. I loved it.

"It's beautiful," I said quietly, looking to Elise, then back to her phone. "Just beautiful."

"They're awesome," Elise agreed. "I've been watching loads of them all morning." She dropped her eyes. "Look at these, too." She leant over and pointed to another batch of videos.

There were countless other ones on there, exactly like the one Elise had just shown me, mainly using either clips or stills of Jasmine from over the years. Some were with slow, romantic music, some with upbeat, quirky music, but each one had been done so well that I was in total awe at both the skill and the time that had been put into them.

One particular fanvid that caught my eye, though, was set against a beautiful, slow song by one of my favourite artists and showed short clips of Jasmine during her few unhappy relationships with men and ended with a gorgeous screenshot of her with Casey, taken from a magazine.

"The Road to Her," I whispered as I watched it.

"It's perfect, isn't it?" Elise leant over and watched with me.

She was right. It was the most perfect, beautiful short video I'd ever seen—the sort I could have happily watched over and over again.

There were comments underneath the videos, too, most of which were complimentary, with viewers saying how much they loved Jasey, and how they couldn't wait until they got together, and how they thought they were going to be the cutest couple in soap history.

"Ignore the bitchy comments on there, though," Elise said. "Do what I do and just focus on the good ones."

I felt weird reading many of the comments and discussions that were underneath as they mainly asked whether Elise and I were gay in real life, and whether we were dating in real life, too. Even though Jasmine and Casey hadn't got together on screen yet, the speculation over us as actresses had already gone into overdrive.

I read those with a mixture of amusement and concern, wondering if Elise was unhappy with what people were saying on there, too.

"The questions about me and you make me laugh, though," she said, almost as if reading my mind. She studied me from the corner of her eye. "Bearing in mind Robbie asked me out…"

I tensed up. "Oh?" I said, as lightly as I could.

"Mm-hmm," Elise smiled. "That would put all speculation to bed, wouldn't it? If I actually went out with him, I mean."

"I guess you'll get that sort of speculation in any storyline," I replied, changing the subject as the video we had been watching finished.

"Yeah, I guess."

Elise put her phone down on the table.

"Are you, uh, are you going out with Robbie, then?" I asked, inspecting my nails.

"I told him no," Elise replied. "But I might change my mind. I haven't decided yet."

"You don't mind all the rumours going round about us, then?" I asked, wanting to move the subject away from Robbie. I got up from the sofa and wandered towards the kitchen. "Coffee?"

"Nope," Elise replied, getting up and following me, her feet padding softly on the carpet. "But yes to coffee." She leant against the breakfast bar and watched as I fetched mugs and coffee, then filled the coffee machine and flicked the switch on the side of it. "Like I'd be dumb enough to date a co-star anyway," she said. "Let alone a girl."

One of the mugs slipped from my hand as I was lifting it and fell with a clatter onto the sideboard.

"So you'd never date Robbie because you work with him?" I asked, my face burning as I hastily picked up the fallen mug.

"Total nail in the coffin for any actor, that," Elise said matter-of-factly. "I learnt that out in LA." She pulled herself up and sat on my breakfast bar. "I mean, for a start, the press would have a blast, wouldn't they? Actors confusing their art with real life? C'mon!"

"And that would bother you?" I asked. "The press?"

"Big time," she said. "Wouldn't it you?"

"No," I said truthfully. "It wouldn't." I thought for a moment. "Maybe when I was younger, but not now."

As I filled our mugs with the freshly made coffee, I thought about what she'd said. Was I really okay about all the supposition about us? I'd answered her question far too readily, but underneath it all, did I mind total strangers discussing my sexuality? An image of Grace suddenly entered my head. I could see her perfectly as if it had only been yesterday since I'd last seen her, rather than the two long years since she'd walked out of my life.

"The questions of whether we're getting it on in real life…" I suddenly said, sipping at my coffee.

"What about them?" Elise watched me over her mug, her face expressionless.

When I saw the look on her face I immediately thought that I'd annoyed her by mentioning it, so I replied quickly to try to explain myself.

"Well, they're funny," I mumbled. "That's what I meant."

"Mm."

Elise's blunt reply and her earlier comments about never dating co-stars suggested that she didn't think it at all funny, making me wonder if she was lying to me when she said she was okay about it. Maybe she really was uncomfortable with all the speculation after all. I mean, some of the comments had been very forthright, saying that Elise and I must be getting it on because of the suggestive stills released by the publicity people at *PR*. In a lot of fans' eyes, that had to make us a couple in real life, too.

I smiled to myself, thinking that if only the fans that had written those comments knew how much Elise had annoyed me in those first few days, they'd never think anything of the sort. But now? I looked at her, sitting on my breakfast bar, and my smile instinctively widened.

"You look happy." Elise's voice roused me from my thoughts.

"I was just thinking how much I enjoy working with you," I replied, shrugging sheepishly.

Elise stared down into her coffee. "We get on okay, don't we?" she said, looking slowly up at me. "Last night was a blast."

"We were wasted last night!" I said, putting my coffee cup down and folding my arms across my chest.

"Indeed," Elise said slowly. She carried on looking at me, almost as if she wanted to say something else, but instead she tore her eyes away and glanced at the clock on my kitchen wall, then hopped down from the breakfast bar.

"I better go," she said with a sigh, walking back to the sofa to collect her bag.

"You don't want to read some more of that magazine article with me?" I asked, following her and pointing down to the magazine, still on my coffee table.

"No," she replied. "I've read it. You keep it." She walked to the door and paused before turning round and looking me straight in the eye for a few seconds. She opened her mouth as if she was about to say something else, just like she had in the kitchen earlier, then closed it again. "See you, then," she said, opening the door and closing it tight behind her, leaving me bewildered and hurt at her rush to get away from me. After all, it had been her that had wanted to come and see me in the first place, hadn't it?

CHAPTER EIGHT

Around a week after our night out at Bobby's, Jasmine and Casey's confession scenes finally aired. The TV channel we went out on had given *PR* an hour's special that evening, with them both featuring extensively throughout the programme, and I was stoked that we'd been given so much airtime and publicity, both for me and Elise—and for Jasmine and Casey.

Once these intimate and heartfelt scenes had gone out, and it was clear to the viewers that Jasmine and Casey were definitely going to get together as a couple, interest in both the story and in me and Elise as actresses absolutely rocketed. I figured they'd rocket even more when the next ones—Jasmine and Casey's first kiss—finally went out.

Ah, their first kiss.

Filming on *PR* was always out of sequence, and I'd known for days, of course, that Jasey's first kiss was ready to be filmed the morning after the confession scenes had aired, and now I was absolutely bricking it.

We'd received the scripts for The Kiss a few days before, and I'll be honest and tell you that I'd read them with a certain amount of trepidation, even though I knew I was being ridiculous. I was worried about making them seem realistic; these would be the first making-out scenes I'd filmed since Jasmine's ill-fated and very short relationship with the boy down the road—whom she'd briefly run away to Scotland with—when she was sixteen, and I wanted to do them justice.

The scene was being shot in Jasmine's bedroom. Elise hadn't arrived on the set yet, so I found myself pacing up and down, playing with my phone and chatting with the cameraman while I waited for her—anything to take my mind off the butterflies that were swirling around inside me. Kevin and Stuart were busy discussing the lighting in the corner of the set when Elise finally arrived from make-up, looking slightly flustered. The sight of her looking flushed and hurried struck me as strange; Elise didn't ever get flustered, right?

"Sorry I'm late," she called over to Kevin, coming over to join me. She sat down on Jasmine's bed and looked up at me, puffing out her cheeks.

"You're not late," Kevin called back. "Don't worry."

"You okay?" I laughed.

"Thought I was going to be late, that's all," Elise replied, kind of tightly I thought.

"You ready for this?" I asked.

"Yeah," Elise replied. "You?"

"Yeah."

"Nervous?"

"A bit, yeah. You?"

Elise thought for a while before answering me. "Very," she finally said.

Elise was nervous? And there was me, thinking she had nerves of steel.

"I hope you haven't eaten garlic or anything." I laughed, cringing at my feeble attempt at a joke, and came to join her on the bed.

She glanced at me quickly then looked away again, staring down at her feet. "I hope you haven't either," she said nervously.

I wanted to say something else but didn't know what. I hated the stiltedness of our conversation, especially after we'd been getting on so well just lately, but I honestly couldn't think of a single word to say to her, so we didn't speak again until Stuart finally—after what seemed like ages—called us to our markers.

We'd already filmed some other scenes in Jasmine's bedroom that morning, where Jasmine and Casey had continued their heart-to-heart about their growing feelings for each other, and the kiss we were about to film now was going to happen immediately after they'd both admitted they liked each other.

These particular scenes were going to be aired as a two-part special, with each programme going out either side of the evening news, so that the kiss would fade out the end of the first episode, and the second episode would then pick up where the first one had ended and have us both still kissing as the opening credits rolled. It was all going to be very technical, as it was important that the continuity was just right and that the kiss lasted the required amount of time to go through one set of closing credits and one set of opening credits.

It was also all going to be very chaste, of course. *Portobello Road* went out before the watershed, so it was important that the kiss could in no way upset the viewers. The script had Casey kissing Jasmine first, and then Jasmine would reciprocate; I'd read it over and over, and although Elise and I had talked the scene over together, discussing how we would both play it, I was still nervous.

The cameras were finally ready to roll; Stuart gave us both one last instruction on how he wanted us to stand, and then we were ready. We had no words to say for the initial take—it was just straight into the kiss, and as Stuart called for us to begin, I immediately tensed up. I glanced at Elise and saw apprehension written across her face, too, so I figured she was feeling just as anxious as I was. That made me feel better somehow.

On our cue, we had to gaze tenderly into each other's eyes for no more than five seconds, letting our eyes roam over one another's faces, before Casey leant in and kissed Jasmine.

I hadn't stood this close to another girl in over two years. The intimacy of Elise, standing barely inches from me—the warmth of her body, the faint aroma of her citrusy perfume, and the look in her eyes—made my pulse start to thud alarmingly in my neck as, almost on cue, an image of Grace flooded my mind.

With the cameras rolling and my heart still beating wildly, I looked deep into Elise's eyes, then closed my eyes as I felt her lips on mine, tight and anxious. I was aware that I was standing with my arms stiffly around her, my body tense in her arms, and my own lips were clamped rigidly to hers, not really sure what they should be doing.

"Cut!"

I jumped slightly as Stuart's voice echoed out across the silent set. He walked over to us, clipboard in hand, and looked at us both kindly. "Could we try that again?" he asked, with rising intonation. "Just try to relax, okay?"

I glanced at Elise and smiled nervously. "Sorry."

She nodded but didn't reply.

We were given our cue to go once more, and again, as Elise leant in, all I was aware of this time was her stiffness and anxiousness and the feel of her dry lips on mine while I stood, dizzy and rigid in front of her, wishing I could do something to make my body relax a bit.

"Cut!"

"You pulled away," she said, stepping back from me. She stood in front of me, hands on her hips, licking her lips then wiping them, as if wiping the sensation of my lips away from hers.

"Did I?" I asked. "I thought you were pulling away from me."

"When I leant in to kiss you, you pulled your head back," she said. "I can't kiss you if you do that."

"Everything okay?" Stuart called over from behind the camera.

"Yup," I called back over my shoulder. "Ready to roll."

We tried again and again, the tenseness of Elise's body against mine and her lack of emotion making it absolutely impossible to be anything other than uptight myself.

"You pulled away again!" Elise swung away from me and walked over to the other side of the set.

"If I pulled away, it's because you're so tense!" I called after her. "You're not making it easy for me to get into it."

She turned and looked back at me, a hurt look on her face.

"Do you girls want a break?" Kevin came over to me and placed a hand on my shoulder. "I appreciate this is unfamiliar territory for the pair of you, so if you want to take five and go and regroup, that's fine."

I didn't want to go and regroup. I just wanted to get this scene over and done with, so that I could get on with all the other scenes I was due to film, and then go home again; the longer we drew it out, the more anxious and uneasy both Elise and I would become, I just knew it. "No, I want to carry on," I said.

Elise still had her back to me, but she took a deep breath, then turned back and rejoined me on our marker. "Let's just do it," she said, smiling and revealing her deep-set dimples, which made my head swim even more than it already was.

Just think of Grace, I suddenly thought. *Just think about how it used to feel with Grace, and imagine it's her you're kissing, not Elise...*

The cameras rolled again, and I desperately thought about Grace, trying to remember how good it used to be when I kissed her, and that really seemed to help. I managed to let my inhibitions go a little, even if I was counting the seconds until Stuart called *Cut!*, and it must have worked as this time Elise didn't instinctively pull away as I kissed her back.

Much to my—and Stuart's and Elise's—relief, that take was a success. The second Stuart called for us to stop, Elise and I immediately parted, both of us automatically taking two or three steps away from each other and avoiding one another's eyes.

"Good!" Stuart came over to us. "That was perfect. Thank you both."

I glanced over to Elise and raised my eyebrows in a *well thank goodness that's over* way. She was still looking uneasy, and I briefly wondered if she hadn't been happy with the take, but figured if Stuart was okay with it, then that would do just fine.

"You two want to take a break for ten minutes?" Stuart was now saying, heading from the set. "It'll be open set for the next few scenes now that we've got the biggie out of the way."

I watched as he walked off, Kevin following him.

"Well, I'm glad we finally got that sorted," I called over to Elise.

"We got there eventually, huh?" Elise walked back over to me.

I looked at my watch. "Coffee?" I asked.

Elise looked at me for a second, then made to walk past me. "Thanks, but no," she said. "I'm just gonna head back to my room for five minutes." She hesitated. "Need to make a phone call," she said, almost as an afterthought. She looked at me again, holding my gaze a while, then smiled tightly and left the set, leaving me standing there—not for the first time since I'd known her—alone and feeling just a bit deflated.

CHAPTER NINE

G uess who's cracked it?" Robbie's face appeared in my dressing-room doorway, grinning from ear to ear.

It was the next day. Elise and I had managed to survive filming our final three scenes the previous day—an open set, just as Stuart had said—and now I was back at the studios the following morning, ready to film some scenes with Bella.

"Cracked what?" I put down the mascara wand I'd been darkening my eyes with and beckoned for Robbie to come in.

"The enigma that is Elise." Robbie rubbed his hands together and threw himself down on my sofa, stretching his legs out in front of him.

He looked like the proverbial cat that got the cream. My skin began to curiously prickle. "And how have you done that?" I asked lightly, turning to face my dressing-table mirror again.

"She asked me out," Robbie said simply.

"But she told me she'd never date a co—" I paused, wand in hand, and looked at his reflection in my mirror. "Didn't you ask her out once before?" I asked, aware that my hands had suddenly gone colder.

"I did, and she said no," Robbie said. "But *she* asked *me* last night. How about that?" He kicked his shoes off and put his feet up on the sofa.

"I see," I said slowly. *Last night. After we'd filmed our kissing scenes...*

"Dunno what made her change her mind," Robbie was now saying. "'Cos when I asked her before she blew me right off, no hesitation."

"Must be your charm and winning smile," I said sulkily.

"Never worked on you, though, did it?" He crossed his legs at the ankle. "Not for the want of me trying, though, hey?"

"So where are you going to take Elise?" I asked, ignoring his comment and conveniently forgetting the number of times Robbie had asked me out over the years.

"We thought a meal, then maybe Bobby's or King's afterwards," Robbie settled back, threading his hands behind his head, and stared up at the ceiling.

"When?" I asked, my voice thick.

"Tonight," Robbie replied, still staring up at the ceiling. "So if she turns up to work tomorrow in the same clothes she has today, then you'll know we hit it off okay." He lifted his head and grinned.

"Well, I'm sure you'll tell me all about it," I said, watching him in the mirror. "Gentleman that you are."

Robbie started to speak, but a knock on my door stopped him. Glad for the interruption, I called out for whomever it was to come in and felt a pleasant twinge in the pit of my stomach when I saw Elise standing in the doorway. She looked from me to Robbie then back to me again, the flicker of something across her face. What was it? Uncertainty? Embarrassment?

"We were just talking about you." Robbie sat up straight on the sofa, eyeing Elise.

"I came to see Holly," she said quietly, still watching Robbie warily.

"About?" I raised my eyebrows.

"Uh, about…we have to go see Kevin," Elise replied, tearing her eyes from Robbie and back to me.

"You go ahead, ladies." Robbie stretched back out on my sofa again. "I'll mind the fort here."

Elise and I walked down the corridor and up the two flights of stairs to Kevin's office in near silence. Part of me wanted to ask her about her date with Robbie, part of me just didn't want to know. I was angry, peeved, and as much as my brain was having a fight with itself over exactly why I felt like that, I think I already knew. Or did I? Part of me was put out because Robbie was my oldest friend on *PR,* but what did that matter? A bigger part of me was upset because Elise had barely just told me she'd never date a co-star, so why now Robbie? Fortunately we arrived at Kevin's office before I had to even think about answering that particular quandary.

When we went in, Kevin was seated at his desk, magazines and papers spread out in front of him.

"My two favourite actresses," he gushed as we approached his desk, making Elise and me glance at one another in a shared knowing look of amusement.

Kevin told us that everyone at *Portobello Road* had been bowled over by the viewers' response to our story, and that magazines and newspapers were queuing up even more than they had been before to do interviews and photo shoots with us both. I didn't need to look at Elise; her excitement crackled across to me like an electrical current all the while Kevin was talking.

"We're getting e-mails coming in daily to the production company from press and public," he said, leaning back in his chair. "They're calling you celesbians."

Elise turned to me, wide-eyed and mouthed, *"Celesbians?!"*

"And others from girls your age saying about how much this has helped them in real life, you know, coming to terms with stuff," Kevin went on. "This has far exceeded our expectations, you two. We're absolutely delighted with the way things are going."

We talked on for a few more minutes, Kevin giving us details of the interview and photo shoot that a women's magazine wanted to run sometime in the next month. With our meeting finally over, Elise and I left Kevin's office and headed back down the corridor of the TV studios, Elise still practically floating on cloud nine.

"Did you hear what Kevin said?" Elise's voice seemed to have gone up by at least an octave. "Celesbians! That's what they're calling us, Holly! Celesbians!"

"Well, it's getting the attention they wanted, at least." I followed Elise back down the stairs.

"And what about the photo shoots?" Elise bumped my arm. "I can't wait to do those! I'm gonna get dressed up and knock 'em all dead."

I glanced at her and figured with a pang that she'd have no problem whatsoever knocking anyone dead. Including Robbie that night.

"And when Kev just said they were getting e-mails in pretty much every day from teenagers, well, jeez!" She spoke really quickly, fumbling in her bag for her phone. "I mean, how fantastic is that?"

"I remember it happened when they did it in *The Escape*," I said. "You remember? Martin and Dexter? Well, apparently the guys that played Martin and Dexter used to get letters from blokes telling them how much they'd helped them."

"The power of TV, huh?" Elise said, jabbing her finger over the phone screen while she walked, presumably texting someone.

Finally she put her phone away and, apparently remembering I was still with her, said, "We so need to go out and celebrate now."

"Celebrate?" I raised my eyebrows, the thought of a night out with Elise sending a swell of excitement right through me.

"Yeah!" She rubbed her hands together in excitement. "After all, it's not every day you get told you're a celesbian, is it?"

I hesitated. "Not tonight, though, 'cos you're, uh, you're going out with Robbie tonight, aren't you?" I kept my voice light, trying to sound as if I was interested.

Elise glanced over then away again. "News travels fast round here."

"He just told me." I waved a hand. "In my room before."

"Right," Elise said. "Well yes, I am seeing him tonight as it happens."

"I didn't know you two liked each other," I said, making a big deal of hitching my bag further up my shoulder to try to act as casually as possible, even though my heart was thudding.

"Neither did I," Elise replied slowly.

We walked a little further on, finally arriving at the set where I was due on in a few minutes.

"How about Saturday, then?" she asked. "Just you and me? After all, it's us who are celebrating. No one else."

Just you and me.

"Saturday's good," I said, already thinking about what I would wear.

"Text me details later?" Elise asked, pulling her car keys out of her bag. "No more filming for me till Saturday now, thank goodness."

"Oh." A brief pang hit me. "Lucky for some. I have three scenes with Bella in the morning."

"Well, think of me having an awesome day off, won't you?" Elise pulled a silly face at me as she passed me and left the set.

"I won't," I joked, watching as she walked away, turning briefly to smile back at me before she turned the corner and disappeared from sight.

❖

I managed to sail through the next day's filming—a Friday—without any hitches. It was a shorter day than normal, and my few scenes with Bella were done and dusted by lunchtime. I was grateful to get home early, especially considering it was Friday, and just chill out in my apartment for the rest of the afternoon.

My mind wandered frequently to Elise and Robbie. Robbie, like Elise, had the day off, so it wasn't as if I could see him and tell by the look on his face whether their date had been successful. They'd been on my mind for most of the previous evening and the whole of the morning, if I'm honest, imagining where they'd gone, what Elise had worn, what they'd spoken about, wondering if they'd hit it off. I wish I'd been able to switch it off, to pretend like I didn't care, but I couldn't. I did care—a lot.

I was just settling down to my second cup of tea and fifth biscuit of the afternoon back at my apartment when my mobile rang. I saw Elise's name flashing on and off the screen in front of me and was enveloped in a surge of happiness because she was ringing me on her day off, coupled immediately with an opposing thought that she might only be ringing me to tell me about her and Robbie. I watched her name come and go, deliberating as to what to do, when I finally gave in and answered.

"Hey!" She sounded pleased to hear me.

"Hey," I replied, walking to my window and looking out. "What are you up to?"

"Nothing much," Elise sighed. "To be honest I've been so tired all day. Why does that always happen when you have a day off?"

"Don't know," I replied absent-mindedly, thinking that if she was home in her apartment then maybe she didn't stay the night with Robbie after all.

"Listen, you wanna go out tonight instead of tomorrow?" Elise asked.

My heart quickened. "Sure," I said, thinking of her and Robbie again. "You're not busy tonight, then?"

"Nope," Elise said breezily.

"Do you, uh, do you want to ask anyone else?" I asked hesitantly.

Please say no. Please say no.

"I don't, no," Elise said. "Do you?"

"No, not at all," I said, probably too keenly.

"Good," she said. "Just me and you will be perfect."

❖

"So, I figured King's would be better tonight than anywhere else," I said to Elise as I met her from the Tube.

"King's sounds good," Elise replied as I approached her across the station hall. She stared at me as I came closer to her, her eyes flickering over me. "You look great," she finally said, catching my eye. "Your hair looks awesome like that."

"Thanks. You do, too."

And she did. Elise looked totally stunning, and it was all I could do not to stare at her like some drooling teenage boy. She was wearing a really neat little black figure-hugging dress, which showed off her curves perfectly, and she looked fabulous in it;

our characters in *PR* just seemed to live in jeans and hoodies, so I guess it wasn't often that I got to see Elise dressed up. She'd worn something equally gorgeous for our night out at Bobby's, but tonight she looked even more awesome.

We'd arranged to meet at eight p.m. and just go for a drink and a dance—no getting wasted or staying out until the small hours— just a drink, to relax and unwind after a difficult few weeks, and to celebrate our success on *PR*.

I was stoked that Elise had noticed what I was wearing as I'd really gone to town on my outfit. I knew exactly why. Plus, I figured it wasn't some promotional night where I had to be slightly more… how shall I put it? Slightly more reserved. This was *my* night out and, although I couldn't go too over the top, bearing in mind the number of paparazzi that hung around just about every bar in central London, I thought I could at least let go just a little.

I'd spent ages on my hair, and with a little tweaking and fine-tuning, it tumbled around my shoulders, framing my face perfectly. I usually wore my hair up or just scrunched it up into a ponytail, so it felt good to have it loose against my neck for a change. I'd gone subtle with my make-up as well, with just a bit of smudging round my eyes and pale lip gloss which perfectly matched the colour of the beads I'd thrown around my neck and which hung messily down my front. I'd gone for the shortest, tightest skirt I owned and paired it with a loose-fitting top; the shoes I'd chosen to go with it gave me height and made me look slimmer than I usually looked and, I thought dryly, would at least make me nearly as tall as Elise, even if just for the night.

As we walked together from the Tube over to King's, my brain kept urging me to talk to Elise about Robbie, to ask her if she'd enjoyed herself the previous night and whether she'd be seeing him again, outside of work. But at the same time, it also seemed to be chanting a mantra of *I don't want to know. I want to know. I don't want to know. I want to know.*

Who knew what the hell I wanted?

When we entered the club, the heat and noise immediately sucked us in. Any thoughts I'd been having about Elise and Robbie evaporated as I walked to the bar, waving to the barman I'd known for years.

"I had a phone call from one of the promo guys this afternoon, by the way." Elise leant towards me and spoke into my ear over the sound of the music.

"Oh?" I greeted the barman. "Wine?" I said, looking at Elise.

"White, thanks." She nodded to the barman. "Sauvignon Blanc, if you've got it."

"So what was the phone call about?" I asked.

"The photo shoot Kevin was on about." Elise lifted herself up onto a stool by the bar, hastily pulling at the bottom of her dress which had ridden up.

"And?" I picked up my drink and took a sip from it, concentrating on Elise's face rather than her legs.

"It's been cleared with our agents, according to Susie, so we're good to go." Elise drank from her glass.

"I can't wait!" I lifted myself up on to my stool, too.

"Yuh-huh," Elise nodded. "And, according to Susie, they were so keen to get us there, they're going to be pushing out the boat, like, *big time.*"

"Champagne and caviar?" I grinned.

"Not quite." Elise pulled a face. "But it's going to be a full day of hair, make-up, clothes…the lot."

"Imagine the pampering we'll get!" I bumped my arm playfully against hers.

"Imagine all the freebies, Hol!" She bumped me back.

"You just called me Hol." I stopped mid-drink and looked at her curiously. "You've never called me that before."

"Did I?" She shook her head. "I didn't mean to. Sorry."

I paused. "No, I liked it."

We looked at each other a while, neither of us sure what to say. Elise broke eye contact first, hastily looking away and down at her drink. She traced her finger round the rim of her glass and stared into it, apparently deep in thought. "Anyway," she finally said, flicking a look back towards me, "it's next week."

"Well, I'm looking forward to it already," I said, kind of stilted.

We sat in silence for a few minutes, sipping at our drinks and looking out around the club, until I couldn't bear the lack of conversation any longer.

"C'mon, drink up." I slapped her arm playfully with my hand. "Let's have a dance."

We both knocked our drinks back and left the bar, picking our way over to the dance floor and melting into the darkness there. We danced together for the next four or five tracks, a heady mix of techno, R & B, and dance which was great to get lost in for a while until, finally, I'd had enough and made my way back to the bar, Elise following me close behind.

A girl and a guy stood where we'd been standing earlier. As Elise nodded to the barman to order us both drinks, I could sense the people next to us staring and whispering to one another, but I ignored it. That sort of thing always happened whenever I went out on the town, either with friends or with other people from *PR*, but it happened more frequently now since Jasey. I'd learnt a long time ago to ignore the stares and the comments, which invariably either ended with some catty remark or a request for a photo on their phone.

I sat up on a stool and turned my back to the two people behind me, focusing on Elise instead, who was now paying for our drinks. I felt a tap on my shoulder and turned round to see the girl smiling at me, the guy now gone.

"Are you…?" she asked, tilting her head and looking hard at me through the gloom of the club. "You are, aren't you?"

I smiled. "Who?" I asked politely.

"Jasmine," the girl said. "Jasmine Hunter."

"Yes," I said simply.

"I thought it was!" the girl said excitedly. "I said to Mark I thought it was you." She waved a hand in the direction of the dance floor, so I guessed Mark had been the guy she'd been with just now.

"You watch *Portobello Road*, then?" I asked.

"Oh God, yeah!" the girl said, her face lighting up. "I love it."

Elise appeared behind me, handing me my drink.

"And are you…?" The girl's eyes widened. "O.M.G! It is! Casey!"

"All right?" Elise casually lifted her chin.

"Can I have a photo?" The girl delved into her handbag and pulled out her phone. "Mark'll be gutted he's missed this!" She swung round and looked out across the club, then back to us.

Elise and I leant our heads closer and smiled awkwardly as the girl took a photo of us both, then waved her hand at the barman and asked if he'd take one of her with us both. The photos over, I nodded politely and turned back to the bar again.

"Nice to meet you, anyway," I said, picking my drink up.

"So are you two, like, you know, seeing each other in real life, then?" the girl persisted.

"No," Elise and I said at the same time.

"And are you both, like, lesbians?"

"No." Elise spoke first, while I remained silent.

"We just play the characters," I said, smiling, thankful that Elise had answered before me so that I hadn't had to.

The girl—I think she said her name was Sarah—then started chatting to me about Jasmine and how she'd always been her favourite character and how she loved all the Jasey stuff. I tried to remain polite, aware that Elise was standing next to me not saying a word, just sipping occasionally at her drink and stifling the odd yawn.

At hardly any point in our conversation did Sarah even mention Casey—only to tell me she thought that she and Jasmine were awesome together. She didn't directly address Elise anymore, either, choosing to focus all her attention on me instead. I didn't mind, if I'm honest, and yes, she was cute if that's what you're wondering. Talking to her was no great hardship for me.

I could sense Elise's growing boredom, but despite me trying to involve her in the conversation, she remained stubbornly silent until, finally, she slammed her drink back in one gulp and wandered away from us towards the dance floor. I watched her go from the corner of my eye, still talking and listening to Sarah, and wished that Elise had made more of an effort to speak to Sarah, too.

"Can I buy you a drink?" Sarah suddenly asked.

"Let me get you one," I said, catching the barman's eye and ordering us two more.

We chattered on a little while more, Mark still nowhere to be seen, and Elise lost to me somewhere in the darkness. I enjoyed talking to Sarah, but all the time I was talking to her I was thinking about Elise, wondering where she'd gone to, fretting that she was pissed off with me for ignoring her on our night out.

I needn't have worried that much, though. About ten minutes after she'd left us, I finally caught sight of her, to the edge of the dance floor, dancing with some guy. She had her arms wrapped round him like she'd known him all her life, and I have to admit my first thought was that she'd probably now appear in all the Sunday papers with a dumb headline like *The Lesbian Has Turned* or something equally stupid.

Sarah was still talking to me, but I wasn't listening to her anymore. I was focused on Elise, snaking her body around this random guy, occasionally glancing over to where I was, then winding herself around him even more when she saw I was watching. I turned my attention back to Sarah, trying to keep up with what she was saying to me, but all the while I was aware of Elise and this guy.

Finally, after nearly half an hour, I'd decided I'd had enough. I was tired anyway, and the night hadn't turned out to be the celebration and relaxation I'd expected. I suddenly longed to be back in my apartment, curled up on my sofa watching TV with the biggest bag of crisps ever invented. I made my excuses to Sarah, politely declining her offer of her phone number and, catching Elise's eye, motioned to her that I was leaving.

She ignored me, instead draping herself even tighter around the guy she was dancing with and finally disappearing into the gloom of the club.

I stood on the edge of the dance floor a while longer, desperately searching for her, but when she was nowhere to be seen, I finally decided to leave her to it. Leaving the club, I hailed the first cab I saw coming down the street, arriving back at my apartment just after eleven thirty p.m., feeling utterly miserable.

My head was swimming, images of Robbie grinning smarmily at me when he'd told me Elise had asked him out, others of Elise with Robbie, and of Elise with the guy in the club swirling round and round in my head like leaves in the wind. I was furious with Elise on so many levels: because she'd made no effort to speak to Sarah with me, and because she'd left me standing at the bar to go and dance with some arbitrary bloke, when this was supposed to be *our* night out and it hadn't seemed to have mattered to her as much as it did me.

Most importantly, though, I was furious with myself for giving in to the gnawing, worrying, churning emotion of utter jealousy that flooded my whole body every time I thought about Elise dancing with that guy. It was a sensation that I hadn't had for over two years, since Grace, and now Elise was bringing it out in me.

I'd fallen for her, hadn't I? Hook, line, and sinker.

Chapter Ten

I jumped as the door to the green room swung open and Elise breezed in. She practically skipped over to me, throwing herself down on the sofa with a thump, then laced her arm around my shoulder. I could smell the faint remnants of what I assumed was last night's alcohol still on her and felt my heart drop.

It was Saturday morning and now I was back at work, mooching around the green room, still hurt and upset from the previous night's events.

"You look happy," I managed to muster up.

"Still a bit drunk from last night, if I'm honest." Elise squeezed her eyes shut and pinched the corners of each eye between her thumb and finger.

"I guessed."

"You left early." She turned her head slightly and looked at me.

"Yeah, I was tired," I lied. I wanted to add a sarcastic *So you noticed that I'd left, then?* but stopped myself.

"You missed some night, though." She laughed softly to herself, as if remembering something.

"Yeah, suppose."

"And I pulled," Elise said slowly.

"Pulled?"

"Yup." She sat up straighter and looked at me from the corner of her eye. "Remember that guy who I was dancing with when you left?"

"Not really." *Of course I did!*

"Well, his name's Stig and, well, after you'd left he bought me some drinks."

"Stig?" I snorted. "What sort of name's that?"

"It's his name," Elise said impatiently.

"Right."

"And, anyway, I went back to his place," Elise said, watching me. "And it was amazing."

"You slept with him." It was a statement more than a question.

"Yuh-huh."

"That was nice for you." I moved away a little from her on the sofa, making her instinctively remove her arm from my shoulders. I don't know why I did it. It just made me feel a bit better, even if my shoulder felt empty without Elise's arm around it.

"Yeah, it was," she mumbled.

"And Robbie?" I asked priggishly. "What about him?"

"What about Robbie?" Elise looked at me sullenly.

"Well, uh, didn't you go out with him the other night as well?"

"And?" Elise replied, pinching her eyes impatiently. "That was just a one-off. I told you—I never date work colleagues."

"Priceless," I muttered back under my breath.

Elise looked surprised. "What?" She asked. "What did you just say? Priceless?"

"Nothing."

"It's nothing to do with you, anyway," she said flippantly.

"Of course not," I replied. "So why tell me?"

"Just making conversation, Holly," Elise snorted. "Chill."

"I'm perfectly chilled," I said archly. "I just don't need to know what you got up to, thanks."

"It was just sex, Holly." Elise shrugged. She drew her knees up to her chest, wrapping her cardigan tight around her, then lay her head back against the sofa and closed her eyes. "It was good sex, too," she murmured, more to herself than to me.

"Mm-hmm." I bit my lip to stop me from saying anything more than that.

"It's what happens in the real world, Holly!" Elise half-opened her eyes and peered at me. "Girl goes out, girl meets boy, girl goes home with boy."

"Not to me, it doesn't," I said, adding a small ironic laugh.

"Are you jealous?" She turned and looked at me in amusement.

"Don't be daft!" I blurted out.

"You are, aren't you?" She shuffled back on the sofa, bringing herself up straighter again, and brought her knees up even closer to her. "You're jealous that I pulled and you didn't."

"You are *so* dumb sometimes, it amazes me!" I shook my head. "Number one, I'm not jealous that you copped off last night. Number two, I don't give a holy shit what you get up to in your spare time, and number three…" I paused. "Okay, there is no number three," I said, feeling stupid. "But if you seriously think I could be jealous of you, then you're even more vain than I previously thought!"

"Vain? Me?" Elise's face fell.

"You. Vain." I glowered at her. "Sometimes I think you invented the word."

"Gee, thanks." Elise looked across to me, her forehead crumpling.

I immediately felt bad. "I just don't really want to hear about your sex life, Elise," I said quietly.

"Sheesh, could you *be* more pious?" Elise rolled her eyes.

I loathed it when she rolled her eyes at me. I didn't want her to roll her eyes at me! I just wanted her to understand that I really didn't want to know about her getting together with some random guy. Because it hurt me more than she'd ever know. I gritted my teeth. "You have *no* idea, do you?" I said.

"No idea about what?"

I took a deep breath. "Forget it." I reached down past her and grabbed my bag, then got up and left the room before she had another chance to speak to me.

Back outside in the corridor, I leant against the wall, trying to make sense of what she'd just told me, trying to fight the awful feelings building inside me every time I thought about her and Stig. I pressed my head back against the wall, staring up at the ceiling.

"Shit, shit, shit!" I muttered under my breath. Elise had slept with some guy, someone whom she'd only met an hour earlier. And, yes, she was right. I was jealous. Jealous as hell, but not because I hadn't pulled like Elise had.

I was jealous, pure and simple, because I wanted Elise.

❖

I don't know why it had taken me so long to see what, in hindsight, had been blindingly obvious for ages. When Bella had first told me all those weeks ago that Robbie had asked Elise out, it had pricked curiously at me. Now I understood why, and when she'd finally asked him out, it had upset me terribly, but then when I'd seen her dancing with that bloke—I mean, c'mon! *Stig?*—it had hit me harder than a runaway train.

Perhaps the reason I'd let her get to me was precisely that: I cared what she thought about me because I cared for her. Okay, so I'd thought her a wholly unlikeable person in the early days, but in the space of a few weeks I'd gone from disliking Elise intensely and being hurt and angry by the way she was with me to being hopelessly and insanely attracted to her. And it scared me to death. What scared me even more was her finding out because I knew what her reaction was going to be—disgust and horror. She'd tell me I was a dumbass for confusing life with art, just like the fans sometimes did, and I guess she'd be right; how could I be so stupid for falling for my co-star, for God's sake? She wasn't Casey, she was that sarcastic, lippy, confident, all-round smart alec Elise.

And I'd never wanted anyone so much in my life.

The worst thing was, now I had to carry on working with her, all while knowing that I liked her. I tried to remember back to a point when my dislike for her had changed. She'd certainly stirred something inside me the night she'd come over and removed the spider from my kitchen, and I'd always secretly liked the way I caught her looking at me when she thought I wasn't looking, but was it during that time that dislike had turned to like, which had then turned to proper falling for her?

Did I just wake up one morning and find that something had programmed my Elise-o-meter from *okay, yeah, she's funny* to *whoa!* overnight? Maybe subconsciously I'd always liked her—had always been fascinated by her. I know I thought she was hot the first time I ever met her, but did that mean I actually—

"Holly?" I flinched as I heard Elise's voice next to me.

I was still leaning against the corridor wall, staring up at the ceiling, totally lost in my thoughts.

"Are you in a mood with me?" Her voice was low and husky. Maybe that was my imagination.

I turned and looked at her, wiping away a tear that I hadn't even realised had been there. "No, 'course not." I smiled and cleared my throat, pulling myself away from the wall. "Are we, uh, are we ready to shoot?" I made a big show of looking at my watch, trying to conceal my miserable confusion.

"Yeah," Elise stood close, looking at me. "You sure you're okay?"

"I've just got a bit of a headache, that's all. It'll go," I lied.

She was still watching me, standing uncomfortably close. My eyes flickered to her face and away again. Something inside told me not to look at her in case she could read my mind. I felt wretched. Was this how it would be from now on? Would I be too afraid to be near her, or to touch her, or to look at her in case I gave the game away?

I looked down at the floor of the corridor then quickly back at Elise. Why did she have to look so damned perfect all the time? Why did she have to stand so close to me?

"So come on, then." I snapped myself out of thoughts that were threatening to run away with me and started to walk away from her and down the corridor. "Let's get on with it."

❖

Stuart, our director for the promo shoots we were doing that day, was wandering about the set with a clipboard clutched to his chest. He looked grumpy and stressed—not a good start to the afternoon.

We had to film some mini-clips for a promo that would go out on TV the next week, advertising a future storyline where Jasey, frightened that Casey's parents know they're seeing each other, talk about leaving home, scared that they're going to be split up. It was going to be a week-long story, going out in a month's time, and would air every night, running alongside another separate storyline involving a doctor's affair with one of his patients.

Our first couple of shots—both done in Jasmine's kitchen—went swimmingly and involved filming a snapshot of a conversation between the pair where they discuss where they could go. The idea behind it was that it would be a teaser to give the viewers an idea of what would be coming up in the story when it finally aired.

It wasn't anything harder than I'd done a thousand times before, but I was really struggling with it. I was blinded by confusion and unhappiness, my mind frequently thinking about Elise and Stig dancing in the club the night before—and worse, which made me repeatedly fluff my lines and miss my cues.

"If you could come in immediately after Casey takes Jasmine's hand, please," Stuart said, as I missed my cue for the fourth time. "There's no pause, Holly. Just a straightaway response to Casey's comment."

"Sure." I was aware of both the cameraman's and Stuart's growing impatience. That didn't make my struggling any easier.

"Ready in three, two, one," Stuart counted me down. "And action."

Why did you ignore me in the club, Elise? I looked at Elise, sitting impassively opposite me at the kitchen set table. *Why did you think it was okay to get with some stranger then tell me about it this morning? Don't you know this is killing me?*

"I can't be without you, Casey." I spoke robotically. "I don't think you realise just what you mean to me." I looked at Elise's hand in mine, then back up to her face.

She stared back at me, her eyes questioning. "Your line," she mouthed when I didn't speak, "not mine."

"Cut!"

The pattern of stuttering and missed cues continued. I could hear Elise inhale deeply each time I corpsed or asked to try something again because I wasn't happy with it. When she wasn't prompting me for my line, she was repeatedly suggesting that I add something more to my scenes—a sigh here, a flick of my hair there—but it was impossible. Finally after about an hour, she broke.

"Are you deliberately trying to make this the longest afternoon in history?" she whispered while Stuart halted filming to talk to the lighting guy about changing some angles.

"I'm sorry." I pulled my hands wearily through my hair. "Not a good day today."

"No." She looked at me, her face dark.

"I said I'm sorry," I repeated, wanting her to tell me everything was going to be okay.

"Maybe concentrate, more than being sorry." She smiled. Was her smile kind? Or forced? I wished I knew.

"I'm trying my best here." My voice was thick. "Just give me a break, will you?"

"And that's your best?" Elise asked dismissively, leaning back in her chair and turning to face away from me.

I stared at her dumbly, my face burning.

"You okay, Holly?" Stuart, still talking to the lighting guy, jerked his chin in my direction.

I paused, still looking at Elise's back.

"Give me a sec, yeah Stu?" I called over to him.

I willed Elise to look back at me, but she didn't. Instead, she sat brooding, resolutely refusing to acknowledge that I was still sitting opposite her, and I figured at that moment she must have hated me. Well, I didn't want her to hate me. I wanted her to like me. What's so hard about that? I wanted her to like me like I liked her, but she was never going to, was she? I couldn't even go there because she was straight. She liked men; she'd proved that over the last two nights. Why the hell would she even ever look twice at me?

Without another word, I got up and walked to the corner of the set, angrily wiping away tears of frustration. I stared at the wall in front of me, listening to the sounds of cameras being moved around behind me and of Stuart barking orders at yet another runner on the set.

I so didn't want to be like this, running away from Elise like a petulant child each time she said something to me that upset me, but I just couldn't help myself. Something in Elise and the way she looked at me brought out the hesitant, uncertain actress in me time and again, and I just didn't know what I could do about it.

A shadow covered me, and I was instantly aware of someone standing right behind me. I flinched as Elise put her hand on my shoulder, closing my eyes as I heard her quiet voice.

"I'm sorry."

I turned to face her. "No, I'm sorry," I said. "Dumb reaction."

"I didn't mean to upset you, you know." She stood in front of me, her hand still on my shoulder.

"You didn't upset me, Elise," I said, taking a deep breath.

"You sure about that?" Elise asked. "I wish I knew what it is I do that annoys or upsets you so much, Holly." She studied my face. "Or why you go running off every time I say or do something that you don't agree with."

"I didn't go running off, Elise," I lied. "I just needed five."

"But you don't like it when I say something you disagree with, do you?" Elise asked gently.

"I don't like you being impatient with me, no," I said.

"Who was being impatient?" Elise looked at me in surprise.

"I don't know," I mumbled, aware that I was being stupid and immature again. "That's how it felt."

"I wasn't being impatient, Hol." She finally dropped her hand from my shoulder.

"Well, it felt like it," I mumbled. I leant against the wall and started picking at a loose thread on my jumper, embarrassed at how I was being with her. How could I explain to her that the only reason I'd fled from the set was because of her? How every criticism she directed my way was like a knife in my heart?

I had to be professional. I was just her co-star, for crap's sake! I mean, how stupid would I look if I told her that I was confusing life and fiction, that the lines between what was real and what we were acting out on screen each night were becoming blurred?

For me, anyway.

Elise finally came and stood beside me, so that we were now both leaning against the wall. "Oh, Holly Eight-Year!" Sighing, she leant her head back against the wall and stared up at the ceiling. I looked across and took in the sight of her fine cheekbones, her soft skin, her cute dimples, and her beautifully long eyelashes fluttering briefly each time she blinked. Here she was, standing so close to me, so close I could practically feel the warmth from her, and there was nothing I could do about it. I was desperate to touch her, willing her to turn and look at me, but still she stood staring up at the ceiling.

"I still don't think you like me very much, do you?" Suddenly she turned and looked at me, making me quickly look away. "Despite everything."

I felt my face flush with embarrassment, as if she'd been reading my mind. "I do," I said, probably more defensively than it should have been. "I do like you."

Didn't she realise that I now knew exactly what I liked about her? Her confidence, her attitude, her balls? Didn't she know that's what turned me on? That's what gave me a reason to get up each morning? That I lived and breathed her exuberance, that it hypnotised me, lifted me, made me feel a better person? I felt alive when I was around her, felt like she and I could do anything. We were invincible—Jasey were invincible in *Portobello Road,* and Hollise could be invincible in real life.

Hollise. Holly and Elise.

I turned the words over in my head as Elise continued to talk, not listening to a word she was saying. I liked the idea of Hollise. Together, Elise and I could do anything—I was certain of that. She'd never have a bad experience with me like she'd done when she'd been in LA.

"I don't like to think I've upset you, Holly," Elise said, interrupting my thoughts. "I didn't mean to." She caught my eye. "I'm sorry."

"Okay." I didn't know what else to say.

"If I was impatient, then I apologise," Elise was now saying. "I know I can be a bit in-your-face—God knows I've been told enough times—but I don't mean to be, certainly not with you. Sometimes it just comes out wrong."

I didn't answer her.

"I just want us to be friends," she said. "Because I like you, and I like working with you."

Friends? Just friends?

"Me, too," I finally said feebly. I waited for her to say something else, but she didn't. Instead, she looked at her watch and sighed.

"Good." She finally pulled herself away from the wall.

"Just give me five minutes," I said to her now. "I'll follow you back over there, okay?" I jerked my chin towards the set.

"Okay," Elise said, running her hand down my arm.

She slowly walked away from me, talking briefly to Stuart as she approached him back on set. I stared at her back, wondering what she was saying to him, then shook my head. I was being stupid, letting her get to me the way she was. She was my co-star, she was straight, she was dating Stig, and she'd never be anything more than just the girl I happened to work with. The sooner I accepted that, the sooner I could move on. She was affecting my work, work that I was damned good at and had been for years.

Well, no more. I was ready now. This time I wasn't going to balls things up.

CHAPTER ELEVEN

After we'd finally finished shooting that afternoon, I didn't see Elise again for the rest of the day, or for the rest of the weekend, either. I was relieved, actually, because not seeing her and not hearing from her for nearly forty-eight hours gave me time to think about things, and a chance to try to figure out the best thing to do, which was easier said than done. The trouble was, I just didn't know what to do. I had to work with her, there was no escaping from that, but I figured the more I kept it totally on a professional level, then the easier it would be to handle.

That meant no going round to her dressing room, no hanging out with her between takes, and certainly no going out clubbing with her at all. It also meant not taking any of her funny moods personally, or taking to heart any of her occasional asides to me during and after filming. I was a professional; I made my living out of pretending to be someone I wasn't, so it should be second nature, right?

Wrong.

All the advice I'd given to myself in the few days I didn't see Elise counted for zip when I returned to work Monday morning and saw her again in the car park, arriving just before me. I sat in my car and watched, hypnotised, as she got out of hers, her long legs unfurling from her seat, and shrugged her jacket on. She was dressed down in a simple jacket-and-trouser combination, but she was still achingly beautiful, I thought.

I saw her spot me, and my heart skipped when she then waved at me and stood by her car, waiting for me.

"Hey!" She looked genuinely pleased to see me as I finally got out of my car and wandered towards her.

"All right?" I tried to act normally, desperate not to focus too much on her face. Instead I rooted around in my shoulder bag for some imaginary thing, only so I could stare down into it and not have to look at her.

Would she be able to tell from the look on my face what I was thinking? Would she be able to detect a change in me?

"Good weekend?" she asked. "Or what was left of it, anyway?"

We started walking together towards the entrance to the studios, and I made sure I walked a good few feet from her so my arm wouldn't brush against her. Stupid, I know.

"Not bad," I replied. "You?"

"It was awesome, yeah." She seemed happy, so I could only guess that she'd either spent it with Stig or that she'd pulled another guy in another club somewhere. Whatever it was, I didn't want to know.

We walked on in silence through the entrance. I deliberately didn't ask her what it was that had made her weekend so awesome, really not wanting to hear about her getting it on with some guy.

"I was in Manchester all weekend," Elise now said as we walked side by side down the corridor to our dressing rooms.

Not with Stig. Please, not with Stig…

"Staying with my parents," she added.

Her parents!

I was practically weak with relief that she hadn't spent the last day and a half under a duvet with Stig.

"It was good to chill out with them for a bit," she said. "It felt as though I hadn't seen them, like, forever." Elise opened the door to another corridor and stepped back, allowing me to pass. "So I've allowed myself to be royally spoilt by Mum and Dad all weekend. It's been great."

"My parents live out in the middle of the countryside," I said lamely. "I don't get to see them so much, either." I wanted to tell Elise that I'd had just as good a weekend as her, but of course I couldn't. I'd barely left the apartment since I arrived home late on the

Saturday after filming our promo shots, choosing to mooch around
in my PJs thinking stuff over and over again rather than going out
anywhere. I just hadn't had the energy, the heart, or the enthusiasm
to do anything other than brood, replaying past conversations I'd
had with Elise, and past confrontations, too. I'd even stood in my
kitchen staring at the spot where the spider had been, just thinking
about Elise and how she'd made me laugh so much that night.

"Did you...did you do the clubs on Saturday?" I asked Elise
tentatively, wanting to know whether she'd pulled again, but
dreading the answer at the same time. "I hear they're awesome up
in Manchester."

"Nah," she said, slowing down as she approached her dressing
room door. "I stayed in and watched a DVD with my mum. How
boring am I becoming?" She bumped my shoulder playfully and I
suddenly felt so happy, it was ridiculous.

"Anyway, see you in make-up in a bit," she said, going into her
room and closing the door after her. I stood and looked at her door
awhile, thinking how stupidly relieved I felt that she hadn't gone to
Manchester with Stig, that she hadn't gone out on Saturday night
and—more importantly—that she hadn't hooked up with another
guy all in one weekend.

I bit at my lip, staring down at the carpet. Was it always going
to be like this? Always wondering what Elise was getting up to?
Being pathetically grateful when she told me she'd stayed in, whilst
getting pathetically upset if I knew she'd gone out? I hated feeling
jealous over her, knowing there was nothing I could do about it.

I wandered on down to my own dressing room, deep in thought.
We had about another half hour before we were due in make-up, so
I got my phone out from my bag and slobbed out on the sofa in
there, surfing the net and catching up with the few e-mails that were
lurking in my inbox.

My eye scanned it, filtering out the junk from the important
in amongst the twelve unread mails in there. As I looked at the
list, I felt a coldness rush down my arm from the phone, across my
shoulders, and down my back. Sitting waiting for me in amongst
all the other e-mails was one from Grace, sent late the night before.

I stared at her name, still in bold. *Grace Thomas.*

I hadn't seen her name for over two years, and now it hit me like a hard slap across the face. She'd never contacted me after she'd disappeared to Madrid—why should she have? She'd moved on the second she'd got on that plane at Heathrow, already thinking ahead to her new life with her new Spanish girlfriend. What had I mattered? Did she care whether I'd spent the best part of six months getting over her, living my life in a daze, throwing myself into my work because I knew if I didn't, my world would collapse around my ears? No, she didn't.

I pressed my thumb on her name and saw her message unfurl before me.

Hey Holly, it began.

How are you? It's been a while, huh? I just wanted to see how you are. How's Jasmine treating you? lol Are you even still in the programme? I haven't kept up with what's been going on over there so I don't know if you're still doing what you did, or if you're even still living in London.

I'm single again. Me and Pilar broke up—

Pilar? That was her name? I never even knew what it was.

I read the rest of her e-mail in a daze, not really taking in the stuff she was telling me about her work, and about how her parents were now living in Ireland, and blah, blah, blah. Her last few lines totally caught my attention, though, so much so that they got me sitting up on the sofa and reading them three times over.

I'm moving back to the UK but staying with my parents over in Ireland until I get myself something sorted in London. I'll be coming through Heathrow on my way over to my parents' place next Friday and I'd really like to see you, Holly. I've missed you—

What the...?

I read the last part again.

I've missed you.

Pity you never missed me all the time you were in Spain, isn't it? I thought savagely as I switched my phone off and flung it onto the sofa.

I thought my head was going to burst. Grace was coming home. More than that, she was coming to London and wanted to see me. Madness! Why now? Why fucking now? As if my head wasn't puddled enough with thoughts of Elise, now Grace was coming in and screwing me up even more by not only telling me she was moving back to the UK, but that she missed me and wanted to see me.

I let myself fall sideways onto the sofa, turning onto my back and, drawing my knees up, lay back and stared up at the ceiling. I didn't know what to do. Did I want to see Grace again, after all this time?

I was so over her.

Right?

Seeing her again wouldn't be a problem.

Would it?

Why did she tell me she missed me? Actually, hang that. Why the hell did she feel the need to contact me—after two bloody years—to tell me that? Was it because she'd broken up with this Pilar girl and felt some need to tell me about it?

I rubbed tetchily at my eyes and glanced up at the clock on my wall. I was due in make-up in five minutes, but there wasn't one part of me that gave a damn right now about make-up, about *PR,* about acting, or about Jasey. All I gave a damn about was thinking about Grace's sodding e-mail. I picked up my phone again and read her message one more time, trying to absorb every word of it.

I'd just finished reading it when a knock at my door pulled my gaze to the clock. Five minutes had passed, which meant it was either one of the make-up girls coming looking for me or someone from the set in a foul mood, wanting to know why I was late. Knowing I should move, but not being arsed to, I remained stretched out on the sofa, numb.

"Holly? You in there?"

Elise. I switched my phone off again and stuffed it into my pocket.

"Yeah," I called wearily.

The door opened a crack and Elise stepped in, already made up and dressed in Casey's clothes—her uni hoodie and a pair of ripped jeans, a large, tatty shoulder bag strung round her shoulders.

"They're wondering where you are," Elise said. "Make-up, I mean. They're waiting for you."

"I don't feel so good," I said, still lying on the sofa.

"Oh?" Elise entered the room and was by my side in an instant, looking worried.

"Nothing serious," I said hastily, embarrassed that she'd felt the need to come to me. "Just a headache."

"Again?" Elise crouched in front of me, an anxious look on her face. "Have you taken anything?" she asked. "'Cos I have some pills back in my room."

I shook my head. "It's not that bad," I said feebly, swinging my legs down and sitting on the edge of the sofa. I put my head in my hands, staring down at my feet and pulling my hands roughly through my hair. Grace and her stupid e-mail would just have to wait for now. What did she want me to say? That I missed her, too? Truth was, I hadn't thought of her for a long time, certainly not since I'd started working with Elise, anyway, and it had only been in the last few months that I'd really known for sure that I was finally over her.

I glanced up at Elise, now standing awkwardly next to me, and my insides dissolved at the sweet, concerned look on her face. So Grace was coming back, was she? Well, tough. This was my life now. Right here, right now. Grace was my past, and she could stay there.

"Shall we do this, then?" I scrambled to my feet and wandered to the door, not daring to look at Elise again on my way past her.

❖

I just about made it through my scenes that morning, despite my mind frequently jumping between Grace and Elise, wondering what on earth I was going to do about everything. Despite telling myself over and again that Grace was nothing to me now, that she could go to hell for all I cared, I'd be lying if I said her e-mail hadn't intrigued me, and that a small part of me wanted to see her again. But I didn't know why. Maybe I wanted closure. Maybe I'd get that from seeing her just one more time. I also knew that if I did meet her, there was the huge possibility that I'd take one look and fall for her all over again, and that, coupled with my confusion over Elise, might just tip me over the edge. But it also might take my mind off Elise, mightn't it?

In the days that followed, Elise sensed there was something wrong, too. How could she not? I was acting weird with her; I was robotic—even I could tell that—because all I could think about was Grace, and the fact that I hadn't replied to her, and that the Friday when she was due to be in London was just a few days away.

We were filming the last scenes of the morning on the set of Jasmine's front room, three days after Grace had contacted me, when I thought I might finally flip. I hadn't slept properly since I'd read her e-mail, waking up in the dead of night just churning stuff over in my head, pacing my lounge, drinking a hot chocolate in the hope that I'd manage at least a few hours' sleep. The lack of sleep and constant gnawing worry eating away at me were making me sullen and quiet, and Elise picked up on it straight away.

"So Jasmine's parents are out in this scene." Stuart paced the floor of the set. "Remember, her parents don't know anything yet, so any chances Jasmine can take to be alone with Casey, she's going to grab them, okay?"

I nodded wearily, sitting down on the prop sofa and tensing as Elise sat down beside me.

"You good to go?" Elise asked, seeing me pinch the bridge of my nose with my finger and thumb.

"Good to go."

"Sure?"

"I just said, didn't I?" I pinched my nose harder.

"Just a short scene, this one, to ease us into lunch." Stuart stood next to the camera, his hand on the cameraman's shoulder. "Scene three, take one. Cue Casey."

Elise took a deep breath, casting a quick glance towards me, then was into her take.

"Every time I close my eyes, I see you," she said, leaning back against the sofa.

"It's like, you got into my head and I can't shake you from there." She turned her head slightly, catching my eye. "And you know what?" she said, "I like you being there."

"You really mean it, Casey?" I shuffled slightly, angling my knees towards hers. "I thought when you said you were going out with that guy from the pub…"

"Lloyd?"

"Was that his name?" I asked. "I didn't catch his name."

"Lloyd means nothing to me." Elise moved closer. "You're the only one that means anything to me now, Jas—"

"Cut!" Stuart waved his arms. "You're too quiet, Holly. Soundman didn't pick up your last line. Can we go from *that guy from the pub*, please?"

Elise and I repeated our lines, but every word I spoke was a struggle. My voice sounded weak and thin, strained by the effort of saying lines I wished I could say to Elise in real life. What was happening to me? Why was my life apparently now playing out in the scripts that I was memorising? How could I have been so stupid as to confuse Jasmine's life with my own?

"Scene two, take one." Stuart's instruction woke me from my thoughts. "Action."

"Sometimes it feels like I've waited my whole life just to find someone like you." Elise spoke her lines effortlessly. "Like everything I went through before, with all the guys who didn't give a damn, was worth it because it brought me to you."

We looked at one another, the cameras still rolling.

"Are you scared?" Elise pulled me to her, adjusting her shoulder slightly as I rested my head against it.

"Truthfully?" I lifted my head slightly and peered at her. "Terrified."

"Me, too." She pulled me closer to her again, allowing me to rest my head back on her shoulder. I loved hearing her heart beating in my ear and the feel of the gentle fall and rise of her shoulder as she breathed in and out. "But it *is* what you want, isn't it?" she murmured softly.

"Casey, I've waited months to hear you say what you just said to me," I said, aware of Stuart giving us thumbs up from behind the camera. I carried on from my script. "When I first knew you, okay, you made me nervous because you were so kick-ass, but then I realised I was only nervous because I liked you."

"You liked me from the start?"

"Not at first." Remembering where we were up to, I looped my arms around her waist, just as it had been written in the script. "You kinda grew on me. Once I realised that kick-ass attitude was all for show, and that underneath it all you were just a big softy," I said, "well, then I stopped being scared of you."

"That's kinda cute." Elise gave a half laugh and gazed down at me.

"Okay, cut." Stuart appeared from behind the camera, peering down at his clipboard, his glasses perched on the end of his nose. "Good job, you two." His voice reluctantly pulled my eyes from Elise's. "Very good." He made a winding motion to a runner nearby. "Quick break for lunch, then we're on to the next scene, okay? Shooting on set three for that one, please. One o'clock sharp."

I was still sitting with my arms looped around Elise's waist. I liked that her arm was still around my shoulders, even though we'd finished the scene. She didn't make any move to go, instead just sitting on the sofa, her head resting against the back of it, her eyes closed.

"I don't want to move," she whispered. She opened one eye and peered down to me. "Do you?"

I breathed in and out slowly, trying to calm myself down, scared that Elise would be able to detect that I was breathing far faster than I should have been.

Finally, grudgingly, I moved my arms from her waist, eliciting a grumble from her.

"Don't," she murmured. "I want to stay like this forever."

"We have four more scenes to shoot this afternoon," I said, reluctantly pulling away. She lifted her arm to allow me to disentangle myself from her, instantly making my shoulder want to feel her warmth on it again. "And lunch in between. No time for lazing about."

"Spoilsport." Elise stretched her arms in front of her and yawned. "Just as I was beginning to enjoy myself, too."

She tilted her head slightly and studied me. "You're quiet today, Hol," she said. "Something on your mind?"

I stood up. "Plenty," I said with a exaggerated roll of my eyes. I moved away slightly. "Look, I'm just going to stay and chill here for five minutes."

"Do you want me to go?" She suddenly reached up and took my hand. "Leave you in peace?"

"No." I let her hand fall away from mine again and turned away from her, staring down at the floor, my arms wrapped tight around myself. "I don't want you to go."

Elise stood up and slowly came up behind me. She gently touched my arm, sending an electric current down the length of it to my fingertips.

"Then I'll stay," she said from just behind me. She stood so close I could hear her breathing, could feel her breath on the back of my neck. I squeezed my eyes shut.

"Talk to me, Holly," she said. "You're not yourself today. I can sense it."

I shook my head. "I'll live."

"Are you stressed?"

"Just a bit." I gave a hollow laugh.

"Then let me help," Elise said.

"I don't think anyone can help me." I continued hugging myself.

"But I can't sort out whatever it is if you won't talk to me, can I?" Her soft voice sounded near me, nearer with every word she said.

"You don't need to sort anything out, Elise," I said.

"Casey would want to help Jasmine if she knew Jasmine was stressing about something." She put her hands on my arms and slowly turned me round to face her. "And I want to help you." She gazed at me, her face etched with concern. "Have I done something wrong?"

"You haven't done anything wrong, Elise." My voice cracked with emotion. "I just have a lot on my mind, that's all."

"Because of?"

"Please," I pleaded, scared that everything would come tumbling out. "Just don't ask, okay?"

"No," Elise continued gazing at me. "I need you to tell me what's bugging you."

"Nothing's bugging me that I want to talk about, honestly," I said quietly.

She wanted to know what my problem was, did she? My problem was Grace coming back into my life and bombarding me with e-mails telling me she missed me when I'd finally gotten over her and fallen head over heels for Elise. I was longing for this straight girl, standing right in front of me looking angry and adorable and sexy all at the same time, and knowing that she didn't feel the same way about me. Why didn't she feel the same way? Why?

I stared at Elise, standing there looking so goddamned perfect with her hands on her hips. I knew I should walk away, ignore my feelings for her, but all I could do was carry on glaring at her, taking in every detail of her beautiful face, while my guts churned up inside, knowing that I could never have her.

CHAPTER TWELVE

I finally stumbled away from Elise, leaving her confused, knowing that just one more look from those dark eyes would have me telling her everything about how I felt about her, and I literally bumped straight into Bella on my way down the corridor.

"Blimey, someone got out of bed the wrong side today," she said, rubbing the arm that I'd just cannoned into.

I looked at Bella, and I guess the expression on my face told her everything because she quickly looked over her shoulder and, without another word, ushered me down the corridor and into our dressing room, shutting the door tightly behind us.

"Someone needs a timeout, I think," she said, sitting me down on the sofa and joining me, putting her arm round my shoulders.

"I don't think even the longest timeout could sort out this mess," I said, staring bleakly at the floor.

"Want to talk about it?" Bella asked gently.

I shook my head, just as there was a knock on the door. It would be Elise, I knew.

"Shall I send them away?" Bella rose from the sofa and headed for the door.

"Would you mind?" I asked, leaning my head back against the back of the sofa and staring blankly up at the dust-covered light fitting on the ceiling.

I heard the low murmur of Elise's voice in the doorway but couldn't see her, as Bella had positioned herself in such a way that blocked my view. I sat back, eyes closed, as they spoke briefly to one another before Bella finally closed the door and faced me.

"Now then, my dear," she began. "Is there anything you want to tell me?"

"I just don't know what to do, Bella," I said. "I really don't."

Bella sat with me on the sofa. I was on the verge of tears but knew if I gave in to them and actually started crying, then I wouldn't be able to stop. Trying to stem them, I sat with my elbows on my knees and concentrated on picking at my fingers and staring down at the floor while Bella rubbed my back.

"Do you want to talk about it?" Bella asked gently.

I shrugged.

"Elise wanted to see you, you know," Bella continued.

"Well, I don't want to see her," I said, still staring numbly at the floor.

"She said you've been uptight all day." Bella spoke quietly. "Is something the matter?"

I rolled my eyes and laughed. "Plenty, Bella," I said. "I've just got some stuff going on that I need to get sorted."

"At work?"

"Yeah, partly," I mumbled. "I'm just finding it hard to work with Elise at the moment."

"Have you two still not hit it off?" Bella asked tentatively. "I thought you were getting on so much better now." She looked at me with a motherly concern.

I sighed and leant back against the sofa, closing my eyes. "We're getting on fine," I said finally.

"But?"

I so needed to talk to someone about it, but I just didn't know how Bella would react. Would she think I was stupid for falling in love with Elise? It was ludicrous, wasn't it? Wanting to act out in real life what I was acting out on screen?

"I can't tell you, Bella," I said. "I don't even know where to begin. It's all such a mess, it really is."

I rubbed my hands roughly over my face, digging the tips of my fingers into the corners of my eyes as if trying to push back the tears that were threatening to spill again.

"Holly, my dear," Bella put her hand on my knee. "I've known you since you were twelve. I've been your other mother since you were twelve. I've watched you grow up from a sweet kid into the loveliest, most beautiful young lady anyone could wish to meet." She smiled kindly at me. "I'm very fond of you, you know, and I'd like to think you could come to me and tell me anything."

"I just don't know if you'd understand, though," I said sadly.

"I have three teenagers of my own at home." Bella nudged me good-naturedly. "I don't think there's much I don't understand about you lot." She thought for a while. "Why was Elise so desperate to see you just now? She looked awful. Really worried."

"Did she?" A small spark ignited inside me, in spite of myself.

"Mm-hmm," Bella nodded, her eyebrows raised.

"I'm totally fucked up in the head at the moment," I said quietly. "And I've been messing up takes a bit too much just lately."

"Okay..." Bella started. "So why are you messing up your takes?"

"Because my mind is constantly on something...some*one*... else," I said.

"Now we're getting somewhere." Bella patted my leg.

"My head's such a mess, Bella," I mumbled. "I just don't know what to do!"

"Are you and Elise fighting over some boy?" Bella suddenly asked. "Is that what this is about? You've both met someone and you both fancy him?"

Oh, if only she knew!

"Robbie?" Bella persisted. "Is it to do with her date with Robbie? Do you like him yourself?"

I laughed. "No," I said. "Trust me, it's not that at all." We didn't speak for a few seconds. I was desperate to talk to her about it but just didn't know where to even begin. I took a deep breath. "I had an e-mail," I said slowly. "From an ex."

"Ugh, the ex's e-mail conundrum." Bella shuddered.

"Exactly," I said. "My ex wants to meet me and I don't know what to do."

"How long ago did you split up?" Bella asked. "I didn't even know you were seeing anyone, to be honest."

"Two years," I said. "And, no. I wanted to keep quiet about it."

"And he wants to see you again?" Bella looked at me with concern. "And you don't know whether you should go and see him? Is that it?"

"Something like that," I muttered, staring down at my hands.

"Do you want to see him?" Bella asked.

Her! Her! Did I want to see *her*?

"I don't know, that's just it," I said. "I haven't replied to the e-mail yet."

"So where does Elise fit into all this?" Bella asked.

"She figured I was stressing over something," I said slowly, "and has been pushing me to talk to her about it."

"And you don't want to talk to her because…?" Bella offered.

"Because if I start to talk to her, I'll never stop." I looked at Bella. "I just don't know what to do," I suddenly said. "Elise barely knows I exist some days, and I want her to."

"You want her to?" Bella leant her head to one side, confused.

"I want her to notice me, Bella," I said quietly. "Because I like her."

"I see," Bella said slowly. "I think." She paused. "Are you telling me what I think you're telling me?"

"The e-mail from the ex," I said, wiping my nose with the back of my hand. "The ex is a girl."

"I see," Bella repeated. "I didn't know you were…you know…"

"Gay? Well, I am," I said quietly. "Always have been."

"Okay," Bella said slowly, processing. "So let me get this right. You like Elise, but she doesn't know it, and now you've also had an e-mail from an ex-girlfriend, and you don't know what to do about it?"

"Yuh-huh."

"You are in a pickle, aren't you?" Bella laughed good-naturedly, wrapping her arms around me and pulling me to her in a bear hug. "And they say soaps are full of drama!"

"Could write a whole year's worth with me, I think." I sniffled.

"And Elise has no idea that you're gay or that you like her?"

"God, no!" I looked horrified. "She's no idea about either, and I want it to stay that way."

I looked down at my hands and started worrying at a piece of skin on my thumb. "I don't feel like I can stay away from Elise anymore," I said numbly. "I want her and I can't have her, and I hate it." I thought for a moment. "I haven't felt like this about anyone since Grace," I said simply. "And it's freaking me out a bit."

"In a good way?"

"Yeah." I sighed. "Elise is all I think about, day and night. It feels good to have my mind so full of a person again, but it's scary at the same time, especially because she doesn't even know."

"But Elise likes men, Holly," Bella said gently. "She went out with Robbie, she now has another boyfriend…"

"Stig," I said miserably. "I know. So she's not going to appreciate me coming to her with declarations of love, is she?"

Bella thought for a moment. "But do you think she'll freak out if you just tell her you're gay to start with?" she asked. "Don't you think she might like to know that? Bearing in mind the scenes you do together?" She paused. "I'm trying to be diplomatic here, Holly."

"Yes, I think she'll flip out if I tell her," I said miserably. I looked down at a screwed up sugar packet on the table that I'd been absent-mindedly playing with. "Elise told me once before that she has a reputation for picking the wrong men," I said. "She told me when she was in the States she had bad experiences with men, lurching from one guy to the next."

"And she's doing the same here?"

"Well she's been going from Robbie, to Stig, to God knows who else." I picked up the sugar packet again and screwed it into a tight ball, tossing it straight back down onto the table. "It's like she's drifting from boyfriend to boyfriend, always looking for the right one but never finding him."

"Because you think he doesn't exist?" Bella offered.

"Maybe."

"And you want to be the one who offers her what she wants?" Bella asked tentatively.

"I know I can," I said simply. "Because it's what I want, too."

"Then you have two options, my dear," Bella said, getting to her feet and placing her hand on my shoulder.

"Which are?" I looked up at her.

"You either take a risk and tell her exactly how you feel," Bella said, her hand still on my shoulder. "No holds barred, the whole pouring out your innermost feelings malarkey."

"Or?"

"Or you ignore your feelings completely and try to forget about her," Bella said. "Concentrate on just being her friend instead."

"Forget her?" I repeated, looking up at Bella.

"Mm-hmm." Bella nodded kindly. She paused for a moment. "And your ex?"

"Grace?" I said. "What about her?"

"Are you going to see her?"

"I don't know," I said. "I've been thinking about her a lot since she e-mailed me and *gah!* a small part of me thinks that if I hooked up with her again, my feelings for Elise would disappear."

"Assuming she wants to get back with you, of course."

"But even if I just go and see her, it might make me forget about Elise," I said hopefully. "It's got to be worth a try, hasn't it?"

"Oh, Holly." Bella sighed. "I wish I could tell you what the best thing to do would be, but I guess only you'll know that."

I jumped as there was a sharp rap on our dressing room door.

"That'll be my call for make-up." Bella patted my shoulder. "I'm due on set shortly."

I watched as she walked to the door and opened it, spoke to the person outside, then closed it again.

"We have some scenes together later this afternoon, don't we?" she asked, fetching her bag from the floor.

I nodded.

"Have a think about stuff quietly for a while," she said, coming back over to me. "And if you want to talk again later, you know where I'll be."

"Thanks, Bella." I smiled up at her. "You won't say anything, will you?"

"Holly, my dear," Bella said, "what's said in this dressing room stays in this dressing room." She leant over and kissed the top of my head, ruffling my hair for good measure, then walked back to the door and paused. "Think about talking to Elise as well," she said. "You don't have to tell her you like her, but it might be an idea to tell her about Grace."

"Maybe," I said. "Maybe not." I got up and joined Bella at the door, suddenly getting a rush of affection towards her and an overwhelming sense of relief that I'd come out to her.

"Bella?"

She turned round.

"Thanks," I said.

"For listening?" Bella grinned. "It's what I'm here for."

"Yeah, thanks for listening, and thanks for, well"—I glanced away, then back towards her—"for being cool with…y'know. Stuff."

"It's what I'm here for," Bella repeated, pulling me to her. I rested my chin on her shoulder, feeling my throat tighten with tears. "You know you can always talk to me, don't you?" she asked. "About anything."

"I know." I swallowed hard. "Somehow I think I'm going to be talking to you a lot in the coming weeks."

CHAPTER THIRTEEN

I filmed all my scenes with Bella without any major hitches that afternoon, much to my relief. Talking to her had really helped make me feel less stressed—but still no happier—than I had in the morning, and I felt ridiculously pleased every time I remembered that I'd come out to her, which, considering Bella was my other mother, was a huge deal for me. I was even more relieved that telling her I was gay had passed over Bella without her batting an eyelid, and I guess a small part of me regretted that I hadn't spoken to her or someone else about it before.

I still couldn't bring myself to speak to Elise, though. I knew I should go and apologise to her for not wanting to see her when she'd come to my dressing room that morning, clearly wanting to see me. I'd seen her around and about the studio since then as she'd filmed two scenes with Robbie on the set of Jasmine's kitchen, but that's all I'd seen of her since the morning, and a small part of me was relieved about that.

I'd decided I wouldn't tell her about Grace, despite Bella's advice. I'd also chosen not to see Grace, either. How could I? I'd checked my e-mails on my phone after I'd finished filming that afternoon and had been frustrated to find another one from her waiting in my inbox. This one just asked me if I'd got her first e-mail—*"because you haven't answered"*—and again suggested meeting up in London at some point during the few days she'd be in the capital. I deleted it straight away.

I mean, how could I go and meet up with someone who could have been so cruel as to break my heart the way she did, and then think it was okay to contact me again, just because she'd split up from the very same girl she'd left me for? What did Grace think I was going to do? Welcome her back with open arms? Not a chance—as far as I was concerned now, Grace didn't exist. I wouldn't reply to her e-mails, either. She could sit and stew for all I cared.

I was heading back out to my car, having finally finished for the day, when I heard footsteps behind me and swung round to see Elise trying to run across the car park in her socked feet, a pair of trainers in her hand. It was a sight that, if I hadn't still been so miserable, would have been funny.

"Holly! Wait!"

I looked at her, dressed down in gym gear, her trainers still in her hand, and my heart bunched up inside me. She looked stunning—she always did: sweatpants sitting cutely on her hips, T-shirt clinging to all the right places, and her hair, well, it hung perfectly across her eyes, just like it always did.

"I saw you leave and I wanted to catch you," she said, lifting her trainers up as if to explain.

"I see," I said, not really knowing what else to say.

"I wanted to make sure you were okay." Elise put her trainers onto the floor and wiggled her feet into them. "I've been thinking about you all afternoon."

"Thinking about me?" A pulse travelled through me.

"Yuh-huh." Elise reached out and slowly took my hand in hers, holding it and rubbing her thumb on my palm. No one had held my hand as tenderly as that since Grace. My skin tingled and my head now reeled at Elise's touch, so I lowered my eyes and stared at the floor, afraid to look at her face.

"I came to see you in your room, too," she said, gently squeezing my hand.

"I know, Bella said," I said feebly, still staring at my feet. "Sorry, I wasn't really up for having company."

"I was worried about you," she said.

"Were you?" I lifted my head and our eyes met.

"Mm-hmm," Elise nodded. "I *can* do worried sometimes, you know."

It was as though someone was sitting on my chest, squeezing the air out of me, as she carried on holding my hand and looking at me the way she was.

"I'm sorry again that I messed up our scenes this morning," I finally said.

"Forget about it," Elise replied. "I just want to know you're okay now. That's all I'm bothered about." She studied me carefully, still holding my hand. Suddenly Bella's words to me about talking to Elise came flooding into my head. Perhaps Bella was right. This might be the perfect time to talk to Elise after all.

I leant against my car, my breathing coming faster. "You know, once, you told me I was a lot like Jasmine?" I started, my pulse thudding.

"Mm-hmm?"

"I think perhaps I'm more like her than you realise."

"You're studying graphic design at Harewood University?" Elise dramatically clutched her chest. "You kept that quiet!"

"No," I said. "Not graphic design."

"That's a serious face," Elise said, dipping her head to catch my eye. "Was my joke that bad?"

"Jasmine and I have something in common," I persisted, and I felt my face flushing.

"Which is?" Elise said, making a winding motion with her hand.

"We both share the same tastes," I said slowly. "Like the same things."

"Cappuccinos with far too much sugar in them, you mean?" Elise held up her hands. "Sorry, another lame joke."

"No." I looked at her. "Not cappuccinos."

"Then…?" Elise prompted.

"We both like girls," I said simply. "I thought you needed to know, that's all."

"Okay," she said simply.

"Are you all right with that?" I asked.

"God, yes." Elise took my hand again. "Totally."

"Sure?"

"Completely sure," Elise said. "I'm glad you told me."

"You are?" I said hopefully.

Elise nodded.

"And you don't feel differently towards me?" I asked feebly. "For being gay, I mean?"

"You really need me to answer that?" Elise raised her eyebrows. "You know I like you, Holly. I like you a lot, so that's a ridiculous thing to even be thinking, let alone saying to me."

She liked me a lot?

"Nothing's changed," Elise said gently. "Why would it?"

I looked up and saw that she was still looking at me, intense blue eyes locked onto mine.

Nothing's changed. Nothing.

"Do you have a girlfriend?" she asked, her voice sounding curious.

I shook my head. "No, not at the moment." I paused. "But an ex is sniffing around again." I looked at Elise, trying to gauge her reaction.

"Is that what's been stressing you out?" Elise asked.

"Mm," I said. "Amongst other things."

"It seems a small thing to be so stressed about." She shrugged. "Exes come and go all the time. It's no biggie."

"Maybe in your world, but not in mine," I said, making her laugh.

"Were you in love?" Elise suddenly asked.

"Yes," I said, taken aback by her forthright question. "Very much."

"That's sweet," Elise said, smiling at me.

"It was." I laughed. "Until she dumped me."

"Ouch."

"Mm," I said. "Ouch, indeed."

"Were you upset?" Elise asked.

"Yes, very," I replied. "Can we change the subject now, please?" I plunged my hands deep into my jeans pockets, squirming at Elise's questions.

"Sorry," Elise said. "I just think it must be nice. Being in love, I mean." She thought for a while. "And not caring what anyone thinks." She leant against my car. "I don't think I'd have the guts to be like you."

"Well, it wasn't common knowledge around here," I said. "I kept it quiet and it worked fine."

"You weren't worried that people would find out?" she asked. "And that people would think differently about you?"

"No," I said honestly. "To be completely clichéd here, if people don't like it, then tough."

"I wish I had your optimism," Elise said.

"How do you mean?" I asked, intrigued by the look on her face as she said it.

"Nothing." Elise looked at her watch and sighed. "Damn!" She delved into her bag for her car keys. "I have to go," she said reluctantly. "Stupid gym session." She gazed at me a while longer, then walked away from me and back towards her car, stopping after a few steps to turn and look at me. "I'm glad you told me," she said, "and you have to believe me when I tell you I'm totally cool with it."

"Thank you." I felt like a weight had been lifted.

"And you promise me you're okay?" she asked again. "I can't be worrying about you when I'm supposed to be working out, you know."

I smiled. "I'm fine, honestly."

The truth hit me. I wasn't fine at all, was I?

❖

Relieved at having come out to Elise, my mind felt slightly less cluttered, allowing me to ignore Grace's second e-mail, prompting her to send me a third one, asking me if I'd received it and repeating that she was desperate to see me before she flew on to Ireland on Friday. She left her mobile number, which I instantly forgot, and urged me to ring or text her, just saying over and over about how good it would be for us to hook up again, if only for a quick drink.

My more relaxed state of mind over Elise had a positive effect on my work, too. We practically sailed through our day's filming the next day, and—thank goodness—wrapped all our scenes up in good time, all without me making a complete hash of any take where Elise had to look at me like I wished she'd look at me in real life. That made such a nice change.

With our scenes for the day now in the can, we both went our separate ways down to our own dressing rooms to change back into our normal clothes. I was just heading back from my room and out to the car park to go home for the afternoon when Elise called down the corridor to me, having changed, too.

"Do you want to grab a coffee before we go home?" she asked. "If I go straight home I'll just spend the next God knows how many hours learning lines, and I don't want to do that just yet."

I stole a look at her, stupidly happy that she wanted to hang out with me. She looked drop-dead gorgeous, too, dressed down in scruffy jeans and a sleeveless top but still lovely all the same. She always had this knack of looking amazing, even when she was dressed casually; it was just another thing to add to the ever-growing list of things that I found attractive about her.

"Sure," I said, "Will the canteen do you?"

"I was thinking away from here." Elise wrinkled her nose. "The place down the road does an awesome macchiato."

"Sounds good to me."

We left the studio and walked the five minutes down to the coffee shop Elise had suggested. It was a bright, sunny day—hot, even—and the road where the coffee place was situated was full of people wandering up and down, looking in shops and sitting under parasols outside the numerous other cafes and restaurants down the same road.

We found ourselves a table outside the cafe and, on Elise's recommendation, ordered ourselves a macchiato each. I was aware of a few people staring at us as we sat down, ignoring a stabbing jealousy in my stomach as two guys watched, open-mouthed, as Elise pulled her chair back and sat down, running her hands through her hair. I was even more aware of a few phones coming out to take surreptitious photos of us, but other than that, we were left to enjoy our coffees in peace, which I was grateful for.

"So we have the interview and photo shoot for *Modern Woman* magazine next week," Elise said, sitting back in her chair and tilting her face slightly to the sun. While I was still watching, she pushed her sunglasses back from her eyes and up onto her head, lifting her fringe from her face. Elise looked effortlessly beautiful, I thought as I looked at her near-perfect profile: the line of her jaw, the smoothness of her skin, her perfect lips, and deep blue eyes framed by thick dark lashes. She turned her head slightly, peering at me through one eye. I cut my glance away, hoping she hadn't seen me staring at her.

Our coffees arrived, much to my relief, bringing a welcome distraction, and I watched as the server brought out sugars and dusted our coffees with chocolate. When he'd finally gone, I spoke. "And then it's Millie's leaving do, as well."

Millie was one of the other actors in *PR* who had decided to move on from the show and try her hand elsewhere. We were, in fine *PR* tradition, taking her out to one of London's swankiest hotels for her farewell party. They were always awesome events, with loads of champagne, loads of food, loads of speeches, and, most importantly, loads of silliness thrown in as well.

"At Morgan's isn't it?" Elise sipped at her coffee and looked mischievously at me. "I'll have to get my glad rags on for that one. Really go to town. There'll be paps there, guaranteed!"

I sprinkled sugar onto my macchiato and stirred it in, an image of Elise in the tightest, lowest-cut dress swimming into my head and back out again. Blowing across the top of my mug, I noticed her still looking at me.

"What?" I laughed.

"Nothing." She leant her head to one side. "Just thinking how nice this is, that's all." She took a drink from her coffee. "You're so right for the part of Jasmine, you know," she suddenly said.

I leant over the table and lowered my voice. "What, because we're both gay, you mean?"

"No, silly," Elise said. "It's a compliment. Take it as one."

"Well, thank you," I said, taken aback. "You think I make a good Jasmine, then?"

"Definitely." She thought for a moment. "You're both kind, funny…good company. There's not many people out there like you and Jasmine."

"That's a nice thing to say." I sipped self-consciously at my coffee.

"I mean it," Elise said. "And I can totally see why Casey would fall for her."

"That's just clever writing by the scriptwriters, though," I said, laughing.

"Maybe," she said, watching me. "But you bring something extra to it as well."

I took a large drink from my cup, my pulse beating rapidly. "Sometimes it feels like the part of Casey was written just for you, too," I said, trying not to stare at her as she licked more froth from her lips.

"I love Casey." Elise put her cup down. "I love being in *PR* with you. It's been the best thing ever just lately, and that's all down to you."

The warmth from the sun, coupled with Elise being right across the table from me, maintaining eye contact all the time she spoke to me and looking so damned hot, were making it near impossible to concentrate on anything but her. Just as I was thinking that if I didn't go inside and order us both another coffee, like, *right now*, I might be tempted to leap across the table to her, a voice sounded beside me, making me tear my eyes away from Elise and look up in surprise.

"Holly?"

I squinted into the sunshine, dazzled for a bit, then froze when I saw a slim figure silhouetted against the sun, smiling down at me.

Grace.

CHAPTER FOURTEEN

G race?" I looked aghast at her. "What the...what are you doing here?"

"I've been waiting for you outside the studio," Grace said, waving an airy hand down the road. "Then I followed you down here."

"You did what?" I stared up at her, open-mouthed.

"Well, if you won't answer a girl's e-mails, then what's she supposed to do?" Grace stood next to me, hands in her pockets. She looked just like I'd remembered, to be honest. Most people change a bit in two years don't they? Different hairstyle, a little weight gain or weight loss—but not Grace. She looked exactly as she'd done the last time I'd seen her when I'd gone to her parents' house only for her to tell me she was leaving me.

Her hair was just as I'd remembered it so many times in my dreams about her and in the days, weeks, and months of longing for her after she'd gone—black as night, hanging in tendrils around her shoulders. I'd always loved her hair, so beautiful, framing her striking olive-skinned face and her gorgeous dark eyes, deep brown, like chocolate that you wanted to dive into and lose yourself in.

"Aren't you going to introduce me?" She nodded her head towards Elise.

I snapped myself from my trance and glared at her. "No, I'm fucking-well not." I scraped my chair back noisily and stood up, making some other people who'd been sitting outside look over at us.

I glanced down at Elise, sitting in silence, watching what was going on.

"I have to go," I said, reaching down for my bag, my hands shaking. "I'm sorry."

I ushered Grace away from the table before Elise could even answer, practically frog-marching her down the road before any wise guy watching what was going on thought to either photograph it or video it on their phone and sell it to some tabloid.

I walked with her, occasionally glancing over my shoulder to make sure no one was following, back to the studio car park, not saying a word to her all the way there.

I was fuming. How dare she think she could come and find me when I'd made it clear—or at least thought I had, by ignoring her e-mails—that I didn't want to see her? Was she so arrogant that she hadn't cottoned on that my lack of contact with her meant I didn't give a damn?

I unlocked my car and told her to get into the passenger side, which she did without a word. I watched her as she settled herself into the passenger seat and looked uncertainly over at me. It was like the last few years had never even happened, and we were both eighteen again, just about to finish school, so full of love for each other and so full of plans.

"Hello would've been nice," she finally said.

"What did you think you were playing at?" I swung round to face her. "Waiting outside the studio, then coming to find me, like some bloody stalker!"

"You're not pleased to see me, then?" Grace raised an eyebrow. "I would have thought after two years you would be."

"I'm not," I said bluntly. "What do you want?"

"I just wanted to see you." Grace shrugged. "I sent you three e-mails but you didn't reply, so I thought I'd come find you, in case you hadn't got them."

"Of course I got them!" I spat. "I chose to ignore them like you've chosen to ignore me for the last two years."

"I just thought it would be good to hang out while I'm in London," Grace said. "Catch up on old times."

"Great idea!" I said. "Maybe we could re-enact the day you pissed off to Spain without a second thought for me."

"I always regretted that, Holly," Grace said.

"Only once Pillow, or whatever her name is, dumped you."

"Pilar, Holly. Her name was Pilar. And she didn't dump me," Grace said. "We just drifted apart."

"And then you thought you'd drift over to me?" I said. "Well, think again."

"That's not what I meant, and you know it," Grace said. "I just wanted to catch up, but I can see you don't."

She looked across to me, one playful eyebrow arched. "You're still looking hot, though, I have to say." She looked me up and down, making me feel uncomfortable.

"Don't mess with me, Grace." I surreptitiously shuffled in my seat.

"Who's messing?" Grace said. "I mean it. You always were hot, though."

"Not hot enough to stop you dumping me, hey?" I turned and glared at her.

We didn't speak for a few seconds after that, the awkward silence filling the car.

"How long are you in London for?" I finally asked.

"Just until tomorrow," Grace said. "That's why I came to find you, 'cos I knew time was running out."

"Time ran out a long time ago." I turned my head from her, desperate not to start crying.

"What I did was shitty, and it was immature of me just to leave you like that," she said. "So I'm sorry."

"Whatever." I didn't look at her.

Grace didn't say anything for a minute. Instead, she stared out through the windscreen of my car, deep in thought.

"She looked nice," she finally said, glancing at me from the corner of her eye. "The girl you were with. Who is she?"

"You really don't watch *Portobello Road,* do you?" I said, turning to face her again. "It's what I'm in. Remember?"

"I know what you're in." Grace shook her head. "But, no, I don't watch it. Not for years," she said. "Not since, well, since you and I were together."

"She's called Elise. The girl, I mean. She's Elise." I loved how her name sounded when I said it.

"And is she your girlfriend?" Grace looked at me curiously.

"No," I snapped. "She's my co-star in the programme."

"She's fit!" Grace playfully slapped my arm.

I didn't answer her. Instead I chewed, childlike, at one of my fingers, wondering just what I could do to get myself out of this situation.

"So are you seeing anyone at the moment?" Grace asked.

"Maybe," I said. "Maybe not."

"I'm only in Ireland for a few weeks, Hol." Grace reached over and touched my leg. I looked down at it for a second, thinking about how much I loved it when Elise called me Hol, and how I'd give anything to be with her right now, rather than stuck in a car with Grace.

"Don't," I said, taking her hand and putting it back on her own leg.

"We could get together when I get back…" Her voice trailed off.

"Or not," I said brusquely.

"Not even for a drink?" Grace put her hand back on my leg. "Come on, it's been two years. Okay, I know we both said some stuff we didn't mean, but…"

I thought back to Elise again, who was going to be wondering what the hell was going on and why I'd left the cafe so suddenly. I knew I ought to text her, say sorry for bailing out on her, maybe even go and find her. She wouldn't still be outside the cafe, surely? She'd have realised I meant it when I said I had to go, and wouldn't be coming back, would she?

"I think you should go now," I suddenly said, ignoring Grace, "before I say something I'll regret."

I waited as Grace finally opened up the door and got out of my car, turning to speak to me through the open door. "I'll call you," she said.

"Don't bother," I replied, leaning over and pulling the door shut.

❖

I returned to work the next morning, desperate to see Elise and to explain about Grace. I'd written out at least three different texts to her the previous night but just hadn't been able to say the right words and hadn't been able to bring myself to send them. I don't know why. Perhaps I knew I wouldn't be able to explain myself in so few words, and that it would be better to tell her face-to-face why I'd just run off like I had. I knew she'd be curious at being deserted like that, and I knew she'd have questions, but I figured they could wait until I saw her again.

I went immediately to my dressing room that morning, my mind full of Elise, passing Bella on the way down to the set, made-up and dressed in her character's supermarket uniform.

"Hey you," she said, stopping as I approached her.

"Hey," I said, reaching over and straightening her name badge.

"You okay?" She rubbed her hand up and down my arm. "Anything more to report since we last spoke?"

"Well, I came out to Elise," I said.

"And?"

"And she didn't freak."

"Well that's a positive." Bella leant her shoulder against the wall. "Did you tell her anything else?"

"You mean, did I tell her I like her?" I prompted. "Not a chance. Telling her I was gay was nerve-racking enough."

"But she was okay about it?" she asked.

"Totally." I leant my shoulder against the wall, too, facing Bella. "It's been such a relief to tell her. My head feels clearer about Elise than it has in days."

"Did you tell her about Grace?" Bella asked.

"See, that's when my head clouds up again." I sighed. "When I think about Grace."

"What happened?"

I moved and leant my back against the wall, my hands in my pockets. "She turned up unannounced at some cafe I was in with Elise yesterday," I said, turning my head to look at Bella.

"Grace did?" Bella's jaw fell open.

"Yuh-huh." I recounted the whole scene from the coffee shop, then glanced at Bella. "Elise knows who Grace is, but I guess I'll still have some explaining to do later, huh?"

"Guess so." She leant over and rubbed my arm again. "Good luck with that."

"Thanks. I'll need it."

Bella looked at her watch. "I'm late," she said. "Again." Her face clouded with concern. "I'm off to film those ghastly scenes where I get accused of stealing from the tills this afternoon." She looked at her watch again, as if the time might have changed in the two seconds since she last looked at it. "Talk to Elise. Tell her that Grace is bugging you to see her," she said. "At least it'll let Elise know why you've been so uptight lately, in case she thinks it's her that's done something wrong."

"I suppose you're right," I said.

"I'm always right." Bella started to walk away. "Talk more about it later, yes? I'll have a large coffee with my name on it in our room by three, I can guarantee it."

I watched her turn the corner and disappear, then pulled myself away from the wall where I was still leaning and headed to my room, entering and closing the door tightly behind me. I sat on my swivel chair in front of my dressing-table mirror and dug my script from my bag, figuring it would be good to get some lines learned while I had few minutes' peace and quiet.

I'd been reading for about twenty minutes—barely taking a single word of it in—when my mobile rang from somewhere deep in my bag. I pulled it out, frowning at the unknown number, and answered, one eye still on my script.

"Well how about that? You kept the same number!" Grace's voice sounded at the other end.

I pulled the phone away from my ear and stared quizzically at it, like you see them do in the movies, then pressed it back to my ear. "Grace?"

"Who else?" She laughed down the phone.

"What do you want?" I asked, irritated that she'd had the audacity to call me. I shook inside, my stomach churning and my brain rebelling against taking in another tiny detail of anything.

"It was so good seeing you yesterday," Grace said. "It got me thinking that I'd like to hang out some more with you, that's all."

I sat up straight in my chair, as if that would make my point more forcefully. "Well I don't want to see you."

"But I just thought it would be cool to hook up again," Grace said. "And when I saw you last night, Holly...jeez! It was like the last two years had never happened."

"Well, they did happen," I snapped.

Grace's voice sounded softly at the other end of the phone. "I told you last night I was sorry, and I really am, Holly. I just want to make amends."

"You can do that by staying away from me," I hissed.

"I don't want to do that," Grace said. "You looked so cute last night, Holly. I mean, oh my God, I must have been mad to—"

"Stop it," I said furiously. "Just stop it right now, okay?"

I jumped as there was a knock on the door outside. Instinctively I killed Grace's call and sat back in my chair, thinking that my head was going to explode at any minute. I put my elbows on the table and rested my head in my hands, mumbling a "Yeah?" to whoever was outside.

"Can I come in?" Elise asked tentatively.

I paused. "Sure." My voice was quiet.

She came slowly into my room, shutting the door behind her and leaning against it, looking awkward.

"I'm glad I've seen you," I said, running my hands wearily through my hair. "I wanted to explain about yesterday afternoon."

"That's why I came to see you," Elise said. "To find out what that was all about."

"It was just something I had to get sorted," I said vaguely. "And I did get it sorted."

"Okay," Elise said, not sounding convinced.

"And…and…well, I'm sorry I left in such a hurry," I muttered. "I was gonna text you last night but—"

"You didn't."

"No."

"Who was the girl?" Elise frowned. "Ex?"

"Yup," I said.

"You sure were keen to get her away from our table," Elise said, watching me and chewing at the inside of her lip.

I thought for a moment, unsure how to answer. "Mm." It was the best I could come up with. Just then my mobile rang on the table next to me again, making my heart jump and beat wildly. I glanced down at it and saw the same number that had rung just before flashing up at me—Grace's number. I stared down at it, willing it to stop ringing.

"You can get that," Elise said breezily. "Don't mind me."

I snatched up the phone and switched it off, flinging it into my bag angrily. "It was nothing important," I said, as Elise looked surprised.

"Her?" She asked.

I nodded.

Elise bent her head and looked up at me. "Wanna talk about it?" she asked. "You know, I don't think I've ever seen someone look as horrified as you did yesterday when she turned up," she said slowly. Elise hesitated. "We should talk about her," she said. "If you're stressed it'll affect your work. That, in turn, would affect my work, and so I think we probably really do need to talk." She pulled herself away from the door and walked over to me, then leant over and took the arms of my chair, turning me around so that I was now facing her. "Open up to me. Tell me about her and we can make it better together," she said, crouching down in front of me, gazing up at me with concern.

"You don't have to make anything better," I said meekly.

"Yes, I do." All the while she spoke, her eyes never left mine. "I want to help you, Hol."

"Where do I start?" I said, breaking the gaze and staring down at my lap.

Her hands were still on the arms of the chair as she crouched by me. She was only a few feet away, our faces close. I could feel the tension rising between us and bit at my lip nervously, wanting to pull away but not being able to.

"Start with telling me about your ex," Elise persisted, putting her hand on my leg, running her thumb over the material of my jeans. My skin prickled under her touch. "She really freaked you out when she turned up out of the blue like that, didn't she?"

I couldn't look at her. She never took her eyes off my face, but I knew that if I looked back into those beautiful, persuasive blue eyes, it would tear me apart.

"Seeing her again after so long was a total headfuck, yes," I mumbled. "And the stuff she's been saying to me lately, too."

Elise watched my every move and expression. "Such as?"

"Just...stupid stuff." I ignored her question, desperate to change the subject so that Elise would stop looking at me like that. "Do you fancy going back to King's sometime?" I suddenly asked. "It was neat, last time we went."

"You're changing the subject." Elise gave a small laugh.

"I know," I said. "So? King's?"

"When?"

"Tonight?"

"I can't, I'm sorry." Elise stood up.

"It's okay." I shrugged shyly.

"Only because I'm going out with Stig tonight," she said quietly. "Any other time..."

I saw a hint of something flicker across her face. What was that?

"Oh." I tried to hide the disappointment from my voice. "No matter."

"It's all arranged," Elise continued. "I can't really cancel, I'm sorry." She hesitated. "Although I'd much rather go out with you, to be honest."

Our eyes met.

"Would you?" I asked, not taking my eyes from hers.

"I would, yes," she said slowly, her face flushing slightly.

My heartbeat quickened. "Things not going so well?" I asked, as lightly as my thudding heart would let me.

"Things are fine." Elise nodded, more to herself, I think, than me. "I just, well..." She took a deep breath. "Never mind."

We looked at each other a moment longer before I broke eye contact first and turned in my seat to busy myself gathering my belongings together, just for something to do. "No worries," I said, trying to keep my voice sounding normal. "There'll be other times."

"I hope so," Elise said, standing up and making for the door. "So are we good?"

"We're good," I said.

"And that really is everything?" She watched me over her shoulder, one hand on the door handle. "There's nothing else bothering you?"

I looked at her, thinking about how she'd been crouching in front of me just before, and the achingly lovely, caring look on her face when her eyes had searched my face for an answer. I remembered the feel of her breath on my face, her immediacy, her closeness, the touch of her hand on my leg.

I thought about everything she'd said to me in the cafe the day before, about how she thought I was kind and nice, and then what she'd just said about Stig and how she'd rather be seeing me tonight rather than him. I remembered the look on her face when she'd said it; it had been a look of intensity, of longing. Did she want me like I wanted her? She wanted to see me tonight, not Stig. She did! She wanted me, not him.

Courage swept through me. *She did.* She definitely wanted me. I could see it in her eyes, the way she was standing, the way she was looking at me. She was pulling me towards her, urging me to come closer.

"No, it's not everything," I said, quietly. "I've something else that's been bugging me for ages." Looking her right in the eye, I got up from my chair and walked towards her, my breath coming faster now, my heart beating madly in my neck, feeling giddy with confusion and longing. If she walked out that door now, I knew I'd never do what I'd wanted to do for weeks.

"As in?" Elise looked confused.

"As in this…" I reached over and, putting my hands on her shoulders, pushed her softly against the door and kissed her, slowly at first, but when she didn't pull away, harder and longer.

The feeling of her lips on mine was all I'd dreamt about over the last few weeks, and I totally lost myself in her, in the feel of her softness, in the taste of her. Just as she began to kiss me back, the hint of her tongue brushing against mine, making the backs of my knees turn to jelly, she pushed me roughly away, looked at me strangely, then turned and left my dressing room without a word, slamming the door behind her and leaving me standing there, utterly stunned.

My lips tingled from the pressure of hers on mine, my tongue still tasted hers. I groaned and pinched my eyes tight shut, pressing my lips together slowly, tasting her, remembering.

What the hell had I just done?

CHAPTER FIFTEEN

I didn't have to wait long for Elise to come and find me. I was sitting in the green room, hugging a cup of coffee, waves of nausea hitting me each time the door opened, expecting it to be her. I wished I could have hidden myself away in my dressing room, but Bella had settled herself in there with a sandwich and the daily paper, and the last thing I wanted or needed was to talk to Bella, so I was forced to retreat to the green room and just wait.

I was sprawled on a chair, a music magazine on my knees that I wasn't even reading, when she eventually entered the room. I watched her as she came in, looked, and then practically froze to the spot when she saw me. Without saying a word, she walked over to the other side of the room, occasionally glancing at me as she did so; I was alone in there apart from Rory, the guy who played my on-screen dad, who was fiddling with his phone in one of the other corners.

The silence was unbearable. I was glad Rory was there, so I wasn't alone with Elise, so that I could delay having the toe-curlingly awkward conversation that I knew we'd have to have, sooner or later. I watched her from the corner of my eye, sitting over by one of the windows, turning her phone over and over in her hands, just staring into space.

Finally, after what seemed like ages but was probably only around five minutes, Rory got up and headed for the door, muttering an "All right?" to me as he passed.

My heart sank.

"We need to talk." The second he left the room, Elise came over to me, putting her hand on the arm of my chair and leaning over me, her low-cut top revealing more than I felt able to cope with right at that moment. "About what just happened."

"It was a mistake," I lied, staring up at her and willing my eyes to keep looking at her face and not at her cleavage, which seemed to be taunting me from inches away. "Sorry."

"A mistake?"

"I misinterpreted the situation," I said numbly, desperately trying to read her mood but not wanting to stare at her.

"You make a habit of kissing your co-stars?" Elise spoke in hushed tones, her eyes darting to the door.

"No." I paused. "I thought you liked me. I obviously got it wrong."

"You girls seen Rory today?" We both flinched as the door to the green room suddenly flew open and Stuart came in. He fished his BlackBerry from his pocket and punched some numbers into it without looking up.

"Uh, he was here just a second ago," I said. My voice sounded reedy and nervous as I sensed Elise still looking at me.

Stuart jerked his head in acknowledgement of what I'd just said and put the phone to his ear. "I'll find him. Cheers." He turned and left the room, talking loudly into his phone as he did so.

"Why did you do it?" Elise asked, the second Stuart had left the room.

"Because I wanted to." I stared up at the ceiling, desperate to avoid eye contact with her. I tried to move, but Elise's hands were back on the arm of my chair again, effectively pinning me down.

"You wanted to?" Elise repeated.

"For ages, yes," I said. I looked at her. "Didn't you realise?"

"I...I," Elise stuttered. "No, of course I didn't."

"All the looks?" I said quietly. "I haven't been able to take my eyes off you for ages! How could you have not known?"

Elise's expression immediately changed. It was one that I hadn't seen from her before. "Ages?" she repeated, her voice catching. She stood up straighter. "I didn't know."

"I thought you might have felt the same," I said. "Bearing in mind how you've been with me, the things you've been saying to me lately."

"About?"

"About how I'm kind and nice, like Jasmine," I said. "And that you could see why Casey would fall for someone like me."

"I meant that, too," Elise said. "But—"

"And the fact you responded when I kissed you just now," I said hesitantly. "Even though you pushed me off. Why did you do that, Elise?"

"I didn't respond." Elise sat on the arm of my chair and ran her hands through her hair. "Or, at least, if I did, I didn't mean to. That's why I pushed you away, because—"

"I felt it, Elise," I interrupted. "I didn't imagine it. You wanted to kiss me as much as I wanted to kiss you."

"Well." She paused. "It can't happen again," she said. "I like guys. You know I like guys."

"But do you, though?" I looked up to find her looking straight back at me. "I didn't get that impression when you were kissing me just now."

"You know that I like guys," Elise said carefully. "The *public* thinks I like guys. I'm photographed—"

"The public *thinks*?" I butted in.

"Knows." Elise emphasised the word. "Every magazine article you read about me talks about *sexy Elise* or *blond Elise*," she said. "It's what the public expects."

"And because you're quoted as being sexy and blond that has to make you a man-eater, does it?" I scoffed. "Get real!"

"Please, Holly. Don't push it, yeah?" Elise lowered her voice. "I don't know what you imagined, but it was wrong."

"Stop talking about the public and about magazines and shit like that!" I said. "And I didn't imagine it. I know the difference between a scripted kiss and a real one. You meant it. You really meant it." I looked at her, still sitting on the arm of my chair.

"I can't do this." Elise slowly shook her head.

"What?" I looked up at her.

"This," Elise said. "I don't know what you want me to say."

"I want you to tell me that I didn't imagine what just happened in there," I said.

"I can't be with you like you want me to." She hesitated, looking at me with a mixture of confusion and frustration. "And I can't tell you that I like you."

"I think that you do, though," I said. "You haven't denied it, and the fact you're still sitting here tells me you want to talk about it."

Still she looked at me.

"Just admit it," I said, knowing that she was close to saying something.

"And what if I do?" Elise replied.

"What? Do like me?" I persisted, a knot forming in my stomach.

"Mm," Elise said. "It changes nothing."

"Really?" My heart sank.

"How many actors do you know that are out and proud?" she suddenly asked.

"Plenty!" I said. "Elise, there are loads of gay actors out there."

"And how many are women?" Elise asked. "I saw it all the time in Hollywood. Once they find out you like women, that's it. I don't want that for me." She turned and looked out the window. "I don't want to be labelled *that gay actress*. I want to be labelled on my merit, not my sexuality."

We stayed silent for a few seconds, each of us processing. "I like you, Elise," I finally said when I couldn't bear the silence any longer. "A lot. I can't just switch that off."

"When I said to you I thought you were like Jasmine, I wasn't lying," she said slowly. "I think you're really nice and I *do* like you—I like you a lot. You're the kindest, most sweet-natured person I've ever met, but I don't know if that means I like you like *that*."

"But you're not sure?" I asked. "I can see it in your eyes that you're not sure."

"I think about you a lot," Elise continued, "and I know I'm happy when I know I'm going to see you. And I know I miss you dreadfully when you're not around. That has to mean something, doesn't it?"

"It does," I said, twinges of nerves fluttering inside me. "Because it's how I feel about you."

"And I've never felt like this about anyone else." Elise held my gaze. "I never felt this way when I was with Stig or anyone else I've ever dated before." She exhaled slowly. "I think I do feel something for you, Hol," she said. "But I'm…I just can't act on those feelings."

"At least you've finally admitted that you do like me," I said. "That I've not been imagining it all." I maintained eye contact. "That's something, at least."

In that moment I knew that something and everything had changed between us. There was a new understanding and a mutual attraction. Anything she'd said to me up until that point was now immaterial, forgotten with the one adorable look she gave me that told me everything I'd been dying to hear.

"I love working with you—working here. I love Jasmine and Casey, and that's all down to you," she said. "If you weren't here, then I know that I wouldn't want to be, either."

"I'm sensing a *but* coming up," I said quietly.

"But it'd be career suicide—for both of us—if we got involved with one another," Elise said simply. "Our careers that we've both worked so hard for would be dead in the water before they've really even had a chance to start. So you and I can't happen. It's as simple as that."

"It's all about the career for you, isn't it?" I said. "Rather than feelings."

"Isn't it for you?" Elise asked. "Isn't this why we do what we do? For ourselves?"

"And you'd sacrifice being with someone just because of that?" I asked.

Elise nodded. "I've sacrificed a lot to get where I am in this life," she said.

"Wow." I sat up straighter, leaning my elbows on my knees. I stared down at the floor. "Even though you know your feelings for me are reciprocated?"

"I'm scared," Elise said. "Scared that I *do* have these feelings for you, scared it'll get out, and shit-scared that it'll mean the end of my career if it *does* get out."

"That's a lot of scareds for what should really be something that makes you happy," I said weakly.

"It's the way I've always been." Elise shrugged. "Career comes first with me. Always has. I don't want to be like that, but I can't help it."

"So where does this leave us?" I asked. "I can't ignore how I feel about you like you seem to be able to with me."

"We carry on as before," Elise said matter-of-factly. "Jasmine and Casey carry on as before. Nothing has to change."

"But everything's changed, Elise," I said, exasperated. "How can I work with you every day knowing that I want you and you don't want me?"

"I didn't say I didn't want you," Elise said quietly. "I just said I couldn't be with you because it would be way too complicated." She breathed out slowly. "Can't you understand that?"

"I'm finding it hard to understand any of this," I said, standing up.

"I can't be with you," Elise repeated. "We have to be professional over this, Hol." She looked over to me, her face impassive. "And that means we just stay as friends. For both our sakes, I'd be grateful if you'd respect that."

CHAPTER SIXTEEN

Girls, focus." Stuart pushed his glasses up onto the top of his head. "Nine retakes in a row does not make me a happy director."

It was the next morning. We were out on location in Hyde Park filming wedding scenes, normally a favourite thing for me to do on *PR* because it meant leaving the confines of the studio to go on location, which always felt something like going on a school trip.

"My bad, Stu." Elise held her hand up. "I came off my marker and it threw me." She glanced at me and mouthed, "Sorry."

I hadn't seen or heard from Elise since our heart-to-heart the previous day. She looked tired, I thought. Tired and defeated, as if every look we exchanged was agony to her.

"Shall we go from my last line?" I said, avoiding eye contact with her.

"From *I wish it could be like this forever*?" Elise walked back onto her marker, her back to me.

I stepped beside her.

"I don't want there to be any awkwardness between us, Elise," I said, glancing back over my shoulder towards Stuart and Laura, our make-up girl, who were standing talking next to the camera. "I still don't understand this decision that you've come to for yourself, but I can work through it," I said. "You said yesterday you wanted us to be professional. I can do professional."

"We both can." Elise wrapped her arms around herself. "When we have to."

"Ready to go again?" Stuart called across, not waiting for our answer. He called the take, pointing his pen at me and nodding me into my cue.

I took Elise's hand and walked with her up a short hill towards a tree in the distance.

"Are you happy, Jasmine?" Elise said her lines slowly.

"Very." I squinted up into the sun. "Are you?"

"How could I not be?" Elise squeezed my hand. "I'm with you, aren't I?"

"And you're not scared anymore?" I asked, aware of the camera moving quietly behind us. "Especially after what Tim said when he saw us?"

"Tim's an idiot," Elise said. "So in answer to your question, no. I'm not scared anymore. I have you, and that's all that matters now."

We stood and held one another's gaze while I did a mental countdown until I heard Stuart call "Cut!" and I knew I could move away from her again.

"Perfect!" Stuart called up the hill to us. "That's in the can."

"See?" Elise smiled weakly. "Professional."

"Do you want to sit over there until the next scene?" I pointed to an unoccupied bench in the sunshine.

"Sure." Elise started walking over to it, not waiting for me.

We sat down, the sun in our faces as we watched runners and make-up girls scurry around a little further down the hill. It was a typical early summer's day, warm and cloudless. Elise and I were both dressed in our smart wedding clothes, having changed in the trailer on arrival. Elise was wearing a stunning summer dress, which showed her long legs off to perfection, and I was in a slightly longer, more flowing one. I had my hair up for these scenes, piled up on my head, with just a few wisps hanging about my neck, while Elise's soft, cropped cut, with her fringe hanging sexily over her perfectly darkened eyes, made her look as gorgeous as she always did.

"Your dress suits you." Elise nodded down towards my legs. "I thought earlier, when we were shooting…"

"Yours, too." I cleared my throat self-consciously. "The blue really brings out the colour of your eyes."

"Thank you." Elise paused. "Holly?"

"Mm?" I squinted against the sun to her.

"There's so much I want to say to you," Elise said, "but can't." She looked down at the grass by her feet. "Thanks for respecting my wishes. You know—about stuff."

"Stuff?" I repeated. "Okay."

"It's hard for me," she said. "I hope you understand that."

"It's only as hard as you want to make it, Elise," I said, instinctively moving away from her on the bench as Laura came over to us.

"See, this is what happens when you sit in the sun between takes!" She fished in a small bag clipped around her middle and pulled out some foundation and a brush, fussing about me, muttering kindly about "reddening skin being a sod to work with." I was aware that Elise had got up from where we'd been sitting, and from the corner of my eye I could see that she'd headed back down the hill to talk and was now chatting with one of the runners, a skinny young guy called Josh. As I turned my head to look at her, I noticed she was looking at me over Josh's shoulder while they were talking, making me immediately turn away and stare right ahead again.

While Laura continued to fuss around me, adding more layers of foundation, instructing me to pout for her while she applied more lip gloss, I peered through the corner of my eye back towards Elise. She was still talking to Josh. As I watched, a gnawing jealousy ate away at me with every laugh and look exchanged between them, however innocent they were. I hated it. I turned my head away quickly as Elise suddenly looked at me over Josh's shoulder again, making Laura frown at me.

"Sorry," I said sheepishly.

"You're good to go." Laura peered at me and nodded, putting her brushes away back in her bag.

As she walked away from me, I slid my eyes back in Elise's direction, but she'd moved away and was now walking towards Stuart.

Seeing Stuart motion for me to come over and join them in the small, tree-lined part of the park that had been cordoned off for filming, ready for our first take of the kissing scene—*oh, great!*—I composed myself, breathing out slowly and trying desperately to gather my thoughts once more.

This would be mine and Elise's first kiss that we'd filmed for a while. It would be uncomfortable, I just knew it. We both knew it. I stood, not too close to Elise, but not too far from her either, listening as Stuart's voice drifted in and out of my earshot.

"So, in the scenes we just shot, Jasey have just left Thomas and Emily's wedding, okay?" Stuart said, reading from a printed sheet. "Off camera, they've wandered further away from the wedding party to be on their own, having talked about Tim, who's just found out that they're seeing each other. Everything's good with them now, and they're both even more loved-up than before, especially having just seen their friends get married, yes?"

Elise and I nodded.

"And in this scene now, they're going to be by that tree there"— Stuart turned and pointed—"and kiss. They talk about how much they love one another, and how they want to be together forever, and then kiss. These scenes have totally got to be all about the intensity of the moment, the love they have for each other, okay?"

I swallowed hard, fighting the swell of panic at having to kiss Elise again, knowing what we both now knew.

"So I need you both standing by this tree," Stuart called out to us, motioning for us to follow him.

We followed him and took up our positions not far from the tree as instructed, looking at one another uncertainly as Laura flicked a foundation brush over first my face, yet again, then Elise's, finally muttering, "Ready for the take," then stepping back away from us.

"So you've hidden yourselves away from the other people in the wedding party," Stuart said, walking back over to the camera, "And you're telling one another just how much in love you both are."

I had to stand now and tell her, as Casey, how much I loved her, knowing how much I liked Elise in real life and with the added knowledge that she liked me, too. The irony of the situation wasn't lost on either of us, I knew, as I looked at Elise's face, etched with tension. All I had to do, I kept telling myself, was look into her eyes and speak Jasmine's lines. Professional to the end. It would be embarrassing, yes, and more than awkward, but easy enough to do, I was sure of that.

"Okay, and cue Casey," Stuart's voice rang out near us. "Action."

On her cue, Elise took my hand, threading her fingers through mine. "Today's been perfect, Jas." She spoke her lines. "Being with you, like this, has made me realise just how much you mean to me."

We walked closer to the tree, still holding hands, and leant against it. I looked at her hand, so perfect in mine.

"It could be like this every day," I said. "You know that, don't you?"

"I really want that." Elise gazed down at me. "You know how much I want that—and want you."

"I've fallen for you in a big way, Casey." I turned her hand over in mine, not daring to meet her eyes. "You're all I think about, from the minute I wake up until the minute I go to sleep. All that stuff with Tim finding out about us really freaked me, but you know what?"

Finally I looked up to meet her eyes, still gazing down at me. She watched me as I spoke to her, looking so lovely that I was practically dissolving inside at the sight of her. "I don't care. In fact, I'm glad he knows because at least it means I don't have to pretend anymore." I brought her hands to my lips, kissing them. "So, yes," I said, "I want it to be like this every day. I want to be with *you* every day."

I was fluid, delivering my lines without missing a beat. I meant every word I said to her; it was almost as if the lines had been written for me, Holly, and I said them perfectly, putting my all into them.

"When I first met you," Elise said, "I knew there was something different about you. You had a spark in you that I'd never seen with anyone else I'd ever been with." She spoke her lines back to me, dropping her eyes to my lips then back to my eyes again. "You got me, you know? Understood me. It was almost as if I'd waited my whole life to find you."

"We don't have to worry what Tim or anyone else thinks, Casey." I brushed her hair from her eyes. "Nothing matters now, except you and me."

"Okay, cut!" Stuart's voice rang out across the park to us, making Elise and me subconsciously step away from each other. "Perfect. Beautiful!"

Stuart spoke to the sound guy while Laura scurried up to us and adjusted Elise's hair for about the thousandth time, teasing and brushing it just so across her perfect face.

"Scene two, take one!" A voice sounded from somewhere behind Laura as she took one final look at the pair of us and retreated once again.

"Back to your markers, please," Stuart called to us, without looking up from his script.

The next scene was our kissing scene. With a quick glance at Elise to try to gauge her emotions, I stepped back onto my marker opposite her and waited for my cue.

"So Casey's just told Jasmine she's everything to her," Stuart said, "and now she's going to kiss her to show her how much she means to her. You both know what to do." He pushed his glasses back up on his nose and gave a curt nod to the cameraman. "Action."

With the sound of blood rushing in my ears, I looked up at Elise, her eyes fixed on mine. A myriad of emotions hit me as I leant in and buried my face in her neck, breathing in the sweet, lemony scent of Elise's perfume. I kissed the soft skin of her neck, sensing Elise swallow as I did so, hearing her breathing getting more ragged with every brush of my lips against her.

I moved my face from her neck and tensed as she reached out and took my face in her hands, then slowly bent her head and moved her lips closer to mine. Memories of kissing her as I'd done in my dressing room immediately came back to me, and the thought of our lips touching again held me back, almost as if I didn't dare let her kiss me now, for fear of what would happen this time. Clearly, Elise was feeling exactly the same way.

"I'm sorry." She pulled her head back just as she was centimetres from me, dropping her hands from my face as she did so. "Can we try again?" She looked anxiously at Stuart, who nodded.

"From when Casey takes Jasmine's face in her hands," he said. "Take two."

We repeated our previous actions; Elise held my face again, stepping closer to me and lowering her head towards mine. She hesitated, her eyes roaming my face, her breath coming in shallow gasps.

"Fuck..." Again, she dropped her hands from my face and stepped back, this time taking two or three steps away from me.

"Cut!" Stuart's voice rang out.

"Elise." I reached out and took her hand, giving it a squeeze. "It's okay."

"It's not," she said quietly, dropping my hand. "I don't think I can do this." She turned and walked a little way from me, just as Stuart came over to us.

"Everything all right?" he asked, glancing down at his filming schedule.

"Fine, Stu," I said, looking over his shoulder towards Elise. "I think she just needs five minutes, okay?"

Stuart frowned. "Okay, five minutes," he said, walking over towards the lighting guy to speak to him.

I wandered to Elise, still standing some way from me. She was hugging herself, staring down at a small beetle that was making its way unevenly over the earth by the trunk of the tree.

"Look at that," she said, pointing down to it. "Keeps falling over on his back, but then just wriggles his legs a bit, then gets up and carries on like nothing's the matter."

"Are you okay?" I said, from just behind her.

"Yeah," she said. "I'm just...tired, I s'pose."

"It's been a long day," I agreed.

"Very."

"You wanna talk about the scene?" I asked. "We've pretty much sailed through all the other stuff."

"The scene's fine," Elise said wearily. "I've no problem with the scene. I just needed a breather."

"Cool," I said, watching her closely.

I watched her take a deep breath, mentally composing herself, then lift her head slightly higher.

"Ready when you are, yeah?" she called to Stuart.

I followed Elise back to our marker by the tree and stood in front of her, taking her hand again, ready to shoot.

"Scene two, take three!" a voice, this time not Stuart's, called out to us.

On our cue, we leant towards one another. Elise looked from my eyes to my lips and to my eyes again, sparking countless emotions inside me that I tried desperately to blot out. I wanted to cup her face in my hands, kiss her tenderly, to taste her lips on mine again. I wanted to kiss her again as Elise, not as Casey, and kiss her properly, lovingly, gently. Like I totally meant it. I was so close to just giving in to everything, wanting to wrap my arms around her and kiss her like I'd kissed her in the dressing room. I wanted her to respond the same way she had, knowing that she had to be thinking the same thing.

But neither of us could.

This time, it was me who pulled away just as our lips were centimetres from one another's, pressing my lips together hard, then pulling my hands irritably through my hair, making Laura immediately come over to me to tidy it up again.

"Thought I was going to sneeze," I mumbled unconvincingly to Stuart as he approached me. "Sorry."

"Shall we try again?" Stuart said patiently as Laura moved away from me again. "Their kiss has to mean everything, so no holding back." He put his hand on my shoulder. "Kiss her like you really mean it, Holly."

I glanced at Elise, standing close to me, staring down at her nails. When she sensed me looking at her she slowly looked back up at me, a strange expression on her face.

I stared back at her, neither of us wanting to be the first to look away. Finally, I dragged my eyes from hers and focused on our marker in the grass by our feet. If I kissed her like I meant it, then she'd know all about it, and so would every other person on the set. I watched as Stuart walked away from us and stood next to the camera, holding his hand up and giving us our cue. I took Elise's hand once more and looked directly at her as Stuart called out some instructions a little way from us.

The second I heard Stuart call, "Action!" and with my head pounding and my breath coming faster with every second, I leant in towards Elise, placing my hand on her neck, pulling her closer to me.

"Kiss me like you really want me," she whispered to me, so quietly I could barely hear her. "I want you to."

I dragged her to me, pressing my lips hard to hers, kissing her hard then soft, hard then soft, running my hand round the back of her neck to pull her even closer to me. She fell into me, her body soft against mine, her arms tight around me, her hands on my back, sending icicles up and down it.

We kissed for what seemed like ages, Elise kissing me back as hard as I was kissing her, just as she'd done back in my dressing room, this time so passionately and forcefully I felt faint.

Finally, we heard Stuart yell, "Cut!" and give us a thumbs up. I pulled away from Elise in an instant, stepping back from her and dropping my arms from her.

"Like that, you mean?" I said.

CHAPTER SEVENTEEN

The scene had to be greatly edited, of course. Okay, so I know Stuart had said for us to give it our everything, but somehow I don't think he meant quite as much as we did. After I'd kissed her—*like I really wanted her*—I'd stumbled away, leaving her still standing under the tree. I didn't need to turn round to see what her face was like; I just knew. I hadn't been professional. Giving in to my longing for her like that had been totally unprofessional but totally unavoidable at the same time.

I wasn't due to film with Elise again for another two days, but if I thought the time away from her would help settle my mind and give me head space in which to think about things, I was mistaken. And that was all thanks to Grace.

Grace had flown to Ireland the day after she'd gate-crashed my afternoon with Elise at the cafe and had spent some time at her parents' cottage in Cork. Now she was coming back to London for a while, staying with an old friend of hers, and looking for work in the capital, which was all well and good, if only she'd stop texting me relentlessly to tell me of her plans. Her messages talked about the same stuff that she'd said to me when we'd talked in my car: that she missed me and still thought about me often and wanted to get together while she was in London.

I replied to a few, telling her I was busy—which was true—but she still kept messaging me. Her texts became increasingly flirty as the days wore on, despite me answering them with barely two words sometimes. It confused me all over again. Her texts suggested that she really meant everything she was saying, and that she genuinely had missed me, and truly did want to hook up with me again. They nearly drove me mad, churning stuff over and over, making me think that maybe, just maybe, she really did mean it this time.

I was reading one of Grace's texts for about the third time when I finally saw Elise again. I was on my way to the green room for a ten-minute chill, walking and reading Grace's message at the same time, when I pretty much walked straight into Elise as she came around a corner. We had one of those awkward moments where you look at each other for a second, which feels like a minute, before one of you speaks.

"Hey," I finally managed to say, hoping she'd reply and not totally blank me. I hastily stuffed my phone into my trouser pocket the moment I saw her and stood, gawkily, in the middle of the corridor.

"Hey," Elise said. "How are you?"

"Good," I replied. "You?"

"Mm." Elise nodded. "Good, too."

We stood in uncomfortable silence for a few seconds, the memory of what had happened the last time we'd seen each other hanging between us uneasily.

"I...uh...I was going to get a coffee, actually." She nodded her head in the direction of the canteen. "You fancy it? Canteen crap today, though. No time to escape!" She looked exaggeratedly at her watch and shrugged.

Relief washed over me at the fact she hadn't snubbed me and, even better, still wanted to hang out with me.

Despite that, I still found myself turning her down. "I don't think that's a good idea, do you?" I said. "I'm trying to keep it professional—on your wishes—so maybe hanging out together between takes isn't going to help." I held her gaze. "It didn't help the other day, did it? Up at the park?" My stomach flipped over at the memory of kissing her under the tree.

Elise's face fell. "Please?" she said quietly. "We can still hang out as friends, can't we?"

"This is tough for me, Elise," I said. "I want to be with you, but…"

"I miss you," she said simply, making me hastily drop my eyes from hers. "I just want to see you."

"Okay," I said, trying to maintain a calm face when I was dancing inside. "One coffee."

We walked together in near silence, occasionally muttering a greeting to another cast member whenever we passed one on our way down there. It was fairly quiet when we arrived, but we still somehow ended up choosing a table in a far corner, both subconsciously wanting a bit of privacy. While I sat at the table and waited, Elise fetched a coffee for herself and a tea for me, then wandered back over to me. It was damn good to see her again. Even if it had only been a few days since I'd last seen her, it had seemed like the longest time ever. Any hope I might have had over that time of trying to get over her disappeared the second I saw her picking her way carefully through the chairs towards me, a cup in each hand, and a look of adorable concentration on her beautiful face, which made my insides totally melt. It's always the simplest things when you're mad for someone, I guess.

She handed me my tea, my hand coming up to take it from her. Our fingers touched as I took the cup that was offered to me, a small drop of tea spilling onto the table as my hand shook slightly from the contact.

Elise gave a nervous half laugh.

"Sorry!"

We both said it at the same time.

"My fault." I put the cup down, afraid that Elise would see my hand still shaking, and took a paper napkin, dabbing it at the small pool of tea. "I'm such a klutz sometimes."

"No, my fault." I saw Elise's face had flushed. "I kinda thrust it at you. Sorry."

We both looked down at the table, painfully aware of the ridiculous situation.

"How are you?" I asked, just for something else to say.

"I've been filming with Pete all day." Elise pulled a face. "Can you imagine?"

"I can't imagine, no." I laughed, rolling my eyes.

"And filming with Millie, too," Elise continued. "Her last day tomorrow, isn't it?"

"It is, yes." I nodded. We carried on like this for a while—just idle, polite chit-chat. I didn't mention again anything about what had happened under the tree on location, as though if neither of us talked about it, then it hadn't happened. But it was there. It just remained this unspoken thing lingering between us, even though it really had happened.

All the while we talked, I kept reminding myself what Elise had said to me about us being friends, but at the same time I couldn't stop thinking about the look she'd had on her face just now when she told me she'd missed me. Part of me was stoked that we could still chat easily just like we'd always done, while another part of me died whenever she looked at me a certain way, or when she played with her hair whilst talking to me, and I wondered if I'd ever be able to cope with just being her friend. At those times, I had a rush of longing and sadness, knowing that it was her who wanted it to be like this—all terribly polite and friendly—but never anything more, and if I didn't want to lose her forever, then I'd have go along with it, however painful.

I wanted to tell her that I'd missed her, too. I wanted her to know that I'd spent every hour of every day since I'd last seen her just thinking about her, wondering how she was, where she was, what she was doing. I wanted her to know that I'd looked at my phone a hundred times in the days since Hyde Park, wanting her to text me, to speak to me, to let me know she was thinking about me as well. But she hadn't, had she?

"So did you see your ex again?" Elise suddenly asked.

"I'm sorry?" I looked at her strangely, flummoxed and jolted from my thoughts.

"Your ex," Elise repeated. "Have you seen her again since that time in the cafe?"

"No," I said bluntly. "She's in Ireland now anyway."

"Ireland?" Elise raised her eyebrows.

"Living with her parents over there," I said. "But she's—"

I didn't get a chance to finish or to tell her that Grace was bugging me to meet her again because Robbie suddenly appeared beside us. I'd been so surprised by Elise asking me about Grace that I hadn't even seen him approaching our table.

"Can I join you?" he asked, sitting down at our table before either of us had answered. That was the end of our conversation on Grace. I glanced at Elise, trying to gauge whether she was pleased that Robbie had joined us, or whether, like me, she resented his intrusion. Her face gave nothing away.

"So this is where you're both hiding!" Robbie opened his can of Coke with a loud fizz. "Is it Millie's last day today?"

"Tomorrow," I said, more sharply than I should have done. "We were just talking about it."

"And you're going to her do, of course." It was more an assertion than an actual question to us both.

"We are." I hoped my blunt replies might make Robbie realise he was an unwanted guest at our table, but he seemed oblivious.

"Did I tell you I got free tickets to see United on Saturday?" Robbie turned his attention to Elise, who listened, expressionless, as he continued to tell her about the football match he was going to.

All the while he was talking, my mind was hissing *shut up, shut up, shut up* over and again, willing him to go away, so that I could have Elise to myself. I just wanted to *talk* to her, to let it be the two of us, no one else. Selfish, I know, but it just goes like that when you're mad for someone, doesn't it?

"Okay, so they're at the back of the stand," Robbie now said. "But a freebie's a freebie whichever way you look at it, isn't it?"

"I guess," Elise replied.

"Did I ever tell you about the last time me and Rory got tickets?" Robbie continued.

All the time he was speaking, my eyes would drift to hers, which would invariably then glance at mine, hold my gaze, then look away again, only to repeat the action a few seconds later. Her hands, cupped round her coffee cup, were so temptingly within reach, that all I wanted to do was lean across and put my own hands round hers, just so that I could feel her skin on mine. When she spoke to Robbie, I was transfixed by the simplest of actions, like when she casually flicked her hair from her eyes or touched the cloth of her bracelet as she spoke, and I sat, mesmerised, just watching her gorgeous lips moving, and listening to her beautiful, husky voice.

I was drawn to more than just her beauty, though. As I watched her, I tried to put my finger on exactly what it was about Elise that I'd fallen for. It wasn't just her hair, sitting so flawlessly across her perfect eyebrows, or her dimples that appeared and disappeared whenever she smiled or spoke; it was more about her character, her intelligence, her wit, and, most tellingly, her confidence and attitude. Even though I'd disliked it when I first knew her, now I knew it was a part of who she was, it was yet another thing that just kept drawing me to her. I loved the way she moved her hair from her eyes even though it always kept falling back; I loved the way she arched her eyebrow when she spoke, and the way she'd walked towards me in the canteen with that look of cute concentration on her face.

There were so many indefinable things about Elise Manford that I really liked, but the only definite thing I did know was that I had fallen for her, totally and utterly. It was killing me, sitting there in that canteen, wanting her and knowing that she felt the same way but had the strength to ignore her feelings for me, whereas I didn't.

"We should go, Hol!" Elise's voice roused me from my thoughts.

"Hmm?" I jerked my head up. "The football?"

"No, the new club in Knightsbridge Robbie's just been talking about." Elise smiled and shook her head just a tiny bit, barely enough for me to notice. "You've been away with the fairies, haven't you, silly?"

"Sure. Club. Knightsbridge. Sounds awesome," I said, draining the last of my now-cold tea and glancing at my watch. "Shit, I have to go. I'm on set in five minutes."

"Lucky you! I'm done for the day." Elise leant back in her chair, linking her fingers and stretching her arms out in front of her.

"Oh." A plummeting disappointment punched me in my stomach because I desperately didn't want her to stay on in the canteen without me.

I looked at her, willing her to say she was leaving for the day—without Robbie—but instead, she asked him if he wanted another Coke, and the sensation in my stomach turned to one of spikes, scratching away inside me. Even if she'd just walked with me back down to my set before going home, it would have given me precious extra time with her. I'd have taken that at that moment.

I scraped my chair back noisily, making a big show of gathering my things, hoping that it would make Elise take notice of the fact I was going. It didn't. Instead, she carried on talking to Robbie, barely acknowledging my quiet goodbye to them both or, apparently, even noticing that I'd left.

CHAPTER EIGHTEEN

Another text from Grace the next morning—the day of Millie's leaving bash—was waiting for me when I woke up. I'd spent a lousy night, unable to sleep, drifting off only occasionally, just to be interrupted by dreams of Elise. In my dreams, we were rowing a boat down the Thames on a bright summer's afternoon and everything was—as it sometimes tends to be in dreams—absolutely perfect.

It was just the two of us, lying together, the warm sun on us as our boat floated down the river to goodness only knew where. It was the sort of dream I'd had so many times since I'd admitted to myself that I liked Elise, but the one I'd had that night had been stronger and more vivid than any of the others. When I woke up and realised that it hadn't been real, my heart sank and I was left with a sudden stabbing of desperate loneliness.

It stayed with me all day as well, you know how they do? Snippets of it kept coming back to me periodically throughout the day, making me either happy or sad, depending on what state of mind I was in at the time. That, coupled with Grace's text sent at some ridiculously early hour and which I resolutely avoided replying to, made my day much harder than it really needed to be. I was both glad and relieved when all filming was finally over and we could kick off at Millie's party.

We went to a hotel called Morgan's in the West End, a smart place where a lot of other actors hung out, both from theatre and television, and the type of place where you were charged a fortune for a bottle of champagne, but no one ever batted an eye about spending that kind of money there. We went there for special occasions: after awards ceremonies, or if we'd wrapped on a particularly arduous storyline and wanted to go out and get hammered to relieve the pressure.

"The paps'll be there tonight, guarantee it," Kevin had said earlier in the afternoon. "So I want you two to arrive arm-in-arm together."

"Do we have to?" I'd asked, worried how Elise would feel about arriving with me.

"The fans will love it," Kevin had said dismissively. "I'm sure you both will, too."

The fans. It was all about the fans, of course, and getting some good free publicity for us all.

Elise looked totally awesome that night, of course, in a stunning low-cut turquoise-blue designer dress that stopped midthigh, showing off her perfect long legs. She was wearing matching shoes and had darkened her eyes, making them even sexier than they normally were—if that was possible. The photographers camped outside the hotel couldn't get enough of the pair of us, calling out for us to turn one way and then another, asking Elise who'd designed her dress, shouting out to me asking who'd done my hair. It was crazy, and we both lapped it up.

Once we'd gone inside the hotel and away from the cameras, we could really let our hair down and start to enjoy ourselves. We wandered into the hotel's nightclub, and I got separated from Elise pretty much straight away, losing her in the darkness of the club as she went to speak to some of the others across the other side of the dance floor. A small part of me thought that was deliberate; I guessed it had been hard enough for her to arrive with me. Why should she then want to spend her evening with me, too?

"You look like a puppy waiting outside a shop for its owner." Bella put her arm around me, handing me a drink. "You've been standing here for ages, just staring into space."

"It's always going to be like this, isn't it?" I stared numbly down into my drink.

I'd told everything to Bella in one particularly messy late-night phone call, pouring my heart out to her way into the small hours, about how I'd confessed my feelings to Elise but that she hadn't wanted to know. It hadn't changed a thing, but the relief of telling her about everything had been palpable.

"If that's what Elise wants, then, yes." Bella pulled me away from the edge of the dance floor and back towards the bar. She lowered her voice as the music dipped. "Or risk losing her as a friend."

Kevin appeared with a microphone, ready to make a speech and presentation to Millie. Ten minutes later, I finally saw Elise, standing across from me, amongst some of our other co-stars, looking so breathtakingly gorgeous, my heart bunched up just at the sight of her. I was desperate to make eye contact with her, so she'd know where I was. When she finally spotted me, her face lit up with happiness. An overwhelmingly intense rush of both relief and love washed over me. Nerves fluttered in the bottom of my stomach as she slowly picked her way across the club towards me, apologising as she bumped into people, waving to others who were evidently offering her drinks, gesticulating to them that she was heading my way. At last she came to stand in front of me, her face shiny from the heat of the club and vast quantities of champagne, still managing to look effortlessly amazing.

I don't think I'd ever seen her look so lovely or so happy, standing there in front of me with a half-empty glass in her hand and her hair sticking up slightly, swaying and giggling so much that she had to put a hand on my shoulder to steady herself.

"I've been looking for you." She bent her head to me, her hair tickling my cheek, and whispered in my ear, "You were just behind me, then you disappeared."

She was looking slightly drunk but still managed to exude this air of ubercoolness that made me want to kiss her right there and then. The fact that she still had her hand on my shoulder and was standing so damn close that we were touching really didn't help matters at all, either. I could smell warm wafts of alcohol on her breath, and the champagne was making her flirty, too, I was sure of it, as she leant in close to me and looked at me long and slow. She ran her hand, which had been on my shoulder, leisurely down the length of my arm, making my bare skin prickle, before finally taking my hand in hers. I gently took hold of it, almost childlike.

"I was looking for you, too," I replied, glancing down at her hand in mine. I knew I shouldn't let her touch me like this, but I couldn't help myself.

"I've been dancing with Pete." She groaned.

"Pete?" Robbie leaned over to us and laughed out loud. "Is he going to be your next one then, 'Lise?"

'Lise?

I caught a look exchanged between Robbie and Elise, one that crushed at my chest. It was a knowing, mutual-understanding look. The kind swapped between people that have shared something in the past.

And it stung like hell.

We turned and applauded, Elise finally dropping my hand, as Millie took the microphone from Kevin and said a few words about how she was going to miss us all and about how excited she was to be taking a new direction with her acting. I listened to her talking, all the while looking at the back of Elise's neck, so perfect and lovely, her strands of blond hair cut neatly against it. How I wished I could have been those strands of hair, nuzzled happily against her skin.

"Shit, here comes Pete again." Elise turned and groaned again as Millie finished her speech and the music started up, making me instantly drop my gaze.

"Allow me." Robbie suddenly grabbed Elise's hand and walked her to the dance floor, nodding to a disappointed Pete as they passed him. Elise turned and looked back over her shoulder, pulling a face at me.

Soon she was dancing with Robbie, leaving me standing there still thinking about her lovely neck and how I'd felt when she'd run her hand down my bare arm. I stared down at the glass in my hand and was suddenly more miserable than I'd ever been in my life. I was nauseous, as if there were rocks in my stomach, and so alone I could have broken down there and then and cried my eyes out. It seemed like everyone wanted a piece of Elise tonight, including me.

I watched the pair of them slow-dance, Elise with her hands on Robbie's shoulders, those same hands that had been in *my* hands just a few minutes earlier, then felt a sensation like a cold knife in my heart as I watched him run his hand up and down her back, finally letting it rest just above the abbreviated hem of her dress. Despite Elise repeatedly moving his hand away, he kept putting it back there. A primeval scream began to build inside me when I saw him do it. I wanted to leap onto his back, pull him off her, and beat him to a pulp. His hand didn't belong there! It should have been me dancing with her, me moving my hips gently against hers, her hands on my shoulders, me putting my hand where Robbie was putting his.

They turned around so that Elise was now facing me. When she saw me watching them dance, she mouthed something to me over his shoulder, pulling a face. I shrugged back at her and peered into the murky darkness of the dance floor as she mouthed it again, but I still couldn't make out what she was saying.

She kept mouthing something over and over in my direction, looking increasingly frustrated as Robbie continued moving against her. I wandered closer to the dance floor and she mouthed it again, slower this time: "Help me!"

I rolled my eyes and shook my head, figuring she was just larking about, and wandered back to where I'd been standing, watching as she disappeared into the darkness of the club once more with Robbie. Finally the music changed to something faster, and the next thing I knew, Elise was standing next to me again.

"I'm done here, are you?" she bent her head towards me and shouted.

"Already?" I shouted back. "We just got here."

Ignoring me, she grabbed my hand and led me from the club, occasionally squeezing my fingers to let me know she was there in the darkness. I liked that.

We left the hotel, this time by the back door to avoid the photographers still grouped out the front, and walked in silence down the road a little way, just grateful to be out in the cool night air after the heat of the nightclub.

"Why didn't you save me from Robbie?" Elise asked as we slowed to wander along the South Bank, the Thames rippling softly alongside us, lit up by the moonlight.

"Seriously?" I looked across at her. "You really wanted me to help you?"

"I didn't want to dance with him." Elise looked back at me. "I was trying to tell you I didn't want to dance with him, but you just rolled your eyes and wandered off again."

"I thought you were kidding, Elise," I said, with a laugh.

"I wanted you to help me," Elise said, suddenly serious.

I was surprised to see her still looking so sombre.

"You looked like you were enjoying yourself, so how was I to know?" I asked. "He had his hand on your arse, I noticed." I looked at her from the corner of my eye.

"You were looking at my arse, were you?" She dipped her head slightly and raised her eyebrow mischievously.

"No. Well, I guess, but that's not what I meant," I mumbled.

"And did you also see me trying to get his hand off me, as well?" Elise asked, turning her head and gazing out across the river. "God, I'm so sick of men mauling me sometimes, it's unreal."

She slowed her pace. "Can we go to yours?" she suddenly said. "It's close. We could walk it from here." She peered up into the night sky. "It's a nice night for a walk by the river," she said quietly.

My place? Why did she want to go there?

"Sure," I stuttered, making a mental calculation of the tidiness of my apartment and figured that two pans left soaking in the kitchen sink plus one odd sock on the bathroom floor didn't equal a squalid mess.

It took us about another fifteen minutes to walk back to my street, and by then, a heavy rain had started to fall, so we ran the last hundred yards to the apartment block's front door.

"So unfit!" I breathed hard as I put my key in the door. "Although how anyone's supposed to run in these shoes is anyone's guess." I lifted my foot, and Elise gave a knowing half laugh. We went up in the lift to my floor in silence, both damp from the sudden rain, and entered my apartment. I watched as Elise wandered about the lounge, whistling quietly in approval when she walked to the large open window and looked at the lights of London shining out in front of her.

"I'll never get used to just how lovely it is here," she murmured, turning back to look at me. "It feels like you can see the whole of London lit up like Christmas lights."

I tossed my keys into a wooden bowl next to the front door, eased my pinching shoes off, and wriggled my feet into slippers with a sigh. The night was over. Time for some comfort.

"I'm gonna fetch myself a towel," I called out. "You want one?" I grimaced as I took a look at my reflection in the mirror by the front door. The sudden downpour had messed up my hair, so perfect and neat earlier in the evening but now sticking up in all directions and beginning to plaster itself most unflatteringly to my forehead.

Elise nodded, then turned back to carry on admiring the view in front of her.

I hurried into the bathroom, hastily kicking a crumpled-up pair of sweatpants into the corner on my way, and returned with our towels. I stood next to her at the window, handed her one, and watched, from the corner of my eye, as she dried her hair and face. She raked her fingers through her wet hair, scraping it back from her forehead, and wiped at the remaining make-up on her face with her towel, the rain having washed most of it away. I watched as she stood gazing out the window, hair swept back from her face, completely unselfconscious about the fact she was now totally free of any make-up. She looked beautiful.

"Are you happy here?" she asked, still looking out the window.

"Very, yes," I replied.

"And...are you happy?" she repeated.

"Yeah, I just said."

She turned and looked at me. "No, I mean are *you* happy? In life? Happy with yourself?"

I shrugged. "I guess." I looked at her, urging her to read my expression, needing her to know I was still struggling with the whole *just good friends* thing, and that I'd be a darn sight happier if she'd give me what I wanted: her.

"Would you be happier still if Grace were back in your life?" She wandered away from the window, looking back over her shoulder to me, and sat, with her towel still in her hands, on my sofa.

"I don't know," I said truthfully, remembering with a pang that Grace had texted me again that morning. "I sometimes wonder if she'd help me…take my mind off things." I stayed rooted to the spot by the window, not wanting to move, my heart beating a bit faster than it was before. "Would you be happier with things if Stig came back into yours?" I asked, turning the tables on her.

"Stig? He was no one," she said dismissively. "He was just company when I felt like I needed it. He took my mind off *things*." She looked steadily at me and my insides lurched.

"Anyway," I said, my voice wavering, "I guess I'll find out about Grace soon enough."

Elise looked up. "I'm sorry?"

I swallowed hard, watching her face intently. "I'm meeting her tomorrow night for a drink."

Okay, it was a lie.

But I'd blurted it before I'd even realised. I have no idea why, but the barely disguised flash of jealousy that spread across Elise's face suggested to me it might have been a good move.

"I thought she'd moved to Ireland." Elise pulled herself upright on my sofa. "You told me she was living in Ireland."

I shook my head. "Only temporarily," I said. "She plans to move back here eventually." I watched her closely. I had the bit well and truly between my teeth; there was no going back now, I figured. "She, uh, she wants to get back with me," I lied, my eyes never leaving her face.

"I see." Elise's face flickered with something new now. Not jealousy this time, but something else. Hurt? Confusion? "And you? What do you want?" she asked.

"I want to forget about you," I said bluntly. "Grace can help me do that."

That could have been partly true. At least Grace wanted me, didn't she? Grace would be the easy option.

"And do you think that's a good idea?" Elise's voice sounded thin.

"It's logical," I said. "Grace wants me. You don't. It's a no-brainer really, when you think about it."

"But you don't want her anymore," Elise said. "You already told me that."

"Still," I said. "I can't keep on waiting in the hope that you'll change your mind about me and you, can I?"

I remained standing by the window, clutching my own towel lamely in my hands. When Elise didn't respond, I wandered over to her, holding my hand out for her to pass me her towel, just wanting to do something to break the uncomfortable silence now hanging in the room.

Our hands touched as she passed me her towel, making me pull mine away as if it'd been stung by static electricity. She looked up at me as I eventually took it from her, holding my gaze for a few seconds, then looked slowly away as I moved past her and over towards my bathroom.

I tossed the towels into the laundry bin and turned to come back out again. Elise was now in the bathroom doorway, leaning against the door frame, watching me closely. "Did I tell you just how nice you look tonight?" she said. "I meant to tell you. I don't know if I did."

"No," I said, taken aback. "You didn't."

"Well, you do," she said, smiling uncertainly.

"Thank you," I said. "Uh, and so do you."

Elise frowned, looking as though she was stopping herself from saying something else. With an exasperated sigh, she ran her hands irritably over her face, rubbing at her skin. "Why did you have to be a girl?" she asked, fixing me with a look.

"I'm sorry?"

"Things would be so much easier if you'd have just been a man." Elise rubbed at her face again.

"Don't," I said, sounding stupid to my own ears.

She was anguished and exasperated and angry all at the same time, as if she was having a thousand arguments with herself inside her head. While she'd been wound up when she'd first told me she liked me, I'd never seen her quite as agitated as this before. "Don't what?"

"Why say that now, Elise?" I asked. "Knowing how I feel about you? It's not fair." I remained rooted to the spot, waiting for her to answer. She didn't. "Elise? Talk to me."

"You know why!" Elise pulled herself upright again. "Because you know that I think that...that..."

"You think...?" I asked, looking straight at her. I took a step closer to her, noticing she was breathing fast. I stopped just in front of her and looked questioningly into her eyes.

She glanced away, focusing on a spot on the floor, as if she couldn't bear to look at me. She was breathing hard through her mouth now, running her thumb over her other hand over and over again, struggling to speak.

"Think *what*, Elise?" I pushed, wanting to take her hand.

"I think..." Finally she made eye contact with me. "That I can't do this anymore," she blurted, turning from me and walking quickly back into my lounge.

"Elise! Can't do what?" I caught up with her, reaching out for her arm and turning her to face me. "What can't you do, Elise?"

"This," she said. "I can't do this." She walked to the door, wrenching it open and stumbling out into the hallway.

I followed, calling, "Elise! Wait! *Elise!*"

I scooped my keys back out of the wooden bowl, cursing as they fell to the floor. I snatched them up, then ran into the hallway, watching as the lift doors slowly closed. I jabbed on the lift's button, urging the doors to open again, but instead, I saw the down arrow illuminate. I punched the button again, more out of frustration than anything else, then hurried down the stairs, my speed impeded by my stupid slippers. By the time I'd reached the ground floor, I saw Elise already out on the pavement, hailing a cab and disappearing into the first one that stopped.

It was too late. She was gone.

CHAPTER NINETEEN

I stared at the door that Elise had just left through, my head in a muddle, my heart flailing wildly in my chest. Taking the lift back up to my apartment, my mind repeated her words over and over.

"I can't do this…"

What couldn't she do?

Me?

Jasey?

Portobello Road?

Back in my apartment, I fumbled for my phone, hidden somewhere in my bag, and rang her. She'd been so distressed—there was no better way to describe her—that I worried she wouldn't get home safely. I sank on my sofa, my mobile clamped to my ear, and listened to it as it rang out, going eventually to Elise's voicemail.

"Elise." My voice sounded strained and panicked. "It's me. Are you…are you all right? I don't know what just happened there, but I need to know you're okay." I paused, hoping she might pick up when she heard my voice, but she didn't. "Call me?" I said. "Just let me know you got home safely, yeah?"

I put my phone down and looked at it, willing it to ring, like you do when you're desperate for someone to contact you. I thought if I stared at it long and hard enough, my message to Elise would get through, she'd pick up and call me back, telling me everything was okay. But she didn't. When I tried ringing her one more time, again getting her voicemail, I sent her a text, telling her I was worried about her, and urging her to text or call me back, no matter how late.

Tired of staring at my silent phone, I wandered to the kitchen and poured myself a drink. I leant against the kitchen unit, cradling my glass with both hands, my mind both whirling and completely blank. I don't know how long I stood there, gazing empty-headed at the floor, before I heard my phone beep from in the lounge. Downing my drink, which had remained untouched until then, I went straight to it and felt a rush of relief as I saw Elise's name flash up in front of me.

"I'm fine," it said. Nothing else. Just, *"I'm fine."*

❖

The ringing of my phone woke me with a start. I peered, bleary-eyed, at my alarm clock and saw that it was three a.m.—I'd gone to bed just an hour earlier, feeling slightly more able to sleep since I'd had a text back from Elise and knew she was okay, but now panic seized me, having been awakened so soon after drifting off. My heart thumped wildly, thinking it was bad news about one of my parents. I blinked at my phone, the backlight on it making my eyes hurt in the pitch black of my bedroom.

It was Elise.

"Elise." I sat bolt upright in bed, pinching my eyes tight shut against the bright glare. "Thank God," I breathed.

"I'm sorry," Elise said. She sounded drunk.

"You all right?" I asked. "I was worried about you."

"I'm sorry," Elise repeated, her voice thick. "I don't know what to do."

I ran my hand through my hair, starting to get alarmed. "What's happened?" I asked.

"I don't know what to do," Elise said again. "Can I come over?"

I leant back, propping myself up on one elbow and looked at the alarm clock again.

"Please?" Her voice was urgent.

"Where are you?" My pulse thudded in my neck.

"Outside."

"Outside where?" I frowned.

"Your place."

I instinctively looked at the window, my breath coming faster. "You're here?"

"Are you going to let me in, or not?" Elise slurred.

"Of course!" I jumped out of bed, hopping on one foot as I pulled on pyjama bottoms that had been cast off, as always, during the night. "Wait, I'll buzz you up."

I cancelled her call and looked at myself briefly in the mirror, running my fingers though my hair, trying and failing to get it to behave before giving up. I pressed the buzzer on the intercom, then replaced it and waited for Elise to knock on my front door.

When she finally came to the door, I was shocked at the sight of her. Her eyes were red and puffy from crying and her hair, normally so perfect, was plastered across her face. She was dressed in a scruffy grey hoodie and baggy blue sweatpants, a total contrast to what she'd been wearing just a few hours earlier and a bit of a surprise to see, considering she always looked so immaculate.

"Blimey, Elise!" I looked at her, stunned, as she meekly stepped in through the door and stood, head bowed, in my hall. "You really aren't okay, are you?"

"I couldn't sleep," she said. "I need to talk to you."

She looked up at me through tear-clogged eyes and sniffed loudly. I stood facing her, not saying a word, just not knowing what to say.

"I could use a drink," she said, breaking the silence.

"Sorry, of course." I stepped back from her and gestured for her to follow me in. I made my way to the kitchen, then paused. "Elise, do you think you might have had enough already?"

"Not nearly enough, no," she said, tears welling in her eyes again.

"Even so." I made my way back to the kitchen, pouring us each a tumbler of water, and returned to the lounge, sitting down next to her on the sofa. I slid her glass across the coffee table towards her. "Want to tell me what's going on?" She stared down into her glass and, with one gulp, drained the water inside.

"Not really," she mumbled.

"Has something happened?" I asked, sipping at my water. "Have you had bad news or something?"

"No," she said quietly. "Nothing like that." She perched precariously on the edge of my sofa, and in her drunken mess she looked like she was about to slide off into a heap on the floor. I put down my glass and went to her, gently extricating her glass from her grip.

"Just been thinking, thassall." She tried to focus on me through bleary eyes.

"Yuh-huh," I said, moving away slightly from her. "That's never a good idea—too much thinking, especially after a skinful!"

"All I want is someone nice," she mumbled. "Someone who'll take care of me." She blinked tears away. "I never meant to go out with Robbie or sleep with Stig, Holly," she said suddenly. "That was never the plan. I just wanted to forget about things."

"Okay," I said slowly, wondering just why she'd think to mention either of them right now.

"And I never meant to push you away like I have been doing," she said. "I'm just so scared."

"Of what?" I asked.

"Why did you kiss me like that on the shoot?" she asked. "And before that? In your dressing room?"

My heartbeat quickened. "You know why," I said. "We've been over this enough times."

"I need to hear you tell me," Elise said.

"Don't do this," I said. "You're drunk. You're only being like this because you're drunk. It's a mistake, Elise."

"I'm drunk, yes," she said. "But sober enough to know what I want, and I know that I want you."

"You don't." I shook my head, ignoring the pounding of my heart. "You've made that perfectly clear."

"I've never said that I don't want you, Hol," Elise said. "Just that I can't be with you."

"Your work," I said bitterly. "I know, I know. Your work is more important to you than giving in to what your heart's telling you."

"I know what my heart's telling me now, though." She gazed at me for the longest time before reaching her hand out and touching my face, tracing her fingers up and down my cheek, sending a shudder through me. No one had touched me like that since Grace. I'd forgotten how nice it was. "And I know what I want now," she said.

"Don't do this," I said half-heartedly, closing my eyes. When I opened them she was still looking at me, her face a mixture of wanting and confusion.

"Do you really mean that?" she asked. She put her other hand on my other cheek and leant her face closer to me, so that her lips were now inches from mine, her warm breath fluttering against my skin.

"No," I said weakly.

"Do you want me to stop?" Elise bent her head and kissed my neck.

"No." My voice was barely audible.

"Good," she whispered back as she pressed her lips to mine and began slowly kissing me, sighing in the back of her throat as I kissed her back. I was unable—and unwilling—to hold back anymore, loving the feeling of her gentle lips on mine, and the taste of her.

Finally, we pulled apart. Elise looked at me and bent her head, touching her forehead against mine.

"Oh, Holly, Holly, Holly," she sighed, breathing out slowly. "Holly Eight-Year."

She kissed me again, her soft lips warm and sweet on mine. As I kissed her back, her hand that had been stroking my face moved down to my leg, running over it, caressing the outside of my thigh, sending shockwaves through me. I was dizzy with longing for Elise, and the more she kissed me, the more my head spun, making me feel as if I was floating up to the ceiling.

"I don't understand," I finally said when she pulled away.

She leant her head against the back of the sofa and studied me carefully. "Don't understand what?" she asked slowly, her eyes fixed firmly on my lips rather than my eyes. Before she could even give me a chance to answer, she leant over again and started kissing my neck, nuzzling into me, tracing her lips and tongue against my skin, pulling my PJ top away from my shoulder, kissing down over it to my collarbone.

"Anything. Everything." I gasped as her hand crept up under my PJ top. I grabbed her hand to stop her and pulled away. "What's changed?"

"All my life," she began, biting at her lip, "I've been worried what other people think."

"But—" I began.

"Shh!" Elise hushed me. "Worried about my public image, concerned about how people see me, scared that it'll affect my career." She looked evenly at me. "It's held me back all my life, stopped me from being who I really am."

"Stopped you?" I reached out and moved her hair from her eyes.

"Sometimes it's stopped me from being with the person I really want to be with," Elise said. "But it's never stopped Casey, has it?"

"Casey?" I asked, confused.

"I'm playing this girl who's not afraid of what people think about her," Elise said. "A girl who knows what she wants and won't let anyone stop her." She breathed in deeply, her breath faltering. "I can be that girl on screen, but I can't be that girl in real life." Elise looked at me, her face pained. "How fucked up is that?"

"Casey's just a character, Elise," I said. "Invented for the amusement of the viewing public."

"But she has what I want," Elise said. "I'm jealous of her because she has something I want."

"Which is?"

"You," Elise replied simply. "She has the confidence to be who she truly is, and she has the guts to be with who she wants to be with in life." Elise closed her eyes. "And you have no idea how much I hate that she has you…and I don't."

"But…" I chose my words carefully. "Your career? Your image?"

"I'm lonely," Elise said simply. "I'm lonely without you, but I still ignored my feelings for you because I thought everything would change if I gave in to them." Her eyes flickered up to meet mine. "But I can't ignore it anymore."

"Nothing needs to change," I said. "No one needs to know a thing."

Elise stood up, holding a hand out to me. As I stood to join her, she pulled me close to her, kissing me slowly, running her hands up under my PJ top and over my bare back, raking her fingernails softly up and down over my skin. Without a word, she took my hand again and led me to my bedroom.

I dropped her hand and watched as she slowly lay down on my bed and beckoned me over to her, but instead of joining her, I remained rooted to the spot in the doorway, unsure whether I should go to her. It was agony. Elise had finally admitted that she liked me, and yet something was still holding me back. She was drunk. Did she really mean it? If I went to her now, there would be no holding back.

"Are you sure about this?" I asked her. I peered at her closely, watching as her eyes slowly got heavier and heavier, and smiled to myself even though inside I was groaning with frustration. "You're falling asleep, Elise," I said.

She held a hand out to me. "No, I'm not." She propped herself up on one elbow and squeezed her eyes shut, then opened them again. "Too much whisky tonight, thassall."

Finally I walked over to her. She reached her arms up to me and knitted her hands behind my neck, pulling me down to her. Gently removing her hands from around me, I leant over and moved her hair from her eyes, softly kissing her forehead.

"You're drunk and tired and confused," I began.

"And horny," she said, interrupting me.

"Maybe so. But...I'm not taking advantage of you in this state," I said firmly.

"Oh, please do." She groaned, her eyes closing.

"No." With a sigh, I went to the end of the bed and removed her Converses, listening as her breathing got longer and deeper with each breath.

I looked at her lying on my bed, her blond hair falling softly onto my pillow, her eyes now shut. My heart ached for her. After gazing at her for a few seconds, I slowly and gently pulled the duvet up around her, making her stir.

"Holly?" She looked at me through sleepy eyes.

"Yuh-huh?"

"Sorry."

"Sorry for what?"

What was she sorry for? For kissing me?

"Everything."

My heart sank. "Okay."

"For almost everything. But not for kissing you just then," she murmured. "I've been wanting to do that for a long time."

"Okay." I tried to sound convinced.

"Holly?"

"Mm-hmm?"

"Don't go."

"I'll just be next door, Elise," I said gently. "You'll be okay."

"Don't go," she said again, struggling to prop herself up on her elbow and look up at me, her eyes heavy lidded, her face crumpling. "I don't want to sleep alone."

I hesitated, still standing at the end of the bed, then eventually crept into bed beside her, pulling the duvet up over us both. Elise turned onto her side, facing away from me, and reached round and took my arm, bringing it across her body and hugging it to herself. I nestled in behind her, spooning her, and wrapped my arms tight around her.

"Thank you, Hol," she said sleepily before turning her head away from me and drifting off to sleep.

CHAPTER TWENTY

When I woke up the next morning, the memories of what had happened the night before slowly began to seep, like morning mist, through my tired, hungover brain. Elise was still lying next to me, but now she faced me, fast asleep, breathing slowly and deeply.

I lay on my back, staring up at the ceiling, wondering if last night had actually happened, that Elise really had done what she'd done, or whether it had all been that damned clichéd just a dream.

She sure wasn't a dream. Her hair, always so perfect and never out of place, was now sticking up every which way; I looked at her lovely, full lips, those same lips that had kissed me the night before with such longing, and I wanted to kiss them again now and keep kissing them, over and over. She truly was beautiful, and I honestly don't think I'd ever wanted someone quite as much as I wanted Elise right at that moment.

I exhaled slowly, studying her one more time as if to check she really was there, then slowly pulled back the duvet and started to get out of bed.

"Holly?" Elise murmured, beginning to stir.

I paused, legs half out of the bed, and turned back to look at her. "Hey."

Elise's eyes blinked open slowly, and I watched as she tried to focus and figure out where she was. "Hey," she said, blinking harder now. She stretched her arms out in front of her and smiled sleepily up at me.

"You okay?" I asked, sitting on the edge of the bed now.

"Mm," she replied. "I think I was quite drunk last night, wasn't I?"

Too drunk to remember that we'd kissed?

"A little bit," I said wistfully. I didn't know if I should say something else, about what had happened, but because Elise hadn't said anything, I didn't feel like I could. Instead I sat in silence, tracing a pattern on the duvet with my index finger while she lay on her back, gazing up at the ceiling, apparently deep in thought.

"En-suite's just there," I said, when it was clear Elise wasn't going to speak. I got up and headed towards the kitchen. "Make yourself at home and all that."

I made coffee in something of a daze, thinking about everything that Elise had said to me the night before while I listened to her pad about in my bedroom, humming to herself as she did so.

A wave of panic washed over me. What if she'd been so drunk she'd forgotten what had happened? What if she thought she just got drunk and crashed at my place—as friends do? Or maybe she did remember it, but she regretted it. She'd gone to the bathroom, and now she was in there thinking about how to tell me she'd made the biggest mistake of her life, wondering just how on earth she was going to get herself out of this situation.

I turned and looked with uncertainty as Elise came into the kitchen and leant against the unit, arms folded across her chest. I hesitated, then turned back to the coffee cups, still empty.

"You okay?" she asked from behind me.

"Sure." I didn't turn to look at her, scared that I wouldn't like the look on her face because it might tell me everything I was afraid of. Instead, I focused on the cups on the unit in front of me, a thousand voices all shouting together in my head to be heard.

What should I say to her?

Should I say anything at all, or wait for her to speak?

I cleared my throat. "Do you remember any of what happened last night?" I peered over my shoulder at her.

She watched me for a moment before a slow, happy expression crept across her face. "I do," she said sleepily.

I remained rooted to the spot, still watching her over my shoulder, the coffee cups still empty. "And do you regret it?" I asked hesitantly.

"Do you?" Elise asked slowly.

I shook my head. "But do you?" I asked again.

Elise walked slowly up behind me and circled her arms around my waist, resting her chin on my shoulder.

"What do you think?" she asked, kissing the crook of my neck.

I leant back into her, practically weak with relief, and put my hands over hers. "Well, I'm glad," I said softly, resting my head against hers. "Last night was awesome."

"We didn't, er, did we?" she suddenly said, pulling her head back and peering at me. "Because if we did, then I don't remember it, and that really wouldn't be good!"

I laughed and turned round to face her, leaning against the unit and tucking a stray bit of her hair back behind her ear. Despite having just got up, and despite being hungover and still being in last night's clothes, she still looked—to me anyway—as hot as hell.

"We didn't, no," I said. "We just kissed." I thought for a moment. "Elise…" I began.

"Holly?" Her voice rose with amusement.

"Does this mean…" I bit at my lip, looking down towards the floor then back to her. "Does this mean you want to be with me?"

"I guess it does," she said. "If you want me, that is?"

Did I want her?!

"You know I want you, Elise," I said, "but—"

"But what?"

"What about everything we spoke about before?" I said. "About you being scared?"

"I've thought about nothing else for days," Elise said. "I've thought about what you said about nothing had to change between us, and maybe you were right all along." She took my hands. "I thought I'd be okay just being your friend, but I'm not," she said. "Something keeps pulling me to you, time and time again. I guess there's only so many times I can ignore my feelings."

"I meant what I said," I said. "We can just carry on as we were before. Just friends to the outside world, but—"

"But more in private?" Elise offered.

"If that's what you want?" I asked hesitantly.

"Being with you is better than not being with you," Elise said simply. She thought for a moment. "Are you really going to go and see Grace tonight?"

"Tonight?"

"You said you were going out with her tonight," Elise said quietly. "Last night, you told me you were meeting up with her."

"I'll cancel," I said.

"I didn't want to lose you to Grace," Elise said again, lifting her eyes to mine. "I would have kicked myself if I'd have let that happen."

"Well, I'm glad you did do something about it to not let that happen," I said.

"I've been such a shit to you lately." Elise squeezed my hand. "I'm sorry." She frowned. "I've just got one thing I need you to know, though," she said.

"Which is?"

"That I need to take this slowly," she said. "I've never felt like this about another girl before." She looked down at our entwined hands. "And it's a bit freaky, to be honest," she continued, "but there's just something about you, Holly Croft, that I can't resist."

"So now what?" I asked.

"I should go, that's what." She groaned.

"I didn't mean that," I said, disappointment burning in my chest. "I meant, does this mean we're, you know?"

"I know what you were getting at." Elise lifted my hand to her lips and kissed it. "And I guess it does." She hesitated. "But I really do mean it, Holly," she said. "Just one step at a time, yeah?"

"Of course," I said. "We can take this as slowly as you want, Elise."

She held my gaze awhile before finally letting go of my hand and walking to the kitchen door. "And now I really should go home and change." She laughed, looking down at herself. "Get out of these clothes. Anyone would think I just slept in them."

CHAPTER TWENTY-ONE

Once Elise left my apartment, I felt wretched. It was as though the minute she walked out the door, all the fun and colour and excitement that always came in with her just followed her straight back out again, leaving my apartment grey and lifeless once more. The rest of my morning just became an irrelevance, counting down the minutes until I could see her back at the studios again.

When I did see Elise at work a few hours later, it was all I could do to stop a stupid soppy grin from spreading right across my face. She looked happy, too, the first time I think I'd ever seen her look truly and deeply contented in the whole time that I'd known her.

I wanted to spend every single second of that day with her, to keep her close to me, to keep remembering that we really were together at last. However, as it turned out, and to my disappointment, we hardly saw anything of each other all morning. Most of my time that day was filled with filming mundane scenes with Bella and Rory in the Hunters' front room, which on any other day would be all pretty unremarkable stuff, but today wasn't just any other day. Today was different, special.

And that was all down to Elise.

We finally had time to ourselves over lunch, when filming stopped at around one p.m. for our break and Elise came over to my set, having finished filming elsewhere in the studio. I'd usually go to my dressing room alone or grab a sandwich and head to the green room and see who was around for a gossip. But today I wanted to be alone with Elise, having that selfish desire to have her all to myself, to just be alone with this gorgeous girl I was crazy about, without having anyone disturbing us.

"Hey you." Elise linked her hand with mine when the set had finally cleared and we knew we were alone. "How was your morning?"

"Agony." I rolled my eyes. "I thought about you constantly."

"I thought about you all morning, too." Elise threaded her fingers through mine. "Kevin's been going on to me about the *TV Today* awards ceremony tomorrow night, and all I wanted to do was think about you."

"The ceremony." I groaned. "I'd forgotten about that."

"Well, you've had a lot on your mind, haven't you?" Elise widened her eyes, making me laugh.

"You'll be okay, will you?" I asked, "Going with me?"

"To the awards?" Elise replied. "Of course! It's work, isn't it?"

"I mean, now things have changed," I said.

"Nothing's changed, remember?" Elise said, casting a look over her shoulder as she heard a noise. She hesitated before she spoke, checking we were still alone. "It's all as we were."

"With added bonuses," I said quietly.

"With *secret* added bonuses," Elise corrected. "Our secrets."

"I wish we could go home right now." I sighed. "It's been hell trying not to tell everyone about us—especially Bella."

"You haven't, have you?" Elise looked horrified.

"Of course not!" I squeezed her hand. "I'm not gonna tell a soul, of course I'm not."

"Sorry." Elise shrugged apologetically.

"I get you when you say no one needs to know anything," I said softly. "This is just between you and me."

"Sorry," Elise repeated. "It's just…well, you know."

"It's fine," I said.

"So," Elise said. "Your dressing room or mine?"

"Well," I said, raising an eyebrow. "I've just seen Bella go off in the direction of the canteen, so I'd say mine."

We dropped one another's hands and walked from the set and down to my room. I occasionally allowed my hand to brush against

Elise's hand or back whenever we were alone or hidden from view. I loved it. Things that I'd wanted to do for ages, just simple things like touch her or be close to her, and I could finally do them now. I thought I'd never be able to keep my hands off her ever again.

Back in my dressing room, there was a brief moment of initial shyness as we both went in, unsure really what to do, a shared knowledge that we were about to pick up where we'd left off the previous night hanging in the air. Elise hung back by the door while I went and sat on the sofa before finally following me and sitting at the other end from me, crossing her long legs and angling herself so she was facing me, putting her arm across the back of the sofa.

"I can't stop smiling," she finally said, after a few seconds of awkward silence. She leant her head sideways against the back of the sofa and gazed at me. "I keep wondering if last night really happened."

"You're not having second thoughts about stuff, are you?" I asked uncertainly. "I know you said this morning, but…"

She shook her head, holding her hand out to me. I took it, linking her fingers with mine. She looked at me a while longer, then got up from the sofa and locked the door, returning to sit closer to me this time.

"Does this feel like I'm having second thoughts?" she asked, cupping my face in both her hands and kissing me, so tenderly and gently that my insides flipped right over. She carried on kissing me, soft and long, then slowed it right down, kissing first my top lip, then my bottom lip, then repeating the same movement over and over until I was nearly going crazy for her.

"Well?" she finally asked.

"Nuh-uh." I shook my head, dazed.

"Good." She got up and sauntered back over to the door, unlocked it, then opened it up. "Now, what about lunch?" she said, leaning against the door frame. "I'm starving."

CHAPTER TWENTY-TWO

Y ou," Elise said, her voice low outside my bedroom door the next evening, "are a tease."

"And what's teasing about making you wait?" I called out from inside my room. "The fans have to wait to see me, the press have to wait to see me, so why can't you?"

"Er, hello?" Elise laughed. "Because!"

"Because?" I taunted.

She opened my bedroom door and walked in, closing it and leaning against it. "Because if I don't see you right now, I think I'm going to die."

"So dramatic," I called from inside my en-suite where I was applying dark eyeliner in the large mirror. "I can totally see why you're an actress."

It was awards night, and I was deliriously happy just to know that I'd be going with Elise. She had just arrived at my apartment after a full day of filming on set with Bella and Rory where it had been impossible to have so much as five minutes alone with her the entire day. Now, I had barely an hour to get changed, dress, leave my apartment, and arrive at the ceremony, taking place in a small arena in central London.

"So?" I stepped out from the en-suite and stood in front of Elise, my arms out to the sides of me. "Will I do?"

I was wearing a dark red dress, cut above the knee, which clung to me perfectly and kept clinging to me perfectly, more so as I walked towards her.

"Whoa," she said, looking at me admiringly. "You look amazing! C'mere." She held her hand out to me and chewed at her lip as I took her hand and went to her.

She pulled me close to her and started kissing my neck, whispering to me how fabulous she thought I looked. When her lips started kissing their way towards my mouth, I reluctantly stepped back, shaking my head and laughing.

"Nuh-uh," I said, moving away. "You're not kissing these lips until later, you."

"You're kidding me, right?" Elise looked hurt.

I pointed to my face. "See this? I've just spent the best part of an hour making it look this fabulous, so if you think you can kiss all this gloss off, you can think again."

Her eyebrow arched. "There's a name for girls like you, you know," she said, pulling a grumpy face.

"Yup, and at the moment it's Miss Perfect, so go get your bag and you can spend the rest of the evening thinking about how much fun you're going to have, kissing it all off later," I said, ushering her back into the hall. "Our car will be here in five, so go!"

Still grumbling, Elise disappeared into the hallway while I followed her. My nerves were really kicking in now, as I knew that in less than an hour we'd be at the arena and in our seats, waiting to hear who'd won what. I'd been nominated once before at an awards ceremony—Best Child, when I'd started on *PR* eight years earlier—but never as an adult. Now, knowing that there would be hundreds of screaming fans waiting for us outside the arena, TV cameras focused on all the arriving cars, and paps shouting out for us, I was absolutely bricking it.

I watched Elise from behind as I followed her, thinking how amazing she looked. More than amazing. She looked absolutely out of this world. She'd gone for an understated cream halter-neck dress, which, like my dress, clung to all the right places, with stunning killer heels, and with just the minimal amount of make-up on, she just oozed class and sophistication. I looked at her and thought that, together, we'd look unbeatable.

"You look hot." I caught up with her and ran my fingers slowly down the side of her dress as she leant over the arm of my sofa to retrieve her bag. "It's going to be agony sitting next to you all evening trying to keep my hands off you!"

"Mm-hmm." She grinned mischievously up at me from under hair flopping artfully over her eyes. "Now you know how it feels."

The TV cameras and paparazzi obviously thought she was hot, too. When we arrived and got out of the official car that had taken us there, there was an almighty rugby scrum to see who could get to us first. We had cameras shoved in our faces, microphones pushed under our noses, and what seemed like a million flashlights going off whenever we so much as turned a certain way or waved to the crowd.

And the crowd! Oh, boy! There were hundreds and hundreds of fans waiting outside the arena, all calling out our names or calling out for Jasey. The noise was incredible and the atmosphere totally crazy, but we both whooped it up, going over to speak to a few of the fans, having our photos taken on various mobile phones, signing autographs, and even, at one point, speaking to one girl's mother when she put her mobile phone into my hand and asked me to. We loved it all.

"Well, they sure love you two, don't they?" Bella was waiting in the lobby of the arena while Rory—whom she'd arrived with— disappeared to speak to Kevin.

I hugged Bella when I saw her, both of us doing air kisses so as not to smudge our make-up.

"Photo hacks hardly batted an eyelid when Rory and I fell out of the car five minutes ago." She put her arm round my shoulders and gave me a friendly squeeze.

"I'm so nervous, Bella," I said, rubbing my hands together for no other reason than it made me feel better to do it.

"You'll knock them dead tonight, whatever happens," Bella said. "You both will." She reached out a hand and rubbed Elise's arm.

We made our way into the arena, where all the *PR* actors were seated together in the first ten or so seats just to the left of the stage, and waited for the ceremony to start. The guy hosting the awards—a stalwart of daytime TV—began with the usual few jokes before starting the serious business of presenting the awards, the first three going to a rival soap, making the *PR* cast glance at one another nervously. When we finally did win an award—for Best Exit—the arena erupted, and I figured we'd all be okay from then on.

Elise and I didn't win Best Couple, nor did I win Best Actress (yes, that girl from the other soap who I just knew would win got it), but I was totally stoked when Elise won Best Female Newcomer. It was like one of those slow-motion moments when you watch the person presenting the award open the envelope and read the name out, like you can't quite believe you've heard it right.

Elise looked to me wide-eyed as the announcement was made.

"Me?" she mouthed.

"You," I mouthed back. I leant over to her. "And you totally deserve it," I whispered in her ear.

Then, all chaos broke out. The audience went wild, applauding and whooping and calling out her name, while Bella, Rory, Robbie, and anyone else who was close enough to us leant over their seats to congratulate her. I pulled away from her, just happy to let her soak up the applause.

She still looked stunned as she made her way carefully up to the stage to collect her award, and I seriously thought my heart might burst with pride. I didn't have a hint of envy—just unadulterated pride and happiness for her, knowing how hard she—well, we—had worked, just lately, to get to this point. It was as though her award was reward for both of us and also recognition of the fact that, in my own way, I'd played some part in Elise getting it.

"Wow." Elise stood on the stage, one hand clasped to her chest, the other clutching the award, which had just been passed to her. "I don't really know what to say."

A small ripple of laughter echoed round the arena.

"No, seriously." Elise looked around her. "I really don't know what to say."

Another ripple.

She looked at her award. "This is awesome," she finally said. "And totally unexpected."

"They all say that." Bella leant over two chairs towards me, nearly losing her balance, and whispered in my ear.

"I have so many people I need to thank for allowing me to win this award," Elise said, gazing down at it. "The writers, of course, for coming up with the Jasey storyline in the first place." She paused, grinning, as a whoop went up from around the arena. "Because without them, there wouldn't be a Jasmine and Casey." She looked at her award again, deep in thought. "The producers and directors, my other cast members, the make-up team for always making me look like I haven't just got out of bed…" Another loud cheer went up, allowing Elise the time to finally make eye contact with me.

My breath caught in my throat at just how gorgeous she looked. She was radiant, confident, and funny, loving every second of being up there on the stage. This was everything she wanted to be: famous and loved by her fans. And as I looked around me, I knew from the reaction she was getting that the crowd in the arena really did love her, just as much, if not more, than they loved Casey.

When I looked back, as the cheering subsided, she was still looking at me.

"*Portobello Road* has changed my life," she said. "In more ways than anyone in this room will ever understand. Everyone except one person, that is." She carried on looking at me. "Holly Croft." She opened her mouth to continue, but stopped as another loud cheer went up, one that seemed to go on forever. I turned and smiled at Bella as she leant over again and patted my leg, giving me a reassuring wink.

"Without Holly Croft," Elise said as the noise in the arena died down, "there would be no Casey and no Jasey—or at least not as we all know and love them." She looked directly at me. "And that's all down to you, Hol." I caught her gaze and held it, hearing the cheers ring out around me again. It was like the room receded at that moment, and it was just me and her. No one else mattered. She was talking to me directly. No one but me.

"I love working with you," she said. "Every day on set with you is a blast, and I can't imagine not sharing it all with you." She looked down at me. "You're funny, smart, fiery, and you're a damn good actress as well, which makes working with you so much easier."

There were a few small laughs from around us.

"I can't imagine not being with you every day," she said. "And if it wasn't for you, then I wouldn't be standing here with this award right now." She lifted the award up higher. "So this is for you, too, Hol. Jasey forever."

The room erupted in deafening cheers as Elise walked away from the stage and made her way carefully back down the steps to the side of it, her award clutched safely in her hand.

It had been an awesome speech and I'd totally read the subliminal message behind what she was saying, even if it had been agony having to sit, totally poker-faced but with just the hint of an enigmatic smile on my face, knowing that the cameras would be fixed well and truly on me. All I'd wanted to do while she was talking was to go up on that stage with her and shout out to everyone in that packed arena just what a wonderful person Elise was, and how much I loved her, and—

How much I loved her?

My heart pounded.

I did. I loved her.

Watching her as she made her way down the aisle back to her seat, I knew that I really did love her, and that I didn't know what I'd do if she wasn't in my life. She had become my life, and hearing her tell an audience of hundreds, in her own way, how much I meant to her, too, just made my heart swell with so much love and pride, I thought I could have burst into tears right there and then.

CHAPTER TWENTY-THREE

Her speech over, Elise returned to sit with me once more, still holding her silver award—a twisted piece of metal which looked a bit like an ice cream in a cornet—but we both tried to ignore that.

"You were awesome," I whispered in her ear once she'd sat down next to me. "And I'm so happy for you."

"I meant every word." Elise raised her voice slightly as a swell of applause for the next award rose up. "This is just as much for you as it is for me."

She placed the award in my lap, and I stared down at it with her, running my fingers over the *TV Today–Best Female Newcomer* words etched into its base. I looked at her and filled with pride. It had taken every ounce of restraint not to kiss her when she had come back to her seat after accepting it, and it was taking every ounce again now. She looked so happy, so proud, and so fulfilled, and I was overwhelmed with happiness to see her like that.

The ceremony ended soon after Elise's award. Photos were taken, interviews were conducted, and Elise was—quite rightly—the centre of attention. Everyone was desperate for a piece of her.

"I've just done an interview with *Just So* magazine, a quick TV interview for tomorrow's *Good Morning* programme, and about five hundred photos for the morning's papers," she said breathlessly, looking round the bar to which the entire *PR* cast had decamped and where they were now taking advantage of the free champagne.

Despite all the champagne and exhilaration of the evening, and how long all the after-ceremony media was now taking, she still looked totally amazing. I glanced at her as she grabbed a drink from a passing waiter and drank it back, her eyes still glinting with happiness. She looked alive and glowing and, to me, just so sweet and lovable I could have happily grabbed her hand there and then and led her straight back to my apartment. But I couldn't. Tonight, Elise belonged to everyone else but me, so I had to be patient and contain my longing for her just that little bit longer. I knew I needed to be content to just watch her network, and that I had to leave her in peace to lap up the attention and focus on the very aspect of her life that she was always telling me was everything to her: her popularity.

"I've still got to do a group shot with all the other winners and get some done with Danny Byers," Elise now said eagerly, putting her drink down on the bar and heading over to the other side of the room. Danny had won Best Male Newcomer.

Her photo call with Danny took place just to the side of where we were drinking, so I could see it all unfold in front of me. She worked the camera well and, to his credit, so did he.

I watched her with a swell of admiration. She was doing the thing she loved to do best in the world and was doing it well. She turned her head this way and that, instinctively knowing which way to stand in order for the photographer to get the best shot. They called out to her, asking for a certain look, thanking her when she obliged. They knew, she knew, and I knew that the photos that would come out of this brief shoot would be out of this world.

My admiration for her was coupled with love, too. I loved her not only for the way she was working the camera to her advantage, but also for the way she knew I was watching and would occasionally glance my way with a reassuring look that said, *I'll be done here soon and then I'm all yours.*

"She's good, yes?" Bella's voice sounded beside me. I'd been so transfixed by watching Elise that I hadn't noticed her come and stand next to me.

"She has something, doesn't she?" I said, my voice thick with pride. "Something special."

"She does." Bella followed my gaze to Elise. "I tell you what, they never photographed me like that when I was her age." She sipped from her champagne flute. "Fat chance they're ever going to now, either." She gave a slightly drunken snort, then put her arm round my shoulders, nearly pulling me off my feet. "You look glowing tonight, by the way," she said. "You both do. I'm very proud of the pair of you."

"Mother Bella." I put my head in the crook of her neck.

"Always," Bella said.

"I just wish…" I shook my head. "Nothing."

"You're smitten, aren't you?" Bella said. "I looked at you when she was accepting the award and I thought to myself, there's a girl who's so in love, I can see it in her face."

"You don't care that I'm in love with another girl, do you?" I asked.

"You know I don't!" Bella looked aghast. "I told you before, love is love. Take it when you can."

"I just wish my love didn't feel so tainted," I said, taking a small sip from my glass.

"Tainted?" Bella asked.

"She makes it feel like that sometimes," I replied, stung with guilt for even having uttered the words, but lighter for it somehow, too. "I just wish she wasn't so furtive about us all the time." I looked over to Elise. "She thinks the world will stop turning if anyone ever found out about us," I said. "Or, rather, she thinks *her* world will stop turning."

"It sounds as though Elise's world is very important to her," Bella said. "Just be patient with her. That sounds like all she needs from you right now. Patience and understanding." She raised her arm in greeting as she spied someone else she knew across the other side of the room, spilling half her champagne as she did so. "Shit!" She put the glass in her other hand, shaking the hand that had just been soaked. "That's going to need a refill, isn't it? Back in a mo'," she said, wandering off in the direction of the bar.

I carried on watching as Elise posed for her final photograph, then stood to one side to allow yet another interviewer to corner her for some quotes for the morning papers. Her eyes drifted to mine and held them briefly as she spoke, then drifted back to the interviewer, her attention focused on him, once more.

Finally, she was finished. She walked quickly over to where I was standing in the shadows, empty champagne glass still in my hand.

"Hey." She ran her hand down the length of my arm, letting her fingers rest on mine, before letting my hand slowly drop.

"Hey." I looked into her darkened eyes and another swell of love for her engulfed me.

"I'm done," she said, puffing out her cheeks "Finally!"

"You've been awesome this evening," I said. "I haven't been able to take my eyes off you all night."

"Nor me, you." Her eyes slowly drifted down the length of my body and back up again. "Hol?"

"Elise?"

She leant forwards, her hair tickling my face. "Take me home," she whispered into my ear. "I think I'll go mad if I can't have you tonight."

CHAPTER TWENTY-FOUR

We did manage to leave the party soon after that, hailing a cab from just outside the arena and ducking into it, away from the eagle eyes of the photographers still hanging around outside. The cab drove quickly through the streets of London, me and Elise sitting in silence in the back of it, occasionally looking across to one another and linking hands in the darkness of the back seat, then turning to stare, unseeing, out our respective windows at the streets rushing past.

We arrived back at my apartment shortly after two a.m., sharing the quickest of kisses in the privacy of the lift for the few moments it took it to get up to my floor. I was barely able to keep my hands off her but knew I had to wait until we were safely inside my apartment, away from anyone seeing us. Somehow, that made it hotter, knowing that I couldn't touch her but desperately wanting to, and that soon I'd have her all to myself again.

Once inside my apartment, Elise closed the door and locked it. Flicking the dimmer-switch on, she turned the lights down low and, with one hand, pushed me up against the closed door, all the while never taking her eyes off mine. I pressed myself back against the door, linking my arms up and around her neck.

"Remember earlier you said I could spend the evening thinking about how much fun I was going to have kissing all your lip gloss off?" Elise murmured, looking down at my lips.

"Mm?"

"Well, I thought about it, like, *all* evening," she said, bending her head and kissing her way across my neck and up to my cheek.

"Even when you were with Danny?" I mocked.

"Yuh-huh," Elise mumbled.

She brushed her lips over my cheek, over my eyes, my forehead, before lightly kissing my lips, pressing hers softly to mine. Still kissing me, she took my hand and pulled me away from the door to the lounge, leading me over to the sofa. She pushed me gently down and laid me back onto the sofa, putting both her hands either side of my head and leaning over me, her hair falling softly onto my face.

"This was all I could think about while I was there tonight," she said quietly. "All the time I was standing there having photo after photo taken, all I wanted to do was get the hell out of there and get you back here alone."

"Really?" I looked up at her.

"Really." She pulled herself off me and, kicking her heels off, wandered to the kitchen. "Do you have any champagne? I think it's time just you and I celebrated, don't you?"

"Fridge," I called from the sofa. "Already opened. Probably flat by now."

She returned a few seconds later with a bottle and glasses. "Who cares?" She grinned, sitting on the sofa next to me.

She pulled the stopper from the champagne, nodding approvingly as she heard a satisfying enough pop, then quickly poured out two glasses.

"To you!" I said, taking the glass that was offered to me. "And your award. You deserve it."

"Maybe," she said, "but without you, I wouldn't have got it, would I?"

I thought for a moment. "True." I grinned. "To us, then!"

I linked my right arm around her right arm and looked at her as we both awkwardly took a sip from our glasses, Elise giggling as some champagne dribbled down her chin, while I enjoyed the sensation of the bubbles pricking like small needles inside my mouth.

I swallowed the ice-cold champagne. "Elise?" A wave of doubt washed over me.

"Holly." Elise looked at me with mock seriousness.

"Are you sure this is what you want?"

"The champagne?" Elise leant her head to one side and widened her eyes. "Yeah, it's what I want."

"Be serious."

Without answering me, Elise unhooked her arm from mine, drained her drink, then slowly took my glass from me. She put both our glasses down on the table and took my hands in hers, then stood, pulling me to my feet, too. Still silent, she looked down at my lips then slowly lifted her gaze back up, until she was looking back at me, as if she was looking right into my soul. She was utterly mesmerising, and I was incapable of resisting her any longer.

"I've never been more sure of anything in my life," she said softly.

There was a pause while we both stood looking at each other, eyes roaming over one another's face, both of us knowing what was about to happen. Elise looked adorable and sexy and loving and vulnerable and a million other beautiful things, and I knew by the look in her eyes that she wanted me as much as I wanted her. I instinctively pulled her to me and kissed her more deeply and urgently and with more longing than I'd ever kissed anyone before, Elise all the while pressing her lips hard back onto mine, running her hands up my back, making my skin prickle against the material of my dress.

"I think you're fabulous," she murmured against my lips. "I want to keep you forever and ever."

Still kissing, she pushed me backwards until I was against the wall of the lounge, then slowly—so slowly—started pulling my dress down far enough until I was able to wriggle myself out of it, lifting my feet and kicking it away to one side.

She held my arms above my head with one hand, whilst her other hand stroked my bare skin, making me catch my breath, giving me goosebumps up and down my arms. She stopped kissing me for a second and looked down at me, her eyes fixed on mine.

"You're beautiful," she whispered.

I freed my arms and clasped them behind Elise's neck, closing my eyes and leaning my head back against the wall as Elise started kissing my throat and neck, then suddenly stopped. I opened an eye and glanced at her.

"Don't stop," I pleaded. "Please."

"So where should I kiss you next?" Elise grinned.

I pointed to my lips. "Here would be a start," I said.

"No, no lips allowed." Elise brushed her finger over my lips.

"Okay," I said, laughing. "Here?" I pointed to my collarbone and instinctively tilted my head back as Elise started kissing it, tracing her tongue over it, nibbling gently at my skin over and over again.

"Next?" she finally said, still brushing her lips over my collarbone.

A shiver ran down my back. I loved the way she was teasing me, touching me. I loved how she was kissing me, so gently and lovingly. Even though she was asking me each time, I knew that she knew exactly where to touch me and how to kiss me, and she knew just how hard or soft I wanted it, making my skin tingle and the blood rush in my ears.

I liked this game. I liked it a lot.

Before I'd had a chance to point to my neck, she was already kissing it. I felt myself getting giddier with each kiss as Elise slowly nuzzled at my skin, just below my ear, her hair falling gently against my skin.

"Next?" Elise murmured, still kissing my neck, before lifting her head and meeting my eyes. The look in her eyes was enough to nearly send me over the edge as I pointed to my stomach, laughing as Elise obediently fell to her knees. She put both hands on my hips and started running her tongue up and down my skin before moving her lips lightly over it, alternatively kissing and licking. I pressed my head back against the wall and threaded my hands into her hair, thinking that I might explode at any minute.

Finally, when I couldn't bear it any longer, I spoke.

"Elise?"

"Mm-hmm?"

"Take me to bed."

CHAPTER TWENTY-FIVE

I never believed I could ever love someone again after Grace left me. She'd taken away every ounce of trust and confidence from me, so that I really thought I'd spend the rest of my life alone. I guess that's what being dumped does for your self-esteem, huh?

But now here I was, the morning after what had been possibly the best—and longest—night of sex I'd ever had, and I thought maybe I was going to be all right, after all. Elise had been amazing and so loving and thoughtful and caring, I thought that if I'd died right there in my bed, I'd have at least died happy.

I woke up entwined with Elise, her head in the crook of my neck, my arms wrapped round her shoulders, my leg hooked up over her hip, just cradling her like I didn't ever want to let her go. I looked down at her, still fast asleep in my arms, hardly daring to believe she was here with me, and felt a surge of love for her. I loved that she wanted me as much as I wanted her, and that she wanted to be with me, not with or Robbie or anyone else. Just me. I brushed her hair softly away from her eyes, leaning down and kissing her forehead, tracing my fingertips up and down her bare arm, reluctantly stopping when I saw her stir. I couldn't wait to spend every single minute of every day with her, or to fall asleep with her at night and then wake up and find her in my bed next to me, just as she was now. I wanted her totally and utterly, day after amazing day. Because she *was* amazing. And she was mine.

She began to wake up, just as I was still gazing down at her, and peered up at me through sleepy eyes. When she saw me looking at her, a smile spread across her face that was so sweet it made my heart soar. She sighed contentedly, a long, deep sigh that only comes with pure happiness, her body tensing and shaking slightly against mine as she stretched and suppressed a yawn.

"Hey," she said, reaching over and stroking my face.

"Sleep okay?" I asked, putting my arm under the duvet and stroking her thigh.

"Eventually." She laughed. "Someone kept me up half the night."

She rolled onto her back, pulling the duvet up, and lay there, gazing sleepily at the ceiling. She pulled her knees up and stretched her arms out above her head, linking her fingers, pushing her hands out in front of her, and stifling another yawn.

"Last night was amazing," I said, remembering, still lying on my side, just watching her, taking in every detail of her perfect face.

"Totally awesome." She broke into a reminiscent sort of smile. "You're awesome, too."

"Do you really mean that?" I asked.

She turned and looked at me, lifting up her elbow long enough to allow me to shuffle over and nestle my head against the crook of her neck, then curled her arm round my shoulders.

"Of course I do," Elise replied, sighing contentedly as I draped my arm across her front, idly running my fingers over her ribs and across her stomach, loving how she squirmed with pleasure every time I ran over a particularly sensitive spot on her skin. "Do you really have to ask that?"

"I'm just checking again," I said slowly, "that you're not having second thoughts about everything."

"About us?" Elise asked. "No, I'm not having second thoughts." She hesitated. "Although…"

"Although what?"

"Just that you know we have to be discreet about all this," she said.

"I know, yes," I said, my heart getting heavy. "You already said, and I already said I will be."

"I'm just paranoid that someone's going to find out." Elise hugged me tighter. "I'm sorry."

"How will anyone know?" I tried not to sigh audibly; I really didn't want to be having this conversation again. Not now. "No one's going to find out."

"Unless someone sees me leaving your apartment later," Elise said quietly. "After having seen me arrive last night."

"Did you see anyone follow us, Elise?" I asked.

"No," she replied meekly.

I propped myself up on one elbow, reaching up to push her hair from her eyes. "And since when have I ever had reporters camped outside my apartment?" I made big eyes at her. "Chill." I thought for a moment. "And, anyway, even if anyone did see you coming here and leaving again, why would they assume we're sleeping together?"

"True." Elise rolled her eyes. "Ignore me," she said. "I'm being stupid."

I nestled myself back into the crook of her arm once more. "You are," I said, squealing as she playfully dug her fingers into my side. "I've slept over at Bella's before now—do you think people will think we're an item?" I squealed again as she dug her fingers in harder.

"Don't mock me," she laughed.

"But you can see how ludicrous it sounds, can't you?" I said, stroking her arm.

"I can," she sighed. "Sorry."

I looped my arm tighter around her, enjoying the warmth and feel of our entwined bodies.

"I could lie like this all day," I whispered into her neck, my eyes getting heavy again.

We lay in silence, wrapped up tightly in each other's arms, Elise's chin resting on the top of my head as we dozed, listening to one another breathing softly.

"We should do something today," I murmured. I pulled myself away and propped myself up on one elbow, ignoring Elise's grumbles about being moved. I looked down at her, tracing a pattern on her collarbone with my fingertips. "Considering we have the day off. What do you think?" I thought for a minute, then remembered my recurring dream about being in a boat with Elise. "You know what I'd really like to do today?"

Elise shook her head.

"Take a rowing boat down the Thames," I said.

"No," Elise said firmly. "I don't think so."

"What?" I said, taken aback by her blunt reply. "Why not?"

Elise looked at me, her face serious. "Because we'll be seen," she said. "We've just been talking about discretion, Hol. What's discreet about taking a boat down the Thames?"

"We won't be seen!" I said. "C'mon, it'll be fun."

"It won't be fun when we're plastered all over the papers in the morning if we're spotted," Elise said.

I stopped tracing my finger across her skin and fell back onto the pillow, staring up at the ceiling.

"Will it always be like this?" I asked. "With you being too afraid to be seen out with me?"

"Don't be cross with me, Hol," Elise said. "I'm sorry." She lay on her back beside me and stared up at the ceiling, too. "Why can't we just hang out here all day?"

"*Hide* out here all day, you mean?" I said. "I don't want to. I just want to spend the day with you doing something different."

"So we spend the day here." Elise patted the bed.

I turned my head to look at her and saw that her face was etched with anxiety.

"What exactly are you scared of?" I asked. "Okay, I was with you up to a point about not being seen creeping out of my apartment at six in the morning with last night's clothes on, but it's not like two co-stars are never seen out with one another, is it?" I pointed out. "We were always being seen out with one another before we actually got together. You weren't bothered then."

"Because back then it wouldn't have been written all over our faces that we were a couple," Elise said, exasperated.

"And you think it is, now?" I sank my head back onto the pillow. "We're hardly hanging signs round our necks, are we?"

"But rowing a boat together?" Elise said. "Could that be more obvious?"

"It's just rowing a boat, Elise," I said. "Not making out on the top of Nelson's Column."

"Don't be like this," Elise pleaded.

"Like what?"

"Grumpy," she said. "Argumentative. I just wanted to have an awesome day with you, that's all."

"So did I," I said. "So come rowing with me! If we see any paps we'll talk to them, tell them it was Kevin's idea for us to be photographed together the day after the ceremony. We'll make it out to be nothing more than a clever public relations move by the people at work."

"And where exactly would we take this boat?" Elise asked. "And, more to the point, do you have any idea how to row one?"

"No idea," I said. "And, uh, no idea, either! Just think about it? It'll be fun."

"And you think we could wing it if we were spotted?" Elise asked. "Maybe even turn it to our advantage?"

"Mm-hmm."

Elise thought for a moment. "Okay, I'll think about it," she finally said, drawing me down to her and pulling the duvet over our heads. "As long as I can have some other fun while I do."

❖

"Can you at least look as if you're enjoying yourself?" I pulled on my oar and frowned.

Elise had given the idea of taking a boat out due thought and—after much persuasion—had agreed to an afternoon of messing about on the river with me. I'd been stoked that she'd finally buckled and had agreed to come—albeit with certain limitations that she had set—so we'd hired a skiff and had set off at a slow pace down the Thames, from a small town just outside London. It was a typically temperate English day, the sort that, despite having the sun shining down, still had chilly wind that made muffling up against it crucial. It was good to be dressed casually after the dresses and heels from the night before. I was cosily secure in a hoodie, jeans, and jacket, with the warmest beanie ever pulled down over my ears. Elise looked lovely, as always, and casual in cargo pants and a big, cosy fleece. As much as I loved her when she was dressed to kill, she looked totally cute dressed down.

"I'm on edge," Elise said, looking around her. "I can't help it."

"Just who's going to recognise us anyway?" I said, looking around as the boat sliced through the water. "You're totally unrecognisable for a start." I waved a hand at Elise's striped hat and matching scarf, which was wrapped up round her face.

She pulled her sunglasses down from on top of her hat and put them over her eyes, pulling them down onto her nose slightly and peering over them towards me. "I just don't feel comfortable out here, that's all."

We rowed on down the river in silence, the slow *plip, plip* of the oars dipping in and out of the water the only sound we could hear. I watched Elise from the corner of my eye as I rowed, at the excruciated look of anxiety engraved across her face, her brows knitted as if she was carrying the weight of the world on her shoulders rather than enjoying a day out with her girlfriend.

My insides tensed up into a tight ball at my thoughts. Her girlfriend? Was that what I really was? Looking at the pained expression on Elise's face, I could tell she hated every second of being out in the open with me on our day off. She was sitting just about as far away from me in the boat as she could manage and kept looking anxiously at the banks of the river as if expecting to see a team of reporters following us. The thought hit me like a fist in my stomach that I really wasn't her girlfriend, and if her insistence that we keep our relationship a secret was anything to go by, I probably never would be. Not girlfriends in the true sense of the word, anyway.

"What are you thinking about?" Elise's voice cut through my thoughts, as if she'd been reading my mind.

"Nothing." I heaved the oars back.

"You so are," Elise said. "I can see it on your face. You were deep in thought."

"I was just thinking."

"I know," Elise said. "I just said." She lowered her sunglasses and looked at me over the top of them. "What were you thinking about?"

"Stuff." I pulled hard on one oar, allowing us to move slightly to the left.

"Too vague." Elise carried on looking at me over her glasses. "Try again."

"You," I said. "I was thinking about you."

We ducked our heads as the boat drifted under a large weeping willow, the soft fronds scraping along the side of the boat as we passed under it.

"Good or bad?" Elise asked.

"I'm not sure," I replied truthfully.

"Oh." Elise slid her glasses back up her nose. "That's not really what I wanted to hear."

"You look like you hate this, that's all," I said. "I don't want you to hate it. I want you to enjoy it."

"I'm fine"—Elise saw me staring at her—"really."

"I wish you'd relax a bit, that's all," I said. "You look like you want me to turn this boat around and go straight back."

"I don't," she said softly.

The look on her face didn't do anything to quell my fears, though. A cloud of despondency scudded towards me every time I looked at Elise's tense, set face, and despite the fact she smiled each time our eyes met, her smile was taut with anxiety. That worried me properly for the first time since we'd got together.

But it was more than just despondency, I thought, as I watched Elise pull her scarf further across her face. A quiet discontent was also growing inside me with every pull of my oars through the water, knowing that my relationship with Elise was entirely on her terms, and not at all on mine. And I just didn't know what I could do about it.

CHAPTER TWENTY-SIX

It'll be a fall back to earth for you today," I said to Elise the next morning. I bumped her hip with mine as I passed her in my kitchen. "After your award, I mean."

Elise was leaning against my kitchen unit, eating a piece of toast. She was wearing one of my favourite T-shirts and nothing else, looking totally adorable, her bare legs stretched out in front of her, and it was taking every ounce of self-control I had in my body not to drag her back to my bedroom there and then.

She shrugged. "I guess. Filming scenes today with Bella will keep me grounded, no danger of that," she added with a grin.

Bella.

If there was one person guaranteed to keep us both grounded, it was Bella. I also knew that Bella was the only person in the world I knew I could go to about my worries over me and Elise.

"Bella knows I like you," I suddenly said, immediately regretting it when I saw the look on her face.

"You told her about us?" Elise paused, toast still in hand. "I thought I said not to tell *anyone*."

I hastily shook my head. "I haven't told her," I lied. "Quit panicking, will you?"

"So what *does* she know?" Elise chewed on her toast and watched me.

"Just that I like you," I stammered. "I told her ages ago 'cos she figured something was up. It was at the same time that Grace was calling me. I was stressed, okay? I needed someone to talk to, and Bella was there for me."

"Well, don't go telling her that we got it on, will you?" Elise stopped chewing again and stared at me. "Bella has teenage kids, doesn't she? They get wind of it and it'll be all over the Internet before you know it."

"I told you I wouldn't," I said. "So I won't." I thought for a moment. "But she'll probably ask me something at some point," I lied, "because I'm not walking round with a face like a slapped arse anymore. She'll work out that something's changed."

"So tell her you're fine about stuff now." Elise shrugged, brushing crumbs from her hands. "Or tell her that Grace has buggered off back to Spain or Ireland or wherever it was she was going, and that you're a lot less puddled about it all now."

I knew I'd been well and truly rebuked. When I didn't answer Elise, she held her arms out to me. "C'mere."

I went to her and let her circle her arms round my waist, linking my own arms round her. She kissed my hair before leaning her forehead against mine and sighed. "Can I come over again tonight?" she asked. "I can bring pizza." She bent her head to catch my eye, smiling when I nodded. She pulled me closer to her again. "It'll be okay, I promise," she said. "Everything will be okay."

But the more I thought about it, the more convinced I became that it really wouldn't be.

❖

I had five scenes to film that day, and they just dragged on forever. I don't know if it was because I just wanted it to be over so I could spend precious time with Elise, or because I was flat, being back at work after an awesome few days, or even because of the gnawing worry I kept getting each time I replayed recent conversations with Elise over in my head. To make matters worse, I didn't get to see Elise until lunchtime, either. She spent her entire morning on the set of the pub, filming with Bella and a few others whose characters in *PR* worked with Bella's in the supermarket, and then was finished for the day, while I had to carry on filming with Robbie for the whole afternoon.

I was hurrying down to the canteen to meet Elise for lunch, already thinking ahead to seeing her again, when I bumped into Bella and Rory coming back from another set.

"I've just seen your girlfriend hotfooting it down to the canteen as well." Rory jerked his head back over his shoulder. "She's either hungry or in a hurry to see someone."

"My girlfriend?" I glanced from Rory to Bella and back again.

"Casey." Rory bumped my arm. "Who else?" He winked as he passed me and ambled on down the corridor.

"He doesn't know, so you can take that deer-in-the-headlights look off your face." Bella put an arm round my shoulders and playfully pulled me to her.

I watched until Rory had reached the end of the corridor and turned the corner before I spoke. "I wish I could tell you that Elise felt like my girlfriend," I said quietly, darting my eyes towards a door as I heard it swing open. "Or that I felt like I was hers."

We both waited as a runner hurried past us speaking quickly into a headset, then disappeared through another set of doors.

"Are you in trouble already?" Bella asked, putting her hand on my arm. "I assumed everything was all right with you two."

I leant a shoulder against the wall and sighed. "It's fine, I guess," I said. "It's just..." I struggled to find the right words.

"Not the hearts and flowers you thought it would be?" Bella offered.

"It just doesn't feel like I thought it would feel," I said simply. "I mean, new relationships are supposed to be exciting and carefree, aren't they?"

"Well it's been years since anyone's lit my fire," Bella said ruefully, "and God knows I've handed out enough matches over the years." She paused. "But from what I remember when I first got together with Tom, yes, it should be all red hearts and stolen kisses for you at this stage."

"Not looking over our shoulders every five minutes or having niggling doubts about every tiny thing?" I folded my arms across my chest and stared moodily at the floor.

"Is that how it is?" Bella asked, tilting her head to one side and looking at me sympathetically.

"Seems to be, at the moment," I said. "She still doesn't know you know, either."

"You think she'll freak if she finds out?" Bella asked.

Before I could answer her, I heard Elise call my name from the far end of the corridor, making me swing round probably more twitchily than was necessary. I watched her saunter down towards me, hands in her pockets, her slim jean-clad legs seeming to go on forever. She had this sexy way of swinging her hips when she walked, almost like how a model walks, and I loved how she did it. But, then, it was like everything else she did—just perfect and classy and, yeah, hot as hell, and I sensed my face flushing just at the sight of her.

Despite all my worries, I still had the awesome swell of pride that I always had when I saw her, which just swelled even more when I saw the look of happiness she had on her face at finding me.

"I was waiting for you in the canteen," she said softly when she finally got to me. She lifted her head to acknowledge Bella. "I wondered where you were."

"I was on my way," I replied, meeting her eye. She held my look and gave me this slow, gorgeous, knowing look. My worries, so intense just a few minutes before, lessened.

"We were just talking about you." Bella reached out and patted Elise's arm. "About how lovely you looked at the awards the other night," she continued before Elise had a chance to see the look of alarm on my face.

"Thank you." Elise adjusted her bag on her shoulder. "I think we all looked awesome that night." She flashed me a quick look.

Finally Bella said her goodbyes and left, allowing Elise and me to be alone, at last. We both stood leaning against the wall facing one another, occasionally letting our fingers brush, dropping them whenever someone passed us or we heard a noise further down the corridor. They were just the briefest of touches between us, but each touch spoke volumes—telling the other we'd missed them in the short time we'd been apart that morning, and that we were glad we were together again.

Finally we pulled ourselves away from the wall and headed down to the canteen, hunger forcing us both to leave our little bubble of togetherness.

"So, plans for the weekend?" Elise asked as we walked back down the corridor. She brushed her hand quickly down my arm. "I was thinking takeout pizza at yours tonight, maybe something similar tomorrow, and"—she glanced over her shoulder and, seeing no one around, whispered—"a lie in on Sunday."

"Or how about pizza at mine tonight and a club tomorrow?" I suggested. "Maybe even dinner first?"

"I was thinking more like us having something at yours tomorrow." Elise pulled her bag up higher on her shoulder. "Rather than going out."

I stopped walking. "We haven't been out since, well, you know." I looked behind me. "Since we got together." I lowered my voice. "We should go clubbing or something, rather than stay in and be boring."

"We could," Elise said slowly, "or we could just stay in. I'm thinking a cosy night on the sofa." She widened her eyes at me.

"Or rather, you're thinking…" I began. I took a deep breath. "Nothing." I started walking again. "Takeout and a sofa snuggle sounds great."

"I'll bring wine." Elise fell into step beside me. "And you can choose the food tomorrow. How's that?"

"Now you're talking," I said, trying to ignore the nagging pull in the pit of my stomach. "Shall we forget the canteen?" I suddenly asked. "And see if my room's empty, instead?"

"Clever thinking, I like it," Elise said, following me back down the corridor to my dressing room. Entering it and seeing that Bella wasn't around, Elise followed me in, then closed the door and leant against it before beckoning me back over to her. As I obediently went to her, she draped her arms over my shoulders and drew me in closer.

"So? Weekend sound good?" she asked, moving her hand briefly to tuck a wayward strand of hair behind my ear.

"Sounds awesome," I said. "But I will need to do some other stuff around my apartment this weekend as well."

"Stuff?" She cocked her head to one side.

"Stuff," I repeated. "Cleaning, fixing things that have been waiting to be fixed for weeks, and—"

"Mm-hmm," she said, looking at my chest, nodding to herself and smiling. "And you'd give up the chance to be with me just so you could do a bit of home improvement?" She glanced up at me, her eyebrow curved quizzically and perfectly.

I laughed. "No, of course not! But I..."

Elise lazily traced a finger up the front of my top, stopped at my top button, and slowly undid it. "You were saying?" she said, undoing the second button and slipping a hand inside. She didn't look at me all the time she was doing it, instead concentrating on where her hand was and what she was doing. I was so giddy at her touch I thought my knees might buckle underneath me at any time.

Elise moved in to kiss me, but the rattle of the door handle made us both jump as if we'd just been stung. I instinctively jerked away from her, hastily buttoning up my top, while Elise sprang back away from the door and leant against my dressing table, her eyes wide.

"Damn door sticking." I heard Bella's voice outside the door then jumped as she shoved at the door and practically fell into the room towards me. "Bloody thing. Oh!" She glanced from me to Elise and back to me.

"I was standing behind the door," I stuttered. "Sorry." I looked at Elise and saw she'd gone bright red.

"I thought you'd gone to the canteen." Bella shrugged off her coat and, flinging it towards her chair, cursed loudly as it missed and slithered to the floor.

"Just going now," I muttered, gathering up my bag and heading for the door.

Bella sat herself down in front of her mirror and grimaced. "The make-up girls can do wonders, I know." She cast a glance over to me. "But, my God, even they're going to struggle with this face today."

"If I don't see you again this afternoon, have a good weekend, Bella," I finally said, not daring to look at Elise. I knew what the expression on her face would be like, and I really didn't want to see it.

"You, too," Bella replied, looking from me to Elise and back again, then turning to face her mirror once more when Elise didn't say anything.

Outside the dressing room, I closed the door slowly behind me and breathed out, long and slow.

"Do you think she noticed anything?" Elise asked, casting an anxious look at the door.

"Doubt it," I said nonchalantly. "You know Bella. An elephant could come into the room and she wouldn't notice." I kept my voice light, even though my heart was thudding against my ribs.

"I don't know." Elise looked at the door again. "She looked kinda suspicious."

"Will you chill?" I said. "Stop being so paranoid all the time." I delved into my bag and pulled out my purse, waggling it at her. "So how about some lunch before you go?"

Elise stared at the floor frowning, evidently deep in thought. "Can we take a rain check?" she suddenly said, jerking her head up and looking at me. "I'm really tired all of a sudden. Think I'm going to skip lunch, go home, and just veg out on my own."

Disappointment burned in my chest. "Sure," I said feebly.

Elise looked as if she wanted to say something but stopped herself.

"You okay?" I asked.

"'Course," she said, glancing around and briefly linking her fingers with mine before quickly letting them drop. "I'll call you tonight."

"Sure," I said again.

❖

Elise didn't call that night, as I somehow knew she wouldn't. I spent most of that evening sitting in the darkness of my apartment, lost in my own thoughts, trying so hard not to let my disappointment and frustration at our situation get the better of me.

I spent a sleepless night during which my head and heart argued with one another constantly, my head repeatedly reminding me that things weren't as I wanted them to be, while my heart told me that just one kiss from her would tell me that everything was going to be okay. Finally, morning arrived, much to my relief. It was a bright, breezy Saturday, the sort of gusty day that makes clouds scoot across the sky like they're being chased by an angry mob. I gave up any thoughts of sleep and got up early, deliberately not switching my phone on, not wanting to have to feel the overwhelming unhappiness that I knew would come if Elise hadn't texted or called me. If I didn't switch my phone on, I figured, then I'd never know whether she had or not, would I? And then I couldn't get disappointed again.

I needed to fill my head with thoughts of something other than Elise; housework, it seemed, would fill that perfectly. Cranking up my iPod as loud as my ears would allow, I set my mind to the dull tasks of tidying up and cleaning, tasks that I'd been putting off for weeks and weeks, primarily because I'd been so busy with filming *PR* that I just hadn't had the time. I spent the morning loading machines full of washing, vacuuming corners of my apartment that I didn't even know existed, and finally changing light bulbs in lamps that hadn't worked in weeks.

It was just after midday when I finally slumped down on the sofa with a coffee and a baguette and I remembered to switch my phone on. I munched on my sandwich, listening as it beeped over and over again. With a sense of anticipation, I flicked my thumb across the phone's screen, wiping breadcrumbs from my mouth, and saw that Elise had rung and texted me six times since the night before. I put my baguette down and read her texts, each one asking me if I was okay and whether she could come over. I listened to her voicemails, all saying the same thing, each one getting more exasperated, and I immediately felt guilty.

I rang her straight back, a pulse of relief running through me when she answered. She didn't sound happy.

"Hey," I said uncertainly.

"Holly." She sounded terse.

"You…uh…you've been trying to get hold of me?" I asked, thinking how lame that sounded.

"Since, like, last night," she replied.

"I had my phone off."

"No shit, Sherlock."

I paused. "You bailed out on me last night," I said. "We were going to have pizza, remember?"

"I'm sorry," Elise replied. "That's why I was ringing you last night—to apologise." She paused. "I rang your apartment this morning, too," she said. "Three times."

I looked at my iPod on the sofa next to me. "Ah," I said quietly.

"I wanted to see if I could come see you today." Elise sounded annoyed. "But seeing as half the day's gone already, there doesn't seem much point."

"You're feeling better than you did yesterday?" I asked. I couldn't help it.

There was silence at the end of the phone, then, "Yeah. Actually…I wanted to talk to you about that."

"Oh yeah?"

"And to make it up to you for ducking out on you like I did."

Relief washed over me. "It's okay."

"What are you doing today?" Elise asked.

"Ugh, just tidying and cleaning and shizz, you know." I looked at the baguette crumbs down my front.

"Can I come over? I miss you." Her voice sounded husky on the phone, making my heart skip slightly.

"As long as you bring a duster with you," I joked.

"See you in about half an hour?" I could hear Elise moving around.

"Look forward to it." I jumped up from the sofa and, passing by the mirror, glanced down at my T-shirt, grubby from cleaning and with a large blob of mayonnaise from my baguette plumb in the middle of it. My hair was sticking up in all directions, and the pair of sweatpants I'd chosen to do vacuuming in at eight that morning had a backside so saggy I was confident I could fit a sack of potatoes in them.

I quickly changed into a low-cut T-shirt and a neat pair of new grey Superdry sweatpants that I hadn't worn yet and that were trendy-baggy, not sack-of-potatoes baggy. I hastily straightened my hair, then piled it up on top of my head and slapped some make-up on. After a quick squirt of perfume, I peered in the mirror again and nodded. Better.

I was just picking up my recently cast-off clothes off the floor when the intercom rang out. It was Elise. Buzzing her up, I unlatched my front door, waiting around behind it for her, getting the now-familiar fluttering of anticipation that I always got when I knew I was about to see her.

When Elise finally appeared in the doorway, she whistled softly and looked me up and down, perfect eyebrow raised in apparent appreciation. I stepped back to let her pass, thrilled at the look she'd just given me.

"Whoa!" She laughed. "You always look this good to do the cleaning?"

"Early birthday present to myself," I said, hooking my hands into my sweatpants pockets and waggling them.

"Birthday, huh?" Elise raised an eyebrow.

"Well early-ish," I mumbled, suddenly hoping she hadn't thought I was dropping hints. "It's on the 14th."

"I know."

"You do?"

"I know everything." She reached across and moved my fringe from my eyes. "And it's your twenty-first if I'm correct?" she said playfully. "At least I have plenty of time to think of a fabulous present and the perfect way to celebrate it with you, hey?" Elise wandered past me into the apartment, brushing her hand up and down my arm as she did so, then stopped at the large window overlooking the river. "I wanted to apologise again for yesterday." She looked back over her shoulder. "That was shitty of me, so I'm sorry."

"I guessed you weren't really tired." I smiled tightly, wanting to be mad with her but not being able to. To be honest, I was just glad she was here.

"I freaked a bit after Bella came in," she continued. "I mean, I know she didn't see anything, but well, I suppose I just wanted to go home and think about stuff."

"Stuff?" I frowned.

"Not about me and you," she said quickly, holding a hand out to me.

I walked over to her and took her hand.

"Just…" She paused. "God, I don't even know, to be honest." She rubbed her thumb on the inside of my hand and gazed at me. "Anyway, I'm sorry," she said again. "Am I forgiven?"

"Always." My throat tightened.

"Good." Elise leant forwards and kissed me slowly. My head and heart began their argument inside me again as I fell into her embrace, lost in her kiss.

Finally she pulled away again. "Now that you've forgiven me," she said, putting her hand into her jacket pocket and pulling out a bright yellow duster, "I believe that you had plans for me today?"

❖

"Okay, bathroom cleaned. I can now see my face in your bathtub," Elise said. "Light bulb in bedroom replaced, suspicious stain on lounge carpet removed, and irritating part of blind that just won't pull down properly now fixed." She flopped down on the sofa and ran her hands through her hair. "*Now* can we get some dinner? Please?"

"Just one more job to do, then I'm done," I said, waggling a screwdriver at her. "I promise."

"Seriously?" Elise groaned. "All work and no play makes Holly a very dull girl, you know."

I grabbed a small stepladder from the cupboard and placed it under one of the spotlights in the hallway. "Seriously," I said, reaching up with the screwdriver to tighten the casing that had been hanging loosely for ages.

Elise was still sitting on the sofa, flicking through the telephone book to find my nearest pizza place. Still with my arms high above my head, I glanced over to her to see her watching me, telephone book cast to one side, a hint of mischievousness on her face.

"I can see your stomach when you do that," she said, idly waggling a finger.

"And?" I puffed, trying to keep my balance and screw the casing in at the same time. "And," Elise said, getting up and sauntering over to me, "it means I can do this…"

She lifted my T-shirt higher, slowly kissing my stomach, making me immediately lower my arms, drop the screwdriver I had in my hand, and double over in a fit of laughter. Still standing on the stepladder, I looped my arms round her shoulders, gazing down at her. She looked back up at me, biting on her bottom lip, and pulled me down from the ladder. Without another word, she started kissing me, hard and urgently, pulling my T-shirt up over my head and flinging it across the room so it ended up in a mangled heap by the front door. She kissed her way across my skin, down my neck, over my shoulders, and across my throat, digging her fingers into my bare back, then started tugging at my sweatpants.

I unzipped her hoodie and pushed it back over her shoulders, watching as she shrugged it off and flung it across the room so that it landed on top of my T-shirt by the door.

"Enough housework," she said, pulling me to the floor. "Time to play."

CHAPTER TWENTY-SEVEN

"Wow!" I gasped afterwards, looking at the mess of clothes flung around the floor. "Who knew chores could be such fun?" I turned to face Elise, our bodies still tangled up together on the floor. She reached out and stroked my face, lifting her head slightly to kiss my forehead.

"I think every weekend should be spent doing chores," she said sleepily.

"Especially if that's the reward at the end of them." I sighed happily, gazing up at the ceiling.

Elise propped herself up on one elbow and looked down at me. She tidied my fringe from my eyes and gazed into them. "I think you're great, you know that?" she said.

"I think you're great, too," I replied, reaching up and touching her face.

"My little Holly Eight-Year." Elise took my hand that was touching her face and kissed it. "I'm sorry again that I went weird on you yesterday," she said, reaching over and grabbing both our tops, handing me mine, and then pulling hers back over her head. "It's just…" She thought for a moment before continuing. "It's like I said before. This is all so new to me. I think it's taking time to get my head around it, and if I do freak out occasionally, then I'm sorry."

"But it's a nice feeling, isn't it?" I asked anxiously. "You do like it?"

She bent her head and kissed me. "It's the best feeling in the world," she whispered.

I sat up, pulled my own T-shirt back on, too, and looked round for my sweatpants, finally locating them dangling off my forty-two-inch plasma. "I wish, sometimes…" I began. I frowned, unsure how to continue.

"You wish…?" Elise prompted.

"Well, you say it's a nice feeling, being with me," I said, turning to face her. "I just wish sometimes you showed it a bit more."

Elise's face fell. "I don't get it," she said. "I can't keep my hands off you, you know that."

I shook my head. "It's awesome when we're alone," I said. "Then I feel like I'm the most special person in the world." I sat on the floor, my knees hugged to my chest. "But you don't want to be seen out with me. That makes me feel like you're ashamed of me or something."

"You know why." Elise inhaled deeply. "We don't need to keep going over it."

"But when we got together, I told you nothing had to change," I said. "But *everything's* changed." I looked at her. "This doesn't feel like a relationship, Elise. It feels like, I don't know!" I buried my head in my hands. "It feels like an affair with a married person. I love you and I'm desperate to be with you all the time," I said, "but it's always on your terms, not mine. It's not fair."

She looked at me, crestfallen.

"You only come round when you want to," I said. "We have sex, it's great, then I suggest we hang out somewhere together and do normal things that couples do, but you don't want to because you're scared." I took a deep breath. "Can you see why I'm constantly having a fight with myself?"

"Do you want to end it?" Elise spoke slowly and carefully.

"No, of course I don't," I said, panicked. "I just want us to be like we were before we got together, you know? Going out, having a blast. Not hiding ourselves away in my apartment all the time."

"I don't know if I can give you what you want," Elise said quietly. "You knew the score right from the start. Why have you started thinking all this stuff now?"

"I suppose it's just that when I was with Grace…" I began.

"Grace?" Elise's voice rose. "What's she got to do with anything?"

"It felt different with her," I mumbled. "That's all I meant."

"Better?" Elise asked.

"No," I lied. "Not better. Just normal." I pulled my hands through my hair. "Probably because she wasn't a star in the biggest soap on TV, who was terrified that her public image would be tarnished if anyone found out she was dating me." I stopped myself when I saw the look on Elise's face. "Sorry," I said, "that just came out."

Slowly, and without a word, Elise got to her feet and pulled her trousers back on. She held a hand out to me, getting me to my feet, and watched as I padded over to retrieve my sweatpants.

"Everything you've said is true, though, isn't it?" she said.

I pulled my sweatpants back up over my hips and nodded slowly.

"So where does this leave us?" Elise held her hand out to me and I went obediently back to her, letting her draw me in to her again.

I melted into her arms, the familiar feeling of comfort and security enveloping me. "It leaves us still without pizza," I said.

"I do want to be with you, you must believe me when I tell you that." Elise wrapped her arms tighter around me. "Do you trust me?"

"I do," I murmured into her hair. "Always." I leant up and kissed her cheek. "Now ring for the pizza, will you? I'm ravenous."

❖

Elise left again early the next morning, saying something about how her staying over was becoming a habit, and about how she was worried that her neighbours in her apartment block would notice she wasn't there as often as she used to be. I didn't argue with her, but now she'd gone, I was alone and lonely. I wandered to my window, shrugging my arms tight around me. Elise's hoodie was still hanging off the sofa where it had been flung earlier. I put it on, zipping it up and wrapping it around myself, loving how it held her scent, knowing that it was the closest thing I had to her right now, and that it would have to be my reminder of her until I saw her again.

Hugging her hoodie tight around me, I stared out over the river, looking across town, watching people scurrying to and fro on the streets below me, wishing one of those people was Elise coming back to see me. A fine rain was falling. Spots of water gathered silently on the windowpane, pausing for a moment before pooling together, then quickly slithering down the glass. I watched the soft rain for a while, feeling confused and lonely and scared and a thousand other wretched emotions, wishing there was someone with me in my apartment right at that moment that I could talk to about everything.

Instinctively I picked my phone up, punching in a number. "Bella?"

"Hey you!"

I immediately felt better at the sound of Bella's familiar, warm voice at the other end.

"What you up to?" I hugged my arm across my chest and cradled my phone under my chin, reaching down to pick up two cups that were still on the coffee table. I stared at the one Elise had drunk from, just half an hour earlier, and wished again that she was still with me.

"Well, it's Sunday, so that means I'm doing precisely nothing!" Bella laughed. "Tom's taken the boys to the football, so I'm putting up my feet, home alone." She paused. "You okay?"

"Yeah, I think so." I wandered into the kitchen, putting the cups into the sink and running some water over them. "Not really, Bella, if I'm honest." I'm not sure what it was that made me say that, but it's hard to tell someone you're okay and sound convincing when inside you know you're not okay, isn't it?

"You want to come over and have a girly afternoon?" Bella asked. "Football doesn't start until four, so we'll be alone until at least eight tonight. If you want to talk, I mean. No chance of being disturbed."

Bella knew I needed to talk, but then, I knew that she'd know that. After all, that's why I'd rung her in the first place, wasn't it? "Would you mind?" I asked, already walking to the door and fetching my keys.

"Of course not." Bella spoke gently. "It's what mothers are for, isn't it?"

❖

I arrived at Bella's, a neat Edwardian terraced house a half-hour train ride from London, around forty minutes after our phone conversation. Although I wasn't sure exactly what I wanted to say to her, I did know that I needed to speak to someone about how I was feeling about Elise and me. Bella was just the person I needed to see to both cheer me up and give me some much-needed motherly advice.

Her house was a scene of chaos—as it had been on the few other occasions I'd been there—but I would have expected nothing less. As I picked my way through an untidy hall, cluttered with muddy football boots, wellies, school bags and at least three cats (there could have been more, but to be honest, it was difficult to see anything through the mess), I suddenly wondered if I should have told Elise I was coming to see Bella, in case she went back to my apartment and couldn't get hold of me.

The thought left my head as quickly as it had entered it as Bella ushered me into her large lounge, shooing yet another cat from the sofa and hastily sweeping some loose fur from the seat before gesturing to me to sit down. I plonked myself down on the sofa, feeling—as I always did—instantly relaxed in Bella's company. While her disorganised and messy house wasn't especially my kind of place, I had to admit there was something comforting about the untidiness and chaos and Bella's wide, friendly smile that made any visitor feel instantly at home.

I sat as Bella made coffees in her kitchen, listening to her clattering cups around and occasionally speaking in a sing-song voice to what I presumed—hoped—was a cat, then pulled myself up straighter as she returned to the lounge with two cups clasped in one hand and a packet of biscuits in the other.

"You sounded down on the phone." Bella handed me a coffee and sat on a chair to the side of me. "Not your usual chirpy self."

I reached over for the offered packet of biscuits and took one, biting into it and wiping a crumb from my chin. "Just a bit low today, thassall," I said. "Fancied some company." I paused. "You didn't mind me coming over, did you?"

Bella laughed loudly. "Good grief, no!" she said. "All I had planned for today was a pile of ironing the size of Mount Everest and, let's face it, who wants to do housework on a Sunday?"

I flushed, remembering Elise's quip about housework at weekends and how my chores had eventually ended up being abandoned...

"Actually, who the heck wants to do housework on any day, come to that?" she said, her voice jolting me from my thoughts of Elise. Bella turned and looked at me. "Enough about me," she said. "What about you? What's up?" She leaned forwards in her chair. "More to the point, why are you hanging out with an old fossil like me when you have a stunning girlfriend you could be hanging out with?"

"You're forty-eight, Bella." I took another bite of my biscuit. "Hardly an old fossil."

"So why aren't you with Elise today?" Bella asked, offering a biscuit crumb to a waiting cat, then tutting when it decided it didn't want it and dropped it on the floor. She kicked the crumb away with her foot. "I'm assuming that's why you're here. To talk about her?"

"I'm having the dilemma of all dilemmas," I began.

"Oh, I hate those." Bella waved a hand in the air. "I usually just have a glass of wine and hope that it'll disappear."

"I don't think it's going to be that easy with this one," I said glumly.

"You know what you tell me will go no further than these four walls, don't you?" Bella said. "If you want to offload—and I'm guessing you do—then you know you can talk to me, okay? A problem shared and all that."

"I know," I said, staring down into my cup.

"So it's Elise?" Bella prompted.

"Who else?" I said.

"Still not the hearts and flowers you want it to be?" Bella reached for another biscuit.

"It's good when we're together," I said. "I just want our relationship to be more open, but she doesn't."

"Because?" Bella asked.

"Because of the usual." I sighed. "Her public image." I thought for a minute. "I hate all the pretence! I just want us to be normal, do all the things other couples do, but she doesn't." I stared down moodily into my cup. "And I really hate that she doesn't."

"I guess Elise has to ask herself what's the worst that could happen?" Bella said. "If people found out?"

I put my cup back on the table in front of me and leant back on the sofa. "The worst that could happen is that her precious career would be at risk," I said. "Well, according to her, anyway."

"You sound bitter," Bella said gently.

"I feel it."

"But your career's important to you as well," she offered.

"It is." I nodded. "It's very special to me." I leant my head back. "But, equally, I know I haven't spent my teenage years making a name for myself just to end up as someone's secret," I said, "or to be with somebody who's too afraid to step outside the door with me in case we're spotted." I swallowed hard. "And I know I haven't matured into the strong, intelligent woman that you and everyone else knows, to now follow Elise around, pandering to her every whim."

"And you'd risk not being with her for that?" Bella asked.

"That's what I need to decide," I said slowly. "She's made my life complete, okay—but at what cost, Bella?"

"Do you love her?" she asked.

I squeezed my eyes tight. "I love her implicitly, yes," I said. "And I guess I'm happy for now to submit to her wishes, but for how much longer?"

"So can't you just enjoy it for what it is right now?"

"But I feel like I'm better than that, you know? And stronger than that." I sighed. "When I was with Grace, it was different. It was fun, exciting. We were young and carefree, and I suppose I enjoyed being Grace's adorable little secret." I looked at Bella. "But now? Now it feels sordid and wrong and I'm struggling to be Elise's guilty secret."

"I suppose there's a small part of me that's inclined to agree with Elise, though," Bella said, choosing her words carefully. "You're both the subject of furious Internet gossip already. Do you really want to be plastered all over the papers and the web?"

"More than we already are, you mean?" I said, smiling as another cat wandered into the room and hopped up onto the sofa next to me.

"But at the moment it's all idle gossip. Speculation. It keeps the ratings up. Kevin and Susie love it and, let's be fair, they've capitalised on it, haven't they?" Bella replied.

"And I never minded any of that, to begin with," I said, stroking the length of the cat's back, making it arch up and purr loudly. "We both loved it. Now it feels, I don't know, wrong. Weird. She's already told me she feels like she's lying to the public." I looked at Bella. "What kind of relationship is it when one partner feels like they're lying?" I frowned. "Actually, what kind of relationship is it when both partners are lying?"

"Both of you?"

"Well, I'm lying to myself, aren't I?" I gently dug my fingers into the cat's fur, loving the vibrations of its purr radiating along its body. "All the time I'm going along with the lie that Elise insists on, I'm not being true to myself, either."

"So what are you going to do?" Bella lifted another cat from her lap and placed it on the floor by her feet.

"I wish I knew," I said miserably. "Do I stay with Elise and carry on living this huge, black lie?"

"When the alternative is…?"

"Giving in to my morals and being true to myself." I looked at Bella. "Which means being totally open about everything."

"And alone," Bella said softly, "but still wanting Elise and being miserable, just so you can pat yourself on the back and say you did the right thing." She put her hand on my leg. "Is that what you really want?

"I wish I knew what I wanted." I sighed. "You're not making my version sound very appealing."

"Just think about it carefully, Hol," Bella said kindly. "That's all I'm saying. Don't be hasty."

Chapter Twenty-eight

I returned home from Bella's shortly before six p.m. to find Elise coming back through the hallway of my apartment block, evidently just leaving.

I'd spent the entire train journey home mulling over what Bella had said but still hadn't come up with the perfect answer. It didn't help the decision-making process, the way my heart did somersaults when I saw the adorable look she gave me as I came through the main door.

"Couldn't stay away, huh?" I said. She'd only left my side four hours earlier, but it seemed like forever.

"I missed you." Elise shrugged, briefly touching my arm. "What can I say?" She looked me up and down, one amused eyebrow arched. "You appear to be wearing my hoodie, missy!"

I looked down at myself, totally forgetting that I still had her hoodie on, and shrugged. "I need some reminder of you when you go and leave me alone, don't I?"

"Keep it." Elise lowered her voice. "Then you can imagine I'm with you even when I can't be with you."

"You want to come up?" I asked, heading for the lift. "I need to cook dinner for myself, so…"

"Dinner sounds good," Elise said, stepping back slightly as the lift doors opened.

I glanced across at her in the short time we were in the lift, her smile matching the one I knew was on my face every time we made eye contact before each of us looked away again. I loved just being with her. I wanted to do normal everyday things with her; I wanted to make dinner with her, to spend evenings out with her, or just to spend lazy afternoons draped across one another on my sofa. But I needed her to want it as much as I did, and be as comfortable with it as I was.

"You look tired." Elise's voice broke the quietness inside the lift. She gave me a long, caring look, which let me know I was so wanted, it was unreal.

The lift arrived at my floor, so I didn't answer her. Instead, we walked the short distance from the lift to my apartment in silence. Before I even had the chance to switch some lights on inside, Elise drew me to her and gave me the softest, sweetest kiss, leaning her forehead against mine.

"Sometimes I feel like I want to kiss you all day long, Holly Eight-Year," she sighed, her breath warm against my face in the darkness.

"So you missed me, then?" I said, our foreheads still touching. "I missed you like crazy the minute you left this afternoon. Hated it, just wanted you back here with me."

"I did." I could just see Elise's face in the gloom of the room. "You have no idea what you do to me, you know that?"

"Well, whatever is it," I said, finally pulling away and switching on the dimmer lights, "you do the same to me."

I walked towards the kitchen, briefly touching her hand as I walked from her. Poking my head in the fridge, I called out a number of options for dinner to Elise, who was now standing by my window in the lounge, gazing, as she often liked to, out across the sparkling lights over and across the river.

"So where did you go after I left today?" Elise called out.

I pulled two steaks out from the back of the fridge and, inspecting the eat-by date on them and seeing they were good for another two days, started to unravel the packaging.

"Just out." I took the cellophane from the steaks and put it in the bin. "What about you? Where did you go?"

"Are you sure you didn't go to a cat sanctuary?" Elise appeared behind me. She looped her arms round my waist and rested her chin on my shoulder. "You're covered in hairs." She dusted my front down, her chin still on my shoulder. "On *my* hoodie," she added, giving me a playful squeeze.

"That was Bella's gang." I groaned, picking a few off my front and frowning. "I lose count of the number of cats she has."

"Bella?" Elise lifted her chin from my shoulder.

"Yeah," I said lightly. "I went to see her."

"Today?" Elise's face darkened.

"Today," I said, feeling Elise release me from her embrace.

"Right," she said. She frowned. "And you wore my hoodie to her house?"

"It's just a few cat hairs, Elise." I flicked my hands over it. "I'll wash it if it bothers you that much."

"But she would have wondered why you were wearing my clothes," Elise said, leaning against the kitchen unit, her arms crossed.

"Like Bella would know it was yours!" I snorted.

"She's seen me wear it at work." Elise waved a hand to the front of it. "It's quite distinctive, Hol." She stared at me. "She might have wondered why you were wearing it," she repeated.

"Elise, it's fine." I took a griddle pan from the cupboard and put it on top of the oven. "It's just a hoodie."

A long, awkward pause ensued.

"You told her, didn't you?"

My throat closed. "About?"

"You know what about," Elise said. "Us."

"No," I replied, heat spreading from my neck up across my cheeks.

Elise didn't answer, instead she remained leaning against the unit. "Did you?" she finally asked again.

For a moment, silence. Then, "Yes, I did. I told her." My stomach plunged the minute I'd said it. The immediate change in Elise's mood and the look on her face told me everything I already knew: she was furious with me.

"I *said* to you!" Elise flung her hands out. "I specifically *said* not to breathe a word to anyone about this!" She stood in front of me, hands now on hips, face white with fury. She chewed angrily at her top lip with her bottom teeth, her jaw tight, her breath coming fast and short.

"But Bella's cool!" I said, hating to see Elise so angry. "She won't say a word. She promised."

"Oh, and that makes it okay, does it?" Elise glared at me, eyes blazing, waiting for me to answer.

"I don't see what the big deal is," I said quietly. "It's not like I announced it to the whole cast, is it?"

"You just don't get it, do you?" Elise started pacing the room, running her hands through her hair. "The fact is I distinctly said I didn't want anyone knowing about me and you, yet you still went and blabbed about it!"

"I didn't blab," I said feebly. "Bella already knew. She's known for a long time." I looked at Elise.

"She. Already. Knew?" Elise emphasised every word. "Since when?"

"Ages," I said. "And she's never said a word to anyone, has she?" I jabbed at the buttons on the oven. "So quit stressing."

"Terrific." Elise wandered out of the kitchen and over to the lounge window.

"Don't go weird on me again, Elise," I said. I came and stood just behind her, putting my arm round her shoulder.

"Don't," she said. She took my hand and removed it from her shoulder, still staring coldly out in front of her.

I was stung by her reaction and stood, fuming. Elise frowned, evidently deep in thought.

I thought I'd try another angle. "Would it really matter if people knew?" I asked quietly.

"Of course it would!" Elise sounded exasperated. "Firstly, what do you think Kevin, Susie—shit, even Robbie!—would say if they knew?"

"I don't think they'd care," I said truthfully. "Kevin would probably be thinking about how it'd increase ratings."

"Fuck the ratings," Elise spat, walking away from the window again.

"What!" I watched as she started pacing the room again. "Fuck the ratings? That's a new one, even for you."

She didn't answer.

"When did you become such a hypocrite?" I demanded.

"Thanks for that." Elise stared at me.

"I love you," I said, stung by her stare, "and I just needed to tell someone else that, rather than carrying it around with me like it's something I should be ashamed of." A shock of realisation instantly went through me at my own words, and I suddenly understood everything. "Is this what this is all about? Are you ashamed of us?" I said. "This has got nothing to do with your career, has it? It's really because you're ashamed that you fell in love with a girl!"

That was why Elise was so furious. She was embarrassed about being with another girl. She couldn't handle the fact she'd fallen in love, and it had been with me. Not with Robbie, or Stig, or Rory, or—heaven forbid—Pete, but me. Holly Croft. She'd fallen in love with Holly Croft—a girl—and she just couldn't hack it.

"I'm not ashamed," Elise said. "I told you a long time ago that this was all new to me, but you just seem determined to rush on ahead and tell people."

"Not people, Elise, person," I said. "One discreet person."

We stood, glaring at one another.

I watched as Elise sat down on my sofa, her head buried in her hands. "If you can't handle being with me," I said, "then maybe you're better off going back to Stig and resuming this normal life that you seem so keen on having because I obviously can't give it to you."

Elise looked up at me from where she was sitting. "After everything we've been through to get to where we are?" she said. "After all the soul-searching and dodging round one another?"

"But I can't be the person you want me to be." I sat down next to her. "If you're not comfortable being with me, then what's the point?"

"But I love you," she said simply. "I'm fighting a battle with myself and I'm asking you to give me time."

"You're asking me to hide away," I said. "To be someone I'm not." I looked at her. "I don't want to spend the rest of my life living a lie."

Elise nodded, then, with a long sigh, stood up. "I'm being unfair, I know," she said, bending to pick up her bag.

"You're not staying?" I asked. I reached up and took her hand. "We can talk through this over dinner. It'll be okay."

Elise looked to the kitchen then back to me. She gave my hand a small squeeze. "It's getting late, so I'll say no," she said. "But thanks anyway. I'm going to go and have a think about stuff for tonight." She pulled me to my feet and drew me to her, wrapping her arms around me. "I'm sorry," she whispered. "I've been a complete shit." She paused. "As usual."

I stroked her hair. "We'll talk again tomorrow, yeah?"

"Tomorrow," she breathed into my neck. "Yeah, tomorrow."

CHAPTER TWENTY-NINE

Monday morning arrived like a welcome distraction for the first time ever in my life. After Elise had left my apartment the previous evening, instead of doing something that would take my mind off her and not let me dwell on things, I'd spent time looking back over old YouTube videos of us both and reading messages on Internet forums about Jasey. That hadn't helped at all. Rather, it had reminded me of just how good Elise and I were together and made me wonder whether I was prepared to risk ruining everything—both for Elise and for me—by insisting we were more open about our relationship.

Today, I figured, was another day. I'd speak to her again at work and ask her over to my apartment again that evening to talk. Talking had to be good, right? We could sort things out if we could just talk them through, I was sure of it.

I was just getting ready to leave my apartment for the studios, shortly before lunch, when my phone rang. Thinking it was Elise, I snatched it up, answered with a cheery greeting, and was already mentally asking her over that evening. I was slightly disappointed, however, when I heard Kevin's voice at the other end. And he sounded anxious. Very anxious.

"Holly?" His voice was high—shrill, almost.

"You all right, Kevin?" I cradled the phone under my chin and pulled the fridge door open, looking for something for lunch later. I peered inside, frowning.

"Not really, in all honesty," Kevin replied. I could hear him moving around while he was talking to me. "Can you come down to the studios as soon as possible?"

"I guess," I said, glancing at the clock on my kitchen wall and shutting the fridge door again. "I'm due down in an hour anyway."

"No, you need to come now, please," Kevin said. "I'll explain when you get here."

A wave of panic suddenly swept over me. "It's not Bella, is it?" I asked, fearful. "Nothing's happened to her, has it?"

"No, no," Kevin said. "Bella's fine. Everyone's fine. I just need you to come in."

"Sure," I said.

"I've gotta go, sorry." And with that, the line went dead.

I unhitched my phone from under my chin and stared at it for a second, slightly put out that Kevin had cut the conversation with me like that, then pulled my mobile from my pocket and flicked my thumb over the screen, finding Elise's name. I sent a short text to her, asking her if Kevin had asked her to come to the studios early, too. Elise, like me, wasn't due on set until lunchtime. I wondered if Kevin needed to see both of us, or just me.

I made it out of London and to the studios in just over thirty minutes, arriving there shortly after ten thirty a.m. The scene when I arrived at Kevin's office was one of total chaos: Kevin and Susie were deep in discussion at Kevin's desk while runners were coming and going every few minutes. Bella was already there, seated just in front of Kevin's desk, idly flicking through the broadsheet she had evidently been looking forward to reading in the cafe, before she was rudely interrupted.

Stuart was on his BlackBerry in a corner of the room, a clipboard cradled in one hand, his glasses perched high on his head. He looked tired and grumpy, shooting me a look as I entered the room and made my way over to Kevin.

"Where's the fire?" I asked, looking round the room and smiling.

Kevin didn't smile back. Nor did Susie.

"Hey, Holly," Kevin said, gesturing to the seat in front of him. "Have a seat."

I sat down warily, casting a quizzical *what the hell's going on* look at Bella, who glanced up from her newspaper and shrugged back at me.

"Thanks for coming in so quickly, both of you," Susie said, glancing up at us from a piece of paper she was looking at on Kevin's desk.

I nodded, wondering what scene it was that they seemed to think Bella and I hadn't done properly. That had to be it, right? Dissatisfaction with something the pair of us had done. Why else would they get us both in?

"We've got some major rescheduling to do." Kevin looked at me over the top of his glasses. "And a mountain of rewrites, too."

"Okay," I said, smiling uncertainly.

"It's going to mean a change to your work pattern for the next few weeks, and I can only apologise for that," Susie said. "Probably some longer hours as well, until we can sort all this out and get things back on track."

"Okay," I said again, looking warily across to Bella.

"Have we done something wrong?" Bella asked, folding the newspaper up neatly on her lap and looking directly at Susie.

I looked from Susie to Kevin and back again. "And what about Elise?" I asked. "Is she included in all this, or is it just me and Bella?"

"You haven't done anything wrong, no," Kevin looked back down to the paperwork on his desk.

"Neither of you have," Susie continued.

"And Elise?" I repeated.

Susie reached across the desk and grabbed a pile of papers. "It's because of Elise we have to do all this," she said, gesturing to one of the runners who came over to her, and handing the papers to her. "Take these upstairs, will you?" she asked her.

"Tell them we'd like them back by two at the latest, yeah?" Kevin called out to the runner's retreating back.

I watched as she left the room, then turned to look at Bella. "I don't understand," I said. "What's Elise done?"

"She's gone, that's what," Susie said sharply. "She's quit *Portobello Road* and left us with a whole pile of trouble."

CHAPTER THIRTY

My mouth went dry at Susie's words. My heart instantly started racing behind my ribcage, and I had to breathe through my mouth, because I thought that at any moment I might pass out.

"Gone?" Bella finally spoke. "What do you mean, gone?"

"Came in at eight this morning to see me," Kevin said, putting his pen down on the desk. "Told me she was taking an extended break with immediate effect."

"For fuck's sake!" Bella threw her hands up in the air and shot a look at me.

"Precisely." Susie pulled a face.

"And, what?" Bella said wearily. "She's just upped and offed, has she? Without a thought for any of us?"

"Apparently so." Kevin leant back in his chair and rubbed his hands over his face.

"Can she…can she do that?" I finally managed to croak.

"No," Kevin said bluntly. "She can't."

"So…?" I looked at Kevin numbly.

"I told her she was in breach of contract," Kevin said. "She told me that she was due some holiday, that she'd cleared it with her agent, and that she was going now."

"And has left us all up shit creek," Susie piped in irritably.

"So it means we have to rewrite all of Jasey's scenes for the next two weeks, which the writers upstairs," Kevin said, jabbing his pen upwards, "are absolutely *delighted* about, as I'm sure you can imagine."

My head was swimming. Elise had gone? Gone where? "But she hasn't quit, as such?" I asked. "She's just taking some leave?"

"Who knows?" Kevin sat back in his chair, a weary look on his face.

"Did you have any idea she was going to do this?" Susie asked me harshly. "Because if she talked to you about taking unplanned holidays right in the middle of filming, we sure could have done with knowing about it sooner than this, Holly."

"No!" I said, aghast, looking frantically from Bella to Susie to Kevin. "I had no idea!"

My breath was coming in gasps, making me hyperventilate. I needed to find Elise, wherever she'd gone to, and convince her—no, *beg* her—not to leave. I knew what it was all about, of course I did. She'd freaked out over everything, and it was my fault. If only I'd kept my big mouth shut and not pushed her about everything, then it would all still be okay.

"Of course she didn't know," Bella said hastily. "Look at her! She's as shocked as we are."

"I have to go." I scraped my chair back noisily and lurched to my feet. "I have to go and find her." Ignoring Susie frantically calling me back to her, telling me I needed to stay around the studios, and Bella following me to the door, trying to stop me, I stumbled from Kevin's office, slamming the door behind me louder than I needed to. Half walking, half running back down the corridor and out to my car, I fished my phone out of my bag and rang Elise, knowing with a sinking heart that the chances of her actually answering were slim.

Where the hell was she? More importantly, how did she think this was an okay thing to do? To just up and leave *PR* without so much as a word to me? And what about breaching her contract? I thought she'd been happy playing Casey. How could she just give up on her character like that? Angrily wiping tears from my eyes, I fumbled the keys into the ignition of my car, fired it up, and sped out of the studio car park, braking sharply to avoid a cat crossing the road and stalling my car in the process. Swearing and banging my hands against the steering wheel in frustration, I started the engine again and rammed the car into gear, my tyres screaming as I raced down the road towards Elise, wherever she was.

❖

I arrived at Elise's apartment choking up with rage, anger, hurt, betrayal—you name it, but the second I pulled into the small communal car park and saw her car parked up, I began to relax a little. I pulled in beside it just as a thought struck me: perhaps she was leaving *PR* for the sake of us. Maybe everything I'd said to her the day before had sunk in, and she'd decided she didn't want to hide our relationship after all. Perhaps she'd done it to protect me—to protect us.

I killed my engine and sat back in my seat, puffing my cheeks out, my heart beginning to slow down again. Would Elise really have done that? I glanced up to the fourth floor of the apartment block—Elise's floor—and thought about what I'd say to her. If she had left the programme because of us, then it was up to me to persuade her to come back, despite everything I'd said to her. Jasey was more important right now for both of us. We'd managed to keep our relationship a secret for long enough already, and I was sure we'd manage to carry on seeing each other in secret until we both felt the time was right to go public.

Following another person in, I entered the lobby of the block and took the lift to the fourth floor, tidying my hair on the way up and wiping at my eyes with a tissue. I didn't want Elise to know I'd been crying; I didn't want her to think I'd panicked and didn't trust her, if the simple answer to her leaving really was that she'd done it to protect me and save our relationship.

I rang on Elise's door, but the look on her face when she saw me standing there didn't exactly fill me with confidence, and every comforting thought I'd had in the lift up to her floor immediately left me again.

"I thought you were the taxi, maybe," she said bluntly. She held the door open slightly to allow me in, shot a look around the hallway outside, then shut the door again.

"Taxi?" I asked, wandering a short way into her apartment and looking around. The irony that this was the first time I'd ever visited her apartment wasn't lost on me.

"You've heard, then?" she said, ignoring my question. She leant against the door, not following me in.

"You could say that," I replied. "Kevin rang me in a complete panic and summoned me over to the studios straight away."

Elise looked at me.

"So, want to tell me what's going on?" I asked. "And why you didn't think to tell me you were having yourself a little holiday?"

"Because I only decided last night," Elise said simply, looking down at her feet. "After I got home from yours."

"Why did you do it?" I asked. "Are you leaving because of me? Because of us? Or just because of you?"

"Because I need some headspace," Elise said, lifting her head to look straight at me. "Like you, I can't handle all the creeping around, all the pretence." She put her hands in her pockets. "And, like you, I feel as if this has all been a lie." She paused. "But, unlike you, I could have lived with that."

"This is all to do with me telling Bella, isn't it?" I said. "Bit of a knee-jerk reaction, though, isn't it? Cutting off your nose to spite your face and all that?"

Elise studied me cautiously. "I can't give you what you want," she said. "I want secrecy, you want openness because you can't pretend to be someone you're not." She took a deep breath. "But that's what we do for a living, Hol! We make out that we're something else, just to please people." She put her hands in her jeans pockets. "I've done it all my life—it's all I know how to do," she said, looking up and catching my eye. "You can't change me."

"So, what?" I shrugged. "You're just going to go, are you? Give up on me?"

"Isn't that what you've been planning to do with me?" Elise asked. "I know you've not been happy. I know you've been having this moralistic argument with yourself for days." She rested her hip against the back of her sofa. "So what do you do? Stay with me and have this fictional life you don't want, or leave me and be true to yourself?" She pulled herself away from the sofa and walked away from me.

"So you're getting in there first, is that it?" I said to her retreating back.

"I just need some thinking time, Hol," Elise said, robotically picking up her coat. "I feel like I can't breathe at the moment."

"Where?" I asked. "Where are you going?"

"Back to the States," Elise replied simply. "I have a friend out there," she said. "I already called him. Said I could crash at his place until I get myself sorted."

The colour drained from my face. I reached a hand out and leant against the back of her sofa, feeling faint. "Him?"

"Him," Elise repeated.

I stared at her, my mouth dry, my heart thudding in my neck. "Don't I mean anything to you?" My voice was thick with emotion. "Okay, so I've fought with myself over what to do, I've thought about calling it a day, but you know what?" I took a deep breath, my voice wobbling, "I thought you were too important to me to just give up on you like that."

"You know you mean everything to me!" Elise said. "I just think this is for the best for now."

"For who?" I asked. "You or me?" I gripped the sofa harder. "And what about Jasey?" I asked feebly. "What about the programme?"

Elise shrugged.

"Are you for real?" I stared at her incredulously. "You bail out on us all at a time when you—well, we—have never been so much in demand?" I asked. "You're throwing away all of this just because you say you can't handle being with me? They're having to rewrite all our scenes because of you!"

"So?" Elise said petulantly.

"What am I supposed to tell people?" I mumbled. I sat down on the arm of her sofa, my legs turning to jelly.

"You don't have to tell anyone anything," Elise said, finally shrugging on her coat and wandering past me.

I watched numbly as she walked into her bedroom, returning a few seconds later with a small holdall. She was perfunctory and uncaring, apparently ignoring the fact I was still perched on the edge of her sofa, in pieces over it all.

"So you're not going to say anything to me now?" I asked as she put the holdall next to the front door.

Elise stopped and turned to me. "I don't know what more there is to say, Holly," she said. "I've made up my mind."

After a few more minutes of watching her in silence, and when it was apparent she wasn't going to say any more to me, I lifted myself away from the sofa and headed for the door. "You know what?" I said, shouldering my bag angrily. "You don't deserve me, and I think I've wasted enough of my life on you, don't you?"

"No," Elise said, leaning against the side unit, staring down at her feet. "I don't deserve you."

"I thought you were cold and emotionless the first day I ever met you," I said, turning to look at her. "Guess I should have stuck by my instincts and stayed the hell away from you." Finally Elise lifted her eyes to me, her face pale and tired. "I was prepared to give us a go, because I thought we had something," I said. "Despite everything, I would never have just given up on you."

Elise didn't answer.

"What, you don't have anything to say?" I said, my hand on the door handle. "Well, thanks a bunch, Elise," I said, fuming. "How fucking callous do you want to be?"

"Life would be so much simpler if you were a man, or if I didn't have to work with you," Elise said, wiping angrily at her eyes. "We wouldn't be having this conversation right now."

"You can't help who you fall in love with," I said numbly, my hand still on the door handle, not quite able to leave her. "You can't tell your heart not to love someone just because they're not your usual type, or because it takes you out of your so-called comfort zone. It doesn't work like that, Elise. That's what makes love so amazing. Because it's so bloody random. It gets you when you least expect it, and no matter what you do to try to ignore it, you can't."

Elise stood, silent, her fingers worrying the buttons on her coat.

"It was bad enough when Grace left me," I said. "But at least she left me because she found something—someone—else. You? You're going because you're a coward."

"Perhaps I am, yeah," Elise said quietly.

"And you think you have an exclusive right to happiness?" I threw up my hands in exasperation. "It's not all about you, funnily enough. It's about me and you, and it's about me and how I'm feeling." I stared down at the floor, fighting the tears that I knew were just one look or one word away. Elise didn't reply this time, and the cold silence that lingered between us was unbearable. "There's nothing I can say that'll make you change your mind, is there?" I finally asked, lifting my head to meet her eyes. "Nothing I can do to make you stay?"

Again, she didn't answer. But she didn't need to.

The look in her eyes told me she'd already gone.

CHAPTER THIRTY-ONE

Holly, I'm so sorry." Bella wrapped comforting arms around me, letting me melt into her warm, soft jumper. "Have you heard from her since you got home?"

I was back in my apartment. An emergency, tear-fuelled phone call to Bella had brought her over after she'd finished filming her scenes over at the studios, and now here she was, her arms around me like the comfort blanket I needed.

I shook my head against her shoulder. "I'd imagine she's halfway over the Atlantic by now," I mumbled.

The hours after I'd left Elise's apartment had flashed past me like speeding cars, and while life carried on as normal for the strangers I'd passed on my drive home, my own life had ground to a halt. I no longer had the ability to function properly. It was as though I was living in a dreamworld, treading water, barely keeping my head above it, constantly gasping for air as if my life depended on it.

"I've spoken to Kevin," Bella said, "told him you're sick today, and probably will be for the rest of the week." She walked me to my sofa and sat me down. "No one knows a thing, so you can stop looking so panicked."

"Her hoodie's still where I left it," I said, getting up and taking it from the back of the chair where I'd hung it up. I gathered it up and buried my head in it, smelling the last remains of the citrusy scent Elise always wore.

"I'm going to say something now," Bella said, getting to her feet and gently taking the hoodie from me, "that you're probably not going to like."

"Which is?"

"Which is that I think we could both see this coming, couldn't we?" Bella said quietly.

"Doesn't make it any easier, though," I said. "No matter how much I tell myself our relationship wasn't going the way I wanted it to, I still feel like shit right now."

"But maybe it's for the best," Bella offered. "You've been tying yourself up in knots about what to do and—"

"Elise has made the decision easier for me?" I finished. "Well, isn't that big of her."

"And I'm sure you hate her right now," Bella continued, "but if she was never comfortable with the whole idea, then was it ever going to last?"

"I do hate her," I said hotly. "I hate her almost as much as I love her, but you know what?"

Bella looked at me.

"It's that love that makes me know that if she walked in through that front door right now, I'd forgive her in a heartbeat."

"But I think you have to come to the realisation that at the end of the day," Bella said, "her career was more important than anything else."

"More important than me, you mean," I said miserably.

"You were fighting with your conscience as well, don't forget," Bella said. "Would you have stayed with her and sacrificed everything you've worked hard for?"

"Why are you defending Elise?" I looked at where Bella had placed Elise's hoodie, the familiar lump in my throat immediately returning. "When she's the one that's turned my life upside down?"

"I'm not." Bella ran her hand down my arm. "I'm just playing devil's advocate," she said, "as always." She looked at me. "You just have to ask yourself honestly if you ever thought you and Elise would be in it for the long run, or whether both your careers would have been too important to risk, even for different reasons."

"Well, I guess I'll never know now, will I?" I said, looking again at her hoodie. "Because from where I'm standing, there's no more Holly and Elise, and there's no more Jasmine and Casey." I took a deep breath. "So where on earth do I go from here?"

❖

I couldn't face leaving my apartment for the rest of the week. I called in sick to work each morning on Bella's insistence that I was in no fit state to resume any vigorous filming schedule until I'd had time to make sense of everything that had happened to me.

She was right. I spent days sitting numbly in the window of my apartment, watching people come and go on the streets below me, or watching the London Eye slowly turn outside, trying to evaluate my life. Often, I'd find myself looking up at the planes that flew in and out of Heathrow right over my apartment every few minutes, stupidly imagining that Elise might be on one of them, and that she was coming home. I'd try to picture her sitting in her seat, then stare blankly at the plane until it was no longer visible, hating it for taking Elise away from me, and hating her for leaving me.

When I wasn't watching the planes, I was crying. When I wasn't crying, I'd torture myself by watching old clips of Jasey or reading fans' messages on forums, speculating over Elise's sudden departure from the show—which had inevitably been leaked to the press by someone from the studios—making the tears that had recently dried up come tumbling back out again. It was ironic, I thought, as I sat slumped in my pyjamas on the sofa, obsessively watching video after video, that Elise hadn't wanted to be plastered over the papers because of our relationship, but her hasty departure had stirred up something of a hornets' nest in the media. My tears weren't just because I loved and missed her. My tears were for a lost opportunity, brought about by my own stupid morals. If only I'd given her what she'd wanted, rather than insisting on being more open when she'd made it clear over and again she didn't want us to be, then I wouldn't be in this mess right now.

I spent time looking at a photo we'd taken in my apartment one time, both of us lying in bed, both devoid of any make-up and with hair sticking up in all directions. Despite how scruffy we looked, we both looked radiant—happy and comfortable in each other's presence. I stared at the picture relentlessly, remembering how she used to call me Holly Eight-Year, thinking about how I'd give anything to hear her call me that again. I took in every detail of her face in the photo, trying to recall all the things we'd talked about the day we took the photo, thinking back to how happy we'd been that day. How had it all gone so wrong?

I followed this pattern of plane-and-video watching and photo-staring for three whole days, until finally, after the fourth day of my absence from work, Bella came back to my apartment, bustling in with a worried but determined and caring look on her face. It was a look that suggested she wouldn't be leaving until she was certain I would be okay to be left again.

"I've been calling your mobile every day for the last four days," Bella said, brushing her hand up and down my arm as I stepped aside to allow her in, "and your landline. Guess you didn't want to be contacted, huh?"

I glanced at my iPhone, switched to silent for the last seventy-two hours, and then to the apartment phone, yanked angrily out from its socket when it was clear that Elise wasn't going to ring me. I looked back at Bella.

"I've not been in the mood for callers." I shrugged, wandering back to the sofa and sinking down wearily into it.

"Have you even stepped outside this door since I was last here?" Bella asked.

I shook my head.

"Or had a shower?" She looked at my crumpled pyjamas and messy hair.

"You know what's ironic about all of this?" I asked, ignoring her question about showers.

Bella sat down beside me.

"That I kept on about how my relationship with Elise wasn't as I wanted it to be," I said, "but now I'd give anything to have any kind of relationship with her." I looked at Bella. "I miss her, Bella," I said. "I miss Casey, I miss Jasmine. I miss everything." I ran my hands through my hair. "I was living this wonderful life, with a wonderful character to play in a wonderful soap. I had a wonderful girl with me who I got to work with all day and hang out with at night, and it still wasn't enough for me." I squeezed my eyes shut and swallowed hard. "And now I've lost it all."

"You haven't lost Jasmine," Bella said kindly. "Everyone's worried about you, you know." She squeezed my hand. "We just want you to come back and carry on doing what you're amazing at."

I felt punch-drunk, like every last ounce of energy had been squeezed from me. My head ached, my eyes were like hard rocks in their sockets, and I was numb all over. But Bella's words to me about work sparked a small feeling of optimism inside me.

"Have you heard from her?" Bella asked.

I shook my head. "Not a word. Nothing," I said. "Have you? Has Kevin, I mean?" I asked hopefully.

"No, nothing either." She sat back on the sofa.

I paused. "Has it caused too much hassle?" I asked. "Elise leaving like that, me not coming in all week?"

Bella patted my leg. "Nothing the writers can't fix," she smiled. "They're annoyed with Elise, yes, but I think they're more than used to us actors and our fragile egos getting the better of us sometimes, then us buggering off and leaving everyone in the lurch." She bumped her shoulder playfully against mine. "They'll cope. They always do." She got up from the sofa and wandered to the kitchen, pausing on her way there. "Let's have no more talk of blame here, okay?" She turned and looked at me. "You have your whole life ahead of you, Holly," she said. "You've got a great career, a good life here in London, and people who love you. Don't let one person ruin all that for you."

I sat and listened to Bella making coffee, thinking perhaps Bella was right, and that it was time I took a shower and joined the real world again. I got up and went to the kitchen, just as Bella was returning with a large mug of steaming coffee and hot buttered toast.

"You're right," I said, smiling sheepishly at her.

"About?" Bella handed me my coffee.

"About everything," I said. "As usual."

I took a piece of toast from the plate, biting into a slice and licking melted butter from my bottom lip.

"Does this mean you feel like you might be ready to come back to work?" Bella asked hesitantly.

"I think so," I replied truthfully. "Might do me better than moping around here, thinking about how well I've managed to fuck up my life, hey?" The words caught slightly in my throat and I hastily took another bite of toast in case Bella noticed.

"And does it also mean you might be up for a night out tomorrow?" Bella bumped my arm. "We do have to celebrate your birthday, you know."

"My birthday," I said on a groan.

"It's the law," she said. "All birthday celebrations are compulsory."

"Oh yes?" I looked at her in amusement. "And whose law says that?"

"Bella's law," she said, taking the second piece of toast from my plate and biting into it. "I'll look after you all night, I promise. Make sure you don't get questioned to death about stuff."

"I think a night out is just what I need," I said wearily. "Might help me forget. Thank you, Bella," I said warmly.

CHAPTER THIRTY-TWO

Elise had been gone exactly six days, nine hours, and twenty-one minutes, but the second I stepped into Bobby's and remembered that the last time I'd been there—with her—it seemed like she'd only left me that morning. Stepping back into that nightclub jolted me back into missing her all over again. I'd thought I'd be spending my twenty-first with her, of course. We hadn't made firm plans, but I'd believed that whatever we did, and however we celebrated it, it would just be the two of us. As much as I appreciated Bella and everyone else taking me out, and as much as I was making an effort to be happy on the outside, a huge part of me was crying inside all evening because all I really wanted to do was be with Elise, on my own, in my apartment, celebrating with her.

"You're thinking too much again." Bella put her hands on my shoulders and steered me towards a table. "You had that faraway look on your face that you always get."

"Just thinking how weird it all is without her here." I sat down and stared around me, trying not to let my mood darken too much. "And missing her all over again."

I'd returned to work that same afternoon and hated every single second of it, for so many reasons.

No Elise. No Casey.

Questions asked. Questions fended off.

It had been awful.

It would be wretched getting into the routine of working without Elise again, as well. We'd been working closely—as well as everything else—for such a long time that to suddenly not have her with me or near me and not knowing when—if ever—she was coming back was utter hell. I frequently thought back to my first meeting with her, all those months ago, and found it curious to think there ever was a time when we hadn't worked with one another because it seemed like Elise had been part of *PR*—and a part of me—forever.

"Try not to dwell on the past," Bella said kindly, "think of your twenty-first as a new start." She hugged her arm round me. "A new start without her."

"She's making that easier for me," I said, not elaborating any further as Robbie placed a bucket of champagne and two glasses on our table.

"Happy birthday, you." He leant across and kissed my cheek. "My spies tell me you had a sack-load of cards from fans this morning, Miss Popular." He squeezed my shoulder.

"Over three hundred and sixty at the last count." Bella looked up and caught Robbie's eye. "That would be precisely three hundred and fifty-nine and a half more than I got this year."

"How do you get half a card, Bel?" Robbie looked quizzically at her.

"It was written on the back of a postcard." Bella shrugged. "Half a card."

Robbie rolled his eyes and, with a final demand that I drink up and enjoy, he wandered off back in the direction of the bar where the others were seated.

Getting cards from fans had been awesome. I'd never received cards on any previous birthdays, and I have to admit, I loved it, giving me the faintest pinprick of something resembling cheerfulness. But that was it, wasn't it? Throughout all of this sorry mess, I was still Jasmine Hunter, and Casey or no Casey, I'd be Jasmine Hunter for many years yet. Even Elise couldn't take that away from me.

"Dare I ask?" Bella said, now we were alone again.

"Ask what?" I replied, pouring champagne carefully into our glasses.

"Did you get anything from her?"

I shook my head. "No text, no card, no e-mail, nothing," I said, sighing. "She knows it's today but she evidently doesn't give a shit."

"So, again," Bella offered, "it's time for you to move on because it sounds like she already has."

"It's difficult." I frowned. "Everything's a reminder. I hated hearing the bitching about her at work this afternoon," I said. "People grumbling about her because she's thrown the schedule into chaos."

"The same people who are having to work longer hours because of what she's done?" Bella sipped her drink. "They'll soon move on to bitching about someone else."

"I hate the way they speak about her, though," I said. "All right, so Elise could be arsey with me in the early days, but she's always been professional and polite to everyone on set, hasn't she?"

Bella nodded. "Can't argue with that." She lifted her glass as she spotted Kevin in the shadows and beckoned him over to our table. "No more talking about Elise. Promise?"

"Promise." I swirled my champagne around in my glass, making it fizz again, and took a long drink.

"I just about remember my twenty-first." Kevin slotted himself into the booth beside me. "But I don't remember drinking as much champagne as you all are!" He raised his glass to me. "Are you having a good one?"

"She is, aren't you?" Bella prompted when I didn't answer.

"It's been awesome." I managed a smile. "Thank you all for coming out with me."

"You're a very highly valued member of *Portobello*," Kevin said. "What's happened isn't your fault. You do know that, don't you?" he asked. "It's Elise that's put us in this mess, not you."

"I know," I mumbled, glancing over to Bella. "Thank you."

"And just because we've had to write Casey out for now," he continued, "doesn't mean we'll be downgrading any of your storylines." He bumped my shoulder. "So don't start thinking you'll have fewer lines to learn than you did a week ago."

"Is this really the end of Jasmine and Casey, then?" I asked hesitantly. "Forever?" The word caught in my throat.

"Just a temporary blip." Kevin waved a hand. "The writers will have her travelling somewhere for the next few months but not breaking up with Jasmine as such." He took a drink from his glass. "We'll cross that bridge when and if we have to."

I stared down into my glass, watching the bubbles play with one another.

"We still have big plans for Jasmine, Hol," Kevin said, draining the rest of his drink. "If anything, the Jasey storyline has told us just how important a character she is." He stood up. "And we'll fight to keep you on board for as long as possible."

I watched him leave our table and head back over to where Susie was talking to Rory, then turned and looked at Bella, my face flushed with pride.

"You see?" Bella leant closer to me. "There's life after Jasmine and Casey, and there's life after Holly and Elise, too." She clinked her glass against mine. "Today is most definitely the first day of the rest of your life."

CHAPTER THIRTY-THREE

"Okay, that's a wrap." Stuart clapped his hands twice and retrieved his clipboard from under his arm, scribbling something down on it. "We're done for the day now, guys." He turned and walked quickly towards a trailer parked up nearby.

"Thank God for that." Robbie drew his hands through his hair. "Who knew a twelve-hour shoot could feel like it was more like a day and a half?"

Just as I'd done when Grace had left me, I'd thrown myself into my work, which was my only salvation. Each day I got up, filmed my scenes at the studios, came home, ate, and slept. Same robotic thing, day in, day out, which was only good because it allowed me to shut out all thoughts of her, while I trained my brain to read scripts in between takes, or found someone to talk to in the green room whenever it seemed like my thoughts were going to drift over to her.

It was midweek and we'd just wrapped on some scenes filmed on location up near Primrose Hill. We were ahead of schedule, which delighted Stuart and meant that I'd now finished all my scenes and wasn't needed again until Monday. A four-day weekend beckoned, which ordinarily would have been something to look forward to; this one, however, filled me with dread because I knew it would be spent alone.

"Do you want to grab a bite to eat on the way home?" I suddenly asked Robbie, the thought of being alone hanging over me. "My treat. I figure we've earned it after the day we've had."

"No can do." Robbie opened the door to the trailer and stood to one side to allow me to enter. "Got a hot date tonight."

"Again?" I said over my shoulder. "Didn't you have a hot date last night, too?"

"And another one tomorrow." Robbie stepped up into the trailer behind me. "What can I say?" He struck a pose, making me groan...and laugh. "Anyway, see you Monday, yeah?" He shrugged his jacket on and left the trailer once more.

"The Adonis that is Robbie Turner, huh?" Bella appeared from behind a door where she'd been changing. She wriggled her sweater over her head, then ran her hands through her static hair. "Irresistible to all female-kind."

"Not all." I sat down and made big eyes at Bella. "You know, I never thought I'd be jealous of Robbie, but I am today."

"Oh?" Bella sat down next to me and kicked her shoes off, sending one clattering across the floor.

"For having something to look forward to all weekend." I sighed. "For having a life."

"You have plenty of friends," Bella said. "Just because you're single again doesn't have to mean it has to be all doom and gloom."

"Yeah, but friends aren't quite the same, are they?" I stared moodily at the floor. "I thought I'd kinda got used to the loneliness after Grace and I broke up," I said. "I thought I was okay with it." I eased Jasmine's shoes off and put on my own much more comfortable boots. "Because you do, don't you?" I looked at Bella. "Then someone new comes into your life and gives you your weekends back, but when they go, you have to get used to the loneliness all over again."

"Until the next new person comes into your life," Bella said, giving my knee a squeeze, "and gives you your weekends back again." She reached into her bag and pulled her phone out, then jabbed at the buttons on it, like she always did with her phone. "Being single when you've been used to having someone around takes some getting used to." She jabbed at her phone again and frowned. "Bloody phone's dead."

I took it from her.

"You ever hear from Grace now?" she asked, watching me as I pressed and held various buttons on her phone.

I shook my head. "Nothing after the last e-mail I told you about," I said. "Guess she finally took the hint, although I was so wrapped up in Elise, I don't think I would have noticed anything anyway." I abruptly stopped talking, Elise's name catching in my throat. "When did you last charge this thing?" I waggled it, grateful to have the chance to change the subject.

Bella shrugged. "I forget."

"I keep telling you that you have to charge it." I handed it back to her. "Your battery's dead, I expect." I rooted around in my bag for my own phone and handed it to her. "Here."

"I just have to ring Tom, make sure he picks the kids up from football," Bella said, clamping the phone to her ear. "He's so forgetful. Drives me nuts. Hello? Tom?"

Wanting to let Bella speak in peace, I got up and walked to the small trailer bathroom, wondering, though, why she had to shout whenever she used a mobile phone. Shutting the door and locking it, I stood in front of the mirror, pulling my fingers through my fringe to move it from my eyes, listening to the muffled voice of Bella still talking outside.

Bella.

She'd been wonderful to me since Elise had left. I'd habitually poured my heart out to her, when I thought things were becoming too much for me, or cried in her arms in our dressing room when something at work pricked a memory of Elise and made everything come flooding back again. Without Bella, I think my life would have come crashing down around my ears weeks ago; she had been the one that had told me I had the strength to get through this, and I didn't know how I'd ever be able to repay her for her kindness.

I covered a wad of cotton wool with cleanser and started removing the heavy make-up that was used on us in order to show up better on camera. When I was done, I leant on the sink and stared at my fresh, scrubbed face looking back at me. I could no longer hear Bella speaking, so I unlocked the bathroom door and went back into the main compartment of the trailer and, finding the trailer now empty, saw a hastily scribbled note on the table in front of the chairs where Bella and I had just been sitting.

Tom forgot the kids. Do you want my husband? Sometimes think I could happily be single. See you Monday.

In haste,
B x

I looked for my phone, but when it was clear that Bella hadn't dropped it behind one of the cushions or left it in a prominent place where I could see it, I realised with a sinking heart that she'd taken it with her.

"Great!" I said aloud. "So not only do I have a weekend on my own, I now also have a weekend without my phone."

I grabbed my coat and bag, hauling it onto my shoulders. With one more quick glance around the trailer, and with the thought in my head that I'd have to go to Bella's in the morning to collect my phone, so at least I'd have something to do, I left the trailer and made my way home.

❖

It was just gone five thirty in the afternoon when the intercom to the apartment rang. The commute getting back across town from Primrose Hill had been tedious, as it always was in the middle of the week.

I was still annoyed about my phone. By now, I thought, it would probably be back at her house, no doubt being batted around her lounge floor by one of her cats. Well, I could wait until the morning to go and collect it. Now I was home, all I wanted to do was kick off my boots, put slippers on my feet, pour myself an enormous glass of wine, and sit and watch TV until either hunger or cramp forced me to move again. It had been one of those days.

The intercom in my apartment rang again, refusing to be ignored. I sighed at its shrill, impatient buzzing and dragged myself reluctantly from the sofa, wincing at my tired, aching legs. There was only one person I knew could ring an intercom like that, and I really hoped she had my phone with her, and I equally hoped that she didn't have any of her children with her.

The intercom rang for a third time, just as I'd reached my door to answer it. Muttering about patience being a virtue, I pressed the button, reaching down at the same time to pull a boot off, kicking it across the floor, and then leaning down to take the second one off.

"Bella?" I waited to hear the familiar, breathy voice of Bella.

"Holly, it's me."

I froze. *Elise.*

"Buzz me up."

Chapter Thirty-four

Icicles cascaded down my back the second I heard her speak. For one split second I felt dizzy and instinctively put my hand out to the wall to steady myself.

"Holly? You there?"

Just hearing her voice again after so many weeks of silence made it seem like I'd just seen her that morning. She'd only said a few words to me, but the sound of her soft, low voice was still making my head spin and my heart thud in my neck. I swallowed hard.

"Elise." My voice sounded reedy, strained.

"Can I come up?" Elise asked.

"Why?" I sounded childish, but I didn't care.

"Please? It's important." Elise said softly.

Without replying, I pressed the buzzer on the intercom. I wandered back into my lounge, my mind racing, imagining Elise in the lift, wondering what she was wearing, whether she was alone or had someone with her—stupid, crazy thoughts like that. I started frantically thinking about what I was going to say to her and how I was going to act towards her, and I jumped at the soft tap on my front door.

I glanced at my reflection in the mirror, adjusted my hair a little, then opened the door. My throat tightened as I saw her standing in front of me, looking just as stunning as she had the last time I'd seen her. Of course, physically she looked the same, a little thinner, perhaps, but same great hair, same beautiful eyes, cute dimples. At the same time, though, there was something different about her. I couldn't put my finger on what it was, but it was as if she was meeker—shyer, almost.

"So? You've seen me," I said, leaning my arm against the door frame, barring her way.

"I need to talk, not just see you." Elise stepped back slightly, looking at my arm blocking the door.

"Oh, *now* you want to talk?" I said.

"Please?"

Finally stepping aside to let her in, I closed the door and leant back against it, watching her as she wandered into the apartment, looking around.

"Any spiders lately?" She turned to me and smiled nervously.

"What are you doing here, Elise?" I pushed back from the door and walked towards the window, glancing across at her as I passed her.

"I came to apologise," she said.

"You came all the way from America to say you're sorry?"

"I gave up on America," she said quietly.

My heart lurched. "Why?"

"Why do you think? You." Elise slowly walked towards me.

I folded my arms tight across my chest. "Why now?"

"I did a lot of thinking while I was away," she said.

"You want a round of applause?"

Not rising to my bait, Elise walked to my window and stared out across the city.

"The view never changes from your window, does it?" She turned her head and looked at me over her shoulder. "I like the consistency about that. I need that."

"Don't we all?" I muttered.

"This is what I'm trying to tell you," Elise said. "I've done a lot of thinking while I was away, and I realised I need stability in my life." Her eyes roamed over my face. "Because I've never had it before. You give me stability." She swallowed. "*Gave.* You gave me stability."

"I make you want to hide from who you really are, remember?" I said. "Isn't that why we both realised it would never work?"

"One day, when I was staying at my friend's apartment in LA," Elise said, ignoring my comment again, "I looked out his window and I realised that everything had changed since I'd last been there." She dug her hands deep into her pockets and turned back to face the window. "But it wasn't the scenery that had changed. It was me." She stared out in front of her. "When I looked out his window, all I wanted was to see London spread out in front of me, not LA," she continued. "Then I realised, it wasn't about the view. Not really. I didn't want to be there anymore. I wanted to stand with you in your apartment and look at the same scene that we'd stood and looked at together countless times." Elise paused, breathing softly. "I wanted you to be standing beside me," she said quietly, "but when I turned round, you weren't there."

"I wasn't there because you were grown-up enough to realise we wanted to live our lives differently," I said, loving how her hair fell around her neck, and fighting the urge to touch it. "I was devastated when you left, but you know what? In hindsight, if it hadn't been you that ended it, then it would have been me."

"And I'm grown-up enough to know how selfish I've been," Elise said, finally turning her back on the window and facing me. "I never wanted to leave, but I didn't see what choice I had. Now I'm glad I *did* go because when I got there, I felt empty, not like when I was last there." She came towards me and sat on the arm of my sofa. "Everything came back to me. I remembered how selfish I'd been when I was living there before. I was selfish because I didn't have anyone else to think about—or to care about. All I had was myself." Elise leant over, resting her arms on her knees. "I was so insular," she sighed, "only caring about me and my career." She looked up at me, holding my gaze. "Everything changed when I came to England and met you, but I never realised it at the time. Never…appreciated it. It wasn't until I was staring out my friend's window that I realised I hadn't left selfish Elise in LA. I'd taken her to London, left with her again, and now she was inflicting her selfishness on someone who she really cares about. You."

"So what are you saying?" I asked, my throat tight. I wanted to be angry with her, but each gaze up at me from under her fringe, each sigh from her, each look of anguish on her face just made me want to go to her and gather her up in my arms. "You just left me! Without a word! I had to hear it from Kevin that you'd gone, for fuck's sake. How could you have done that to me?" My eyes pricked with tears.

"I'm saying that I'm sorry for everything I've done, and that I want to try again," Elise replied, her face sincere.

"Jesus, Elise. How can we be together?" I asked. I leant against the wall, my legs feeling like jelly. "We want different things. I want us to be open as a couple. You want total secrecy. How would it ever work?"

"Something happened when I was in LA," Elise said slowly, "that made everything so much clearer."

"Right," I said, my heart thumping even more wildly than it was before. *Please don't tell me you hooked up with a guy when you were there.* I swallowed hard. "So what happened when you were away?" I asked, dreading her answer.

"I had my very own eureka moment," she said, "which got me on the first plane back over here."

I shook my head. "I don't understand."

Elise stared down at the floor, absent-mindedly turning one of the cloth bracelets on her wrist. "My agent over there," she said slowly, "called me one day, asked to see me."

"To offer you work?"

"More like, to offer me men." Elise shrugged.

My stomach plunged. "Other actors?" I managed after a few seconds, the words nearly choking me.

"Yeah." Elise didn't look up. "He produced this file, full of headshots of actors," she went on, "ones who are further up the greasy pole than I am. You know the type?"

"I know, yeah," I replied. "Young and perfect, just the sort of guy your agent wants you to be seen with." I looked at her, trying to read her reaction to my words.

She finally lifted her head and looked back at me, her face expressionless. "Do you know what he said to me?" she asked. "Do you know what the fuck he suggested?"

I shook my head.

"He told me to look through the photos and choose the one I thought I'd look best with." She threw up her hands. "Can you believe it? He actually asked me which one I wanted to hook up with."

I let myself slowly slide down the wall until I was sitting on the floor, then brought my knees to my chest, clasping my hands round them. "Hook up as in…?" I asked weakly.

"How do you think?" Elise sprang up from the sofa, her hands shaking. "As in, go to premieres together and be visible. My agent said I'd look good with any of them, but he wanted to give me a choice," she scoffed. "He told me to make out for the cameras with them. He said it would help get my face known in good old Tinseltown, and that it wouldn't do the actors' credibility any harm to be seen out with the *cute English chick*." She emphasised the last words.

"And what did you say?"

Elise ran her hands through her hair. "What do you think?" she cried, her eyes filling with tears. "Do you really think I'd be that shallow?"

"No, I…" I dropped my gaze. "I'm sorry."

"He offered me work, as well," Elise continued, "said that most of the guys in his grubby little portfolio were in soaps or TV movies—that kind of thing." She sat down on the floor next to me, our shoulders touching. "He said he could get me work in the same programmes." Elise turned her head and fixed me with her adorable eyes. "Every character he offered me was the same shallow piece of nothingness that couldn't even hold a candle to Casey."

"So?"

"I realised nothing would ever compare to what I have here with you." She paused. "What I *had* here. No character could ever be as good as Casey, no bit part in some cable-channel soap could ever match up to what I had on *Portobello Road*." She put her hand to my cheek, bringing my head round to face her. "And the thing that makes it so fucking awesome here is that not only do I have an incredible character to play, but I get to play her opposite you."

"But you'll always be worried about what other people think, won't you?" I tried to keep the wobble from my voice. "That'll always stop us. I can't live like that, always running scared."

"I won't be. I promise." Elise's hand stayed cupping my face.

"You will, Elise," I said quietly. I squeezed my eyes shut, forcing a tear to spill down my cheek. Elise wiped it away with her thumb. "It'll always be like that," I whispered. "You worrying about what people think, or what they might say, because of your career. That's the difference between us." We held each other's gaze. "I don't care what people think."

"No." Elise shook her head, tears filling her eyes, too. "I've thought about nothing else since I've been away." She took her hand away from my face and wiped her eyes with the inside of her wrist. "If being with you means I lose my career, then the career wasn't worth having," she said earnestly.

"You say that now…"

"I just want to do ordinary things with you, Holly." She put her hand on my leg and stroked it. "I want to go to sleep with you every night and wake up with you every morning. I want to row a boat down the Thames with you, eat picnics in the winter with you. I want to rid your kitchen of spiders and spend silly afternoons picking your socks up off your bathroom floor and fixing spotlights that we both know won't work." She was half laughing and half crying by now.

I stared at her, feeling as though someone was squeezing my already bunched-up heart and draining every last ounce of blood from it.

"I don't care what I do, Holly, as long as it's with you." She wiped at the mascara running down her cheeks, smearing it even more.

"I don't want to go back to a life without you because without you I don't have a life. Can't you see that?" Tears were now cascading down her face, Elise no longer bothering to wipe them away. "I don't want to be Brad Bentley's pretend girlfriend, when I can be your real girlfriend."

"Brad who?" I smiled.

"Exactly." I felt Elise relax against me.

I gazed at her, not daring to move. It was as if I was in one of the dreams I'd had so many times since Elise left. I half expected to wake up and find that none of the last twenty minutes had actually happened.

I squeezed my eyes shut and opened them again. She was still there. Perhaps this wasn't a dream after all.

"So?" Elise took my hand. "What do you say? Can you forgive me?"

CHAPTER THIRTY-FIVE

"This is everything I've wanted to hear for such a long time, but how do I know you mean any of it?" I looked at Elise, tears starting to prick at my eyes again. "How do I know you won't get cold feet the first time someone sees us out together and go running off again?"

"I won't," she said slowly, lifting my hand to her face and kissing it. "I promise you, I won't."

"I don't know if I believe what you say anymore, though," I said. "That's the trouble. I just don't know if I can trust you again."

"Can't you at least try?" Elise asked, her eyes pleading.

"I don't know," I said, my resolve starting to waver. "I don't know what's the right thing for me to do."

"What's right is that I love you!" Elise said. "And I know it's going to take you time to trust me again, but I'm begging you. Just give me one more chance. I want to prove to you that I mean everything I'm saying right now."

I linked my fingers through hers.

"And how will you do that?" I asked, hypnotised by the feel of her skin against mine. "I won't let you hurt me again."

"I'll never do anything to hurt you again," Elise said.

"If everything you're saying is true, then prove it to me," I said suddenly. What I was about to say was a risk, I knew, but I needed to know that Elise meant what she was saying to me.

"How?"

"You just said you wouldn't care if you lost your career because of me."

"I did," Elise said, "but—"

"You know I'd never ask you to risk that," I said. "You know as well as I do that you belong in front of the camera, that's what you live for. I could never expect you to put all that in jeopardy for me. But I really don't think that you admitting to our relationship is going to harm your career, at least not over here."

Elise started to speak but I hushed her. "If you're willing to turn your back on LA because your agent wanted you to make a name for yourself by hooking up with nameless guys, then I think you're ready to come back to *Portobello Road* and be open about our relationship." My heart was thumping out of control behind my ribs, my breath coming short and shallow as Elise and I stared at each other.

To my surprise, a slight smile tugged at the sides of Elise's mouth.

"I'm one step ahead of you," she said.

"What do you mean?"

"I contacted some magazines," Elise said slowly. "All the big ones."

"And said what?"

"Invited myself to be interviewed," she said. "Told them I had a scoop about my private life."

"About...me and you?" I leant back and looked at her quizzically.

"No, about me," Elise said simply. "Your name doesn't have to come in—"

"But I want it to!" I interrupted. "This is exactly what I want—openness about me and you."

She reached out and took my hands in hers. "Life's about being with the person who makes you laugh, who makes you happy, who makes you feel special, and that's what I'm going to tell them." She dipped her head and looked up at me through her fringe. "It's about being with the person you can't stop thinking about, the person who gives you a squishy feeling inside when you know you're going to see them," she said. "The person you can't imagine living without. The person you truly want to be with." We held one another's gaze. "I truly want to be with you, Holly, and soon the whole country will know that, too."

I leant into her. I knew one more look from her was all that it would take.

"Sometimes it just takes someone to be an arsehole before they realise what they've lost," she said softly. "And I have been."

"Have been what?"

"An arsehole."

"You got that bit right," I said, glancing at her, the hint of a smile on my lips.

"I've missed that, too." She rested her head on my shoulder.

"Missed what?"

"Your smile," Elise sighed.

My smile deepened. "You'd do all that for me?" I asked.

Elise shook her head. "I'd do it for us," she said simply. "Everything I've ever wanted in a person is sitting right here next to me. Everything."

I rested my head on top of hers.

"You're funny and sweet and adorable and lovely and you're all I want," she said, her breath fluttering against my neck. "You're my Holly Eight-Year, do you know that?"

I raised my head away from hers.

"You mean that?" I asked.

"Every word." She lifted her head off my shoulder and our eyes met, the look of complete love and longing on her face pulling me in to her, totally captivating me.

I let her take my hand, the feel of hers so warm and soft, making me feel safe again.

Slowly and tentatively she put her arm round my shoulder and pulled me to her. Her face was now millimetres from me, her warm breath on my skin, her lips almost touching mine.

"Please," she finally said, her voice low and quiet. "Just let me try again?"

Her words disappeared as my lips met hers. I was lost in her; the weeks of despair just drifted away as I kissed her back. I shivered as she slowly kissed me, the sensation of her tongue against mine sending tingles up and down my spine, and melted at the touch of her soft lips, her body pressed against me, her hand reaching up under my T-shirt and stroking my side as she kissed me, over and over again.

Finally, she pulled away and wrapped her arms tight against me again, as if she never wanted to let me go. I leant into her, Elise warm against me, her breath in my hair, all my feelings of love for her that I once thought I could ignore just flooding back again because they'd never gone away in the first place.

"I'm so sorry," she said, her voice muffled in my hair. "You have no idea just how much I love you."

"I do love you, too, Elise," I said, tracing a finger up and down her arm. "I've never stopped loving you."

She cupped my face in her hands and kissed me again, softly and slowly. "I've been such an idiot," Elise said, kissing my face, my eyes, my hair, my forehead. "Such an idiot." She took my hands in hers and pressed them to her lips. "No one else matters, Holly," she said. "All that matters from now on is us, and soon everyone will know just what you mean to me, too."

She stood up, holding her hand out for me. I let her pull me to my feet and lead me over to my window. Elise stood behind me, her arms linked around my waist, her chin resting on my shoulder as we gazed out at the early evening lights flickering into life across London.

"My whole life's been one big act, Holly," she said. "I'm tired of trying to be someone I'm not, so this time, I'm playing it for real." She softly kissed my neck. "Are you with me, my little Holly Eight-Year?"

"Always, Elise," I said. "Always."

EPILOGUE

I settled back in the boat, the warmth of the wood, heated by the midafternoon sun, hot on my bare arms. Squinting up into the sunshine, I shielded my eyes with my hands as I watched the swallows quickly swoop and dive over the water's surface, which sparkled in the sunshine.

Idly dangling a hand over the boat's edge, I dipped my fingers in and out of the cool water and thought about everything that had happened to me over the last few months.

I was ridiculously, utterly, totally, absurdly happy.

"Perfect, isn't it?" I muttered sleepily.

I turned my head and gazed lazily at Elise, lying next to me, head tilted towards the sun. She lifted her sunglasses and glanced at me, a contented look spreading across her face.

"Perfect, just like you," she said.

"Smooth!"

Elise propped herself up on her elbow and smiled down at me, tracing her fingers across my face.

"Read it to me again." I linked my fingers behind my head and closed my eyes. "Especially the bit in the middle. I liked that best."

"We only just read it!" Elise laughed but still reached behind us, making the boat rock slightly, and picked up the magazine. "The same bit as before?"

"That's the best part, isn't it?" I opened one eye and looked at her.

"Not the photos?" She pulled her sunglasses down the bridge of her nose and peered over the top of them at me, one eyebrow raised.

"Just read it!" I flapped a hand at her and settled down again, waiting for her to start.

Elise lay down next to me again, holding the magazine above her head to shield herself from the sun. "Okay, wait." She ran her eyes over the page. "Here we are: *It's true love! Actress Elise Manford tells us how her love for co-star Holly Croft grows deeper every day...*"

"I could lie here and listen to you say that over and over, you know?" I turned my head and smiled.

"*Following her exclusive interview with this magazine last month, in which popular* Portobello Road *actress Elise Manford revealed that she was dating co-star Holly Croft, Elise now talks about how being with Holly both in real life and on screen has changed their lives.*"

"I love that photo of you." I pointed a lazy finger at the page. "Read some more?" I asked, adding, "Please?" when I saw Elise mock-roll her eyes behind her glasses.

"Let me see..." She studied the article. "Okay: *Elise (19) told us: 'Holly is everything to me, and I have to pinch myself every day at just how lucky I am to have her in my life...'*"

"I love that bit," I said quietly.

Elise read on. "'*Our popularity has rocketed since we first went public about our love for one another, and we've both received so many messages of love and support from people telling us how happy they are for us. We're ecstatic at just how amazing our fans all are!'* Isn't that the truth?" Elise puffed her cheeks out.

"And didn't I always tell you it would be okay?" I said, reaching out and stroking her leg.

"*In the last month the public has taken the real-life couple to their hearts, culminating in Elise winning Best Actress at last week's Go Soaps! awards and, with Holly, also scooping the Best Couple award...*Ha!" Elise put the magazine down and propped her herself up on her elbow, taking my hand and threading her fingers through mine. "What a night that was, hey?"

"The way things are going," I said, "there'll be lots more nights like that, too."

"And we'll be together for each and every one of them," she said before leaning down and giving me a long, lazy kiss that seemed to go on forever.

"It really can be like this all the time, can't it?" I said dreamily when she finally pulled away, gazing back up at her.

"It can be like this forever and always," she said. "I told you before, now I've got you, I'm never letting you go ever again."

"Hollise forever?" I asked, pulling her down to me again.

"Hollise forever," Elise grinned.

About the Author

KE Payne was born in Bath, the English city, not the tub, and after leaving school she worked for the British government for fifteen years, which probably sounds a lot more exciting than it really was.

Fed up with spending her days moving paperwork around her desk and making models of the Taj Mahal out of paperclips, she packed it all in to go to university in Bristol and graduated as a mature student in 2006 with a degree in linguistics and history.

After graduating, she worked at a university in the Midlands for a while, again moving all that paperwork around, before finally leaving to embark on her dream career as a writer.

She moved to the idyllic English countryside in 2007 where she now lives and works happily surrounded by dogs and guinea pigs.

Soliloquy Titles From Bold Strokes Books

The Road to Her by KE Payne. Sparks fly when actress Holly Croft, star of UK soap Portobello Road, meets her new on-screen love interest, the enigmatic and sexy Elise Manford. (978-1-60282-887-2)

Kings of Ruin by Sam Cameron. High school student Danny Kelly and loner Kevin Clark must team up to defeat a top-secret alien intelligence that likes to wreak havoc with fiery car, truck, and train accidents. (978-1-60282-864-3)

Swans & Klons by Nora Olsen. In a future world where there are no males, sixteen-year-old Rubric and her girlfriend Salmon Jo must fight to survive when everything they believed in turns out to be a lie. (978-1-60282-874-2)

The You Know Who Girls by Annameekee Hesik. As they begin freshman year, Abbey Brooks and her best friend, Kate, pinky swear they'll keep away from the lesbians in Gila High, but Abbey already suspects she's one of those you-know-who girls herself and slowly learns who her true friends really are. (978-1-60282-754-7)

In Stone by Jeremy Jordan King. A young New Yorker is rescued from a hate crime by a mysterious someone who turns out to be more of a something. (978-1-60282-761-5)

Wonderland by David-Matthew Barnes. After her mother's sudden death, Destiny Moore is sent to live with her two gay uncles on Avalon Cove, a mysterious island on which she uncovers a secret place called Wonderland, where love and magic prove to be real. (978-1-60282-788-2)

Another 365 Days by KE Payne. Clemmie Atkins is back, and her life is more complicated than ever! Still madly in love with her girlfriend, Clemmie suddenly finds her life turned upside down with distractions, confessions, and the return of a familiar face... (978-1-60282-775-2)

The Secret of Othello by Sam Cameron. Florida teen detectives Steven and Denny risk their lives to search for a sunken NASA satellite—but under the waves, no one can hear you scream... (978-1-60282-742-4)

Andy Squared by Jennifer Lavoie. Andrew never thought anyone could come between him and his twin sister, Andrea...until Ryder rode into town. (978-1-60282-743-1)

Sara by Greg Herren. A mysterious and beautiful new student at Southern Heights High School stirs things up when students start dying. (978-1-60282-674-8)

Boys of Summer, edited by Steve Berman. Stories of young love and adventure, when the sky's ceiling is a bright blue marvel, when another boy's laughter at the beach can distract from dull summer jobs. (978-1-60282-663-2)

Street Dreams by Tama Wise. Tyson Rua has more than his fair share of problems growing up in New Zealand—he's gay, he's falling in love, and he's run afoul of the local hip-hop crew leader just as he's trying to make it as a graffiti artist. (978-1-60282-650-2)

me@you.com by KE Payne. Is it possible to fall in love with someone you've never met? Imogen Summers thinks so because it's happened to her. (978-1-60282-592-5)

Swimming to Chicago by David-Matthew Barnes. As the lives of the adults around them unravel, high school students Alex and Robby form an unbreakable bond, vowing to do anything to stay together—even if it means leaving everything behind. (978-1-60282-572-7)

365 Days by KE Payne. Life sucks when you're seventeen years old and confused about your sexuality, and the girl of your dreams doesn't even know you exist. Then in walks sexy new emo girl, Hannah Harrison. Clemmie Atkins has exactly 365 days to discover herself, and she's going to have a blast doing it! (978-1-60282-540-6)

Cursebusters! by Julie Smith. Budding psychic Reeno is the most accomplished teenage burglar in California, but one tiny screw-up and poof!—she's sentenced to Bad Girl School. And that isn't even her worst problem. Her sister Haley's dying of an illness no one can diagnose, and now she can't even help. (978-1-60282-559-8)

Who I Am by M.L. Rice. Devin Kelly's senior year is a disaster. She's in a new school in a new town, and the school bully is making her life miserable—but then she meets his sister Melanie and realizes her feelings for her are more than platonic. (978-1-60282-231-3)

Sleeping Angel by Greg Herren. Eric Matthews survives a terrible car accident only to find out everyone in town thinks he's a murderer—and he has to clear his name even though he has no memories of what happened. (978-1-60282-214-6)

Mesmerized by David-Matthew Barnes. Through her close friendship with Brodie and Lance, Serena Albright learns about the many forms of love and finds comfort for the grief and guilt she feels over the brutal death of her older brother, the victim of a hate crime. (978-1-60282-191-0)